THE
REAPPEARING

THE
REAPPEARING

A Novel

David Orsini

Other Books by David Orsini

The Weaver of Plots

Schemes, Disguises, & Traps

Vanishing by Degrees

The Ghost Lovers

The Woman Who Loved Too Well

The Subtleties of Seduction

Bitterness / Seven Stories

CONTENTS

"Three things are necessary for our salvation: to know what we ought to believe, to know what we ought to desire, and to know what we ought to do."

—Saint Thomas Aquinas

CHAPTER ONE
ENTERING THE NIGHTMARE

I want to tell you the truth. I need to explain when the story involving Tyler Danforth and me heaved up our lives and threw us away, flung us upward at first into long corridors of darkness and swiftly afterward into the nearly endless falling down and down again and again into the depths of a nightmare.

So I begin.

Once again, I see Tyler and me in his Ferrari, a GTC4 Lusso. Its gleaming metallic blue blends well with its sleek chassis and its luxury interior. It has a powerful V-12 engine, and it rides like a comet. I know. Tyler has allowed me to drive it on many occasions, because I am his girlfriend, Rachel Hayworth. I never drive the car at its top speed, which is two hundred fourteen miles an hour. But, whenever I take hold of the steering wheel of that Ferrari, I race with relentless fury across a local drag strip, an eight-mile track that is usually deserted at six o'clock on Saturday mornings.

On the evening that I want to tell you about, Tyler is driving his Ferrari. It is not the beginning of our time together, his and mine. That beginning occurred six months earlier. But this particular evening, the eighth of October, is a beginning of a different sort. It pushes happiness out of our reach.

"This has been a tremendous night," Tyler says as he drives me home after our high school's autumn dance. "One of my best ever."

His words, bonded with heartfelt emotions that surprise him, make his husky voice sound even huskier.

"It has been tremendous for me, too," I tell him. "I'll never forget this night."

Light of heart and supremely happy, Tyler flashes a gleaming smile that makes this moment perfect. His dark hair, strong cheekbones, and long, tapering jawline allow him to look older than his sixteen years. He is more grownup than most of our peers, more mature and confident. Self-aware and self-possessed, Tyler is not embarrassed when I admit that I shall never forget this night. Nor is he intimidated by my wily attempts to gain possession of his will or of his soul and of all his plans for the future. Tyler knows how to navigate his freedom. Even in this early phase of his manhood, he easily accepts my remark that I shall never forget this night in which he escorted me to our school's autumn dance. Tyler is a casual realist. He perceives the world around him with earthbound awareness and with incisive understanding of his friends and his rivals. My telling him that he has accompanied me through an extraordinary evening sounds to his ears like a natural thing. He knows that I have enjoyed this night, even without my saying so. But that I have said so pleases him.

"Good to hear," he answers me. "I like to know when my charm is working."

My fear that this night's happiness will be merely fleeting prods me to say more. I need Tyler's assurance that his elation is more than a momentary sensation. Uncertain of myself, though, I choose the wrong words because they reveal my distrust of the new happiness that he has brought into my life every day of these six months we have known each other. Through all of my troubled years, before Tyler came to lift me out of my darkness, I was searching for the unexpected visitor or the chance happiness that would rescue me. I was searching for more than a rescuing visitor or the influential blessing that he might bring with him. I was searching for a way to rescue myself.

Tyler has become my moral compass, my ethical guide. His choosing me to be the special girl in his life continues to astonish me. But his choice has not surprised most of our classmates. Good students though they are, with materialistic goals and familiar dreams of success in the workplace, they observe only the surface of things. They fail to explore the clouded meanings of an ambiguous remark or of an ambivalent action. When they became aware that Tyler had chosen me as his girlfriend, my classmates regarded our pairing as appropriate and even inevitable. They focused on my looks rather than on my character.

They agreed that my willowy figure, golden blonde hair, and light blue eyes made me an ideal partner for Tyler. They had never properly interpreted my disguised self-centeredness, my concealed indifference toward my classmates' problems, and my hidden contempt of every peer and adult who wanted to clip the wings of my freedom.

Nor do my classmates understand even now that Tyler has saved me from myself. In these six months of our romantic friendship, he has become the most essential person in my life. Yet, if I told him so, he would frown with disappointment.

"Don't be a copycat," I imagine him advising me. "Don't be a carbon copy of anybody and certainly not of me. Be yourself, as honest and authentic as you can be."

Tyler has never spoken those words to me. But his behavior has set the bar high for my reformation. His compassion for others and his many charitable deeds have provided the templates for my new, personal code of conduct. With him, I have worked as a volunteer in soup kitchens in the desolate and nearly forgotten sections of Blue Ridge City in Connecticut, far from the affluent, gated community where we live. With him, while visiting local hospitals, I have read stories to convalescing children, and I have tutored these same children in elementary school math and science. On many weekends, he and I have worked with senior citizens in nursing homes on art projects that challenge their creative use of clay, plaster, collage, drawing, and printmaking.

Always, Tyler has been the beacon guiding and accompanying me to these good deeds and to an honest caring about the wellbeing of other people.

Tyler is the most popular junior at Blue Ridge High School. He is a star athlete, having excelled as a goalie for our school's winning hockey team and as a pitcher for the school's top-ranked baseball team. He is also an honor roll student who plans on becoming a physician. He is, first of all, an altruist. He cares about his fellow human beings. His future studies include a major medical school and an internship at an equally major hospital. Eventually, he wants to serve as a physician for the needy and the aged.

I tell you all these things as a way of explaining my unease when Tyler declares that he will remember this special night. Despite his quiet mentoring of me, I believe that I am not good enough for him. I have more than a little acquaintance with the self-serving behavior and the prideful, rebellious nature that for so many years suppressed my potential goodness. It is only two months since Tyler gave me his hockey pin, the emblem telling everyone who notices I am wearing it that Tyler has chosen me to be his girlfriend. In these six, life-changing months since we first met, I have become an altogether different person. Or so I keep telling myself, disconcerted nevertheless whenever I fall back to my old, self-centered habits.

Now I prod Tyler with another question, searching for the certainty that only a seer who has knowledge of the future could grant me.

I push my way forward. I put a lilt in my voice. I try to convince myself that my mood is as lighthearted as Tyler's.

"A year from now, will you remember this night?"

With his keen-sighted driver's eyes on the dark road ahead of us, Tyler answers without hesitation.

"Sure I will. It's been very special."

"What about two years? Will you still remember?"

For a moment, he ponders the question. Then, after offering me once more a gleaming smile and the bright blueness of his eyes that reveal his serious response, he answers me.

"Two years is a long time away. Maybe other nights will be even more memorable."

"Maybe," I say, disappointed because he has no way of knowing whether the far-flung future or even the next two years will keep us together.

"Of course they will," he says. "There will be plenty of other great nights for us. You and I are just starting our adventure. We're making our way in the dark."

Silence overtakes the both of us, though only for a moment.

I change course. I navigate in a different direction. I try to be witty.

"People often get lost in the dark," I tell him. "Sometimes, they never find their way back."

As though my words rouse some evil spirit that has been observing us, jealous of our young and inexperienced love, the darkness rises suddenly over us—a gigantic ascension moon-tinged and alive, a dangerous, murky power rushing upon us.

Without any warning, as though they are a blaze of lightning, quick flashes are igniting this ascending power and the moonlit, October air. Blinding flares of headlights signal the immense danger that is leaping upon us. For one split second I glimpse the Maserati racing wildly upon us, just before it hits our Ferrari head-on and shudders with the heave and heft of its fury. Right then and suddenly, on this autumn night that has brought Tyler and me so much merriment and a joy that has left me awed and even astonished—right then and altogether suddenly, while we are driving away from our high school's autumn dance, a crash is shaking the darkness with furious and metallic explosions. I catch sight of the Maserati catapulting into an eddying darkness that eludes the glow of the moon. For just an instant, as though some supernatural transaction is allowing me to see beyond ordinary vision, my startled glance shows me the screaming face, rugged body, and spattering blood of a red-haired man flung through the sharp, ragged glass of the windshield. Out of control, the car zooms beyond my seeing at the same time that I hear the screech of its tires and explosive bursts like a bomb.

The impact of the Maserati hurls our Ferrari into a nearby farm field with out-of-control velocity. Our air bags have not deployed and have left us imperiled. Window glass is shattering outward and propelling its shards into moon-touched fields of corn and sweet potatoes. Already, Tyler is slumped over the wheel of his sleek car, his dark-haired, battered head bleeding and his blue-eyed gaze closed now to my seeing, lost as his whole body is to the quick-witted consciousness that makes him the special person he is to me. It is as though some black magic spell has been cast upon us. Over and over Tyler's Ferrari spins across the fiery darkness, gyrating and somersaulting inside the rising folds of the mild-seeming night that is so quickly betraying us. Everything spirals away from us, swiveling into a confusion of scattering objects that include my blue, sequined purse, Tyler's Apple iPhone, and the white corsage that a few hours earlier he had pinned to my ocean-blue, knee-length party dress that paired so well with the navy-blueness of his suit.

In the swirl and sweep of rapid motion, I feel my body springing free of my seat belt and being lifted toward the soft leather of the roof. I feel Tyler's big-boned muscularity thrown against me—pitched more than thrown, heaved up more than pitched—in lopsided trajectory. I hear the windows smashing apart. The front passenger door and the rear door behind my seat shoot out of their hinges and fly away. The horn is blaring, and sparks are rising from the hood of the car. The Ferrari flips and flips once again, barreling and somersaulting and burrowing into the thick darkness of the cornfields. Oil and gasoline fumes overtake the air. More sparks flare up, followed quickly by ricocheting explosions.

Then, as though a circus cannon were firing aerialists high into the air, some force or fury within those fumes lift up our bodies, Tyler's and mine, and with echoing blasts of power throw us out of the Ferrari. Our heaving figures shoot through the open space where the passenger door had been. Blind Chance grants us this escape hatch, this unexpected portal or gate through which our bodies rush past the exploding Ferrari and land with thudding roughness upon the furrowed path near moon-touched ears of corn and in the midst of hazy human figures racing toward us.

Blood is spilling from my forehead and dripping out of my left ear. I try to rise, but the sharp pain piercing my right shoulder and the sharper pain throbbing from my dangling, left leg halt even my smallest movement. In the distance, about twenty feet away, I sight Tyler's blood-smeared, pale face and his lanky, athletic body. No longer does he possess an unblemished physique. The whole, commanding form of him lies twisted and inert, like that of an infantryman grievously wounded on a battlefield. I try to call out his name, but the sound dies in my throat. I begin crawling toward him, fearful that the crash has killed him. The pain that has overtaken my body is unbearable and pushes me into the blackout of nothingness.

How long the blackness holds me its prisoner, I cannot tell. Nor can I count the number of minutes that pass before the voices of a man and a woman call me out of the blackness. The voice of the man is as deep as it is raspy. It is a voice like my Uncle Trevor's that speaks only necessary words. The woman's voice is soft like my Aunt Deborah's, steel-true and self-controlled. I try to lift my head toward these tall, shadowy figures kneeling before me in a field of autumn corn and covering my pain-racked body with the warmth of a thick blanket. But the blood that is dripping from my forehead and hurrying across my half-closed, blue eyes blinds my sight of them.

I try to speak, but my swollen lips and the voice that is suddenly lost to me cannot speak or even cry out my fear and my pain.

Now, while the Ferrari goes on exploding and the rising, fuel-fed flames singe and crackle the breeze-tossed air, I hear the man and the woman speak. They choose careful, matter-of-fact words. There is no fear in their voices or in their words. They have had, I imagine, a long acquaintance with the joys and gifts of the world and with its unreliable promises and its dangers.

"The girl is in a bad way," the man says. "But she may pull through."

The woman does not dispute her husband's opinion. Nor does she agree with it. But Tyler's injuries have given her pause.

"What about the boy?"

"He'll need a miracle to bring him back," the man says.

Whether this man and his wife have more to say, I will never know. The throbbing ache in my forehead and the pain in my dislocated shoulder and in my broken leg grow more and more intense. The pain throws away the sound of their words. Yet I am determined to remain conscious until I see a medic from the city hospital trying to rescue Tyler. The blaring siren of an approaching ambulance tells me I will not have to wait any longer.

In the next instant, a wiry medic in a green hospital uniform is hurrying toward me. My eyes, crusted with dried blood, see the vague reality of this possibly youthful man. My uneasy mind is telling me that he might be a ghost, a Guardian Spirit made visible to those imperiled human beings whom Death is carefully observing. I, in turn, observe him—this efficient medic who works to assuage some of the pain that, with whiplashing fury, has taken possession of my body. The medic measures my pulse. He cauterizes the wounds to my bleeding forehead. He encloses my broken leg within a temporary splint. He washes away the crusted blood that is blinding me. All this while, I feel myself slipping out of consciousness, plummeting into the nightmare that is concealing the horrors waiting to spring upon me. But I do not surrender to this unceasing pain. I do not give myself to the nightmare that some relentless Fate has prepared for me. Only when the medic has washed the crusted blood from my eyes do I consent to this nightmare. It is now, after I catch sight of a taller medic trying to revive Tyler, that I permit the darkness to swallow me up. Only then, uncertain and terrified at the same time, do I hurry inside the nightmare that has always been waiting for me.

CHAPTER TWO

SLEEPING PRINCES

"You've got to soldier through this thing," my father says. "You can't allow it to defeat you. No Hayworth has ever been a coward. Not the men. Not the women."

He stands before me, hardhearted and arrogant. He is an especially tall adversary, six foot four inches. The unsentimental tone of his deep voice and the silver-gray color that has so naturally intertwined with his raven-black hair grant him the same leader's distinction that he brings to his role as the CEO of a major cable corporation that oversees pristine and influential offices in New York, Chicago, Boston, Philadelphia, Los Angeles, and Honolulu. I know first-hand. I have occasionally visited two or three of those offices, careful always to place myself with Miss Harrison or Mrs. Macgregor or Miss Flanagan, my father's most essential, no-nonsense secretaries. Once, while vacationing in Hawaii with my mother, who is an actress, and her entourage of agents and publicists, I even surveyed my father's corporate boardroom that is located on the twenty-fourth flour of one of the tallest buildings in Honolulu. No meeting was in session on that morning. But I did observe the gleaming, well-polished surface of the impressive, long table in that room and the rich leather upholstery of the chairs that were waiting with precise uniformity on each side of the table to serve the commander of the room and his regiment of ambitious officers. On that occasion, my father was not present. Nevertheless, I heard in the deepest corner of my imagination, his harsh, grating voice delivering his militant litany of directives to those same ambitious executives. Here, in this luxurious hospital suite within Blue Ridge Medical Center two years after my visit to that Honolulu boardroom, I hear the same grating voice spewing forth its harshness and its advisory message.

"Bear up. Bear up," my father tells me, delivering his words as though they belong to a carefully crafted memo that he is sending to one of his junior executives. "The faint-of-heart never won any battles worth mentioning."

I resent his lecturing. I dislike his impatience. I detest his insinuation that I am a weak-willed daughter who requires his fatherly counsel. A prisoner of these twelve long weeks of convalescence in a hospital environment, I *am* struggling with hopelessness and depression. I have endured surgeries on my legs, arms, and shoulder that have slowly healed. I have soldiered through the recurring headaches from the concussion to the left side of my head. I have struggled through the ragged breathing that has been the aftermath of a collapsed lung. I have tolerated the pain from my life-threatening injuries. I have accepted my losses. With tight-lipped determination, I have been making the hard journey to my recovery. Though I have tried to conceal my wretchedness, though I have often brought a smile to my conversations with my parents, though I have insisted more than a few times that I have accepted all the bleak things that have happened to me, my father sees through me. He detects the fault line in my armor, the crevice in my rock-like toughness. Nevertheless, with the willful insolence that has returned to me since the accident, I push aside his impatience and his insinuation.

"Don't worry about me," I answer him. "I'm no crybaby. Stuff happens. Life kicks you around. You kick back."

"Now you sound like a Hayworth," he says, imagining that his arrogant words have worked as a fuse to spark my dormant courage.

"Of course she does," my mother says.

She stands next to my father, carefully assessing my emotional state and the slow process of my healing.

"It's not every girl who can come through the ordeal into which you've been thrown. Just think of it. You'll be out of this place in a couple of weeks. You'll get your real life back."

For this hospital visit, my mother has allowed herself a stylized, informal look. Her perfectly coiffed blonde hair is pulled neatly back to make a coil at the nape of her neck. She is wearing a black high-neck sweater; black cropped, cigarette trousers; and black ballet pumps. She has removed her camel Batwing-style trench coat and with her signature, elegant poise placed it across one of the visitors' chairs a few feet away from the bed in which I am sitting up. I am not in the mood to hear her pep talks. They are part of her artifice, the carefully designed image that she has fashioned to represent the ideal woman she believes she has become. This contrived ideal is her brand. It reflects her unfailing ability to adapt to the latest fad, the current newspeak, and the most influential trend. She is, after all, Shawna Hayworth, the actress known for her glamour and her versatility. She has starred in popular musicals on New York stages and in equally successful dramatic films with global appeal. In this moment she has made a special effort to visit me here in the private rehabilitation wing of the hospital. She has summoned precise words and maternal intonations to convince me that I am making a complete recovery from the accident that grievously injured me and that has locked Tyler Danforth inside a coma. Because she wants to intensify the message that she is bringing to me, she finds new words to reinforce her belief that, as if she were a fairy godmother waving a magic wand in one of her films, she can send my sorrow scattering. She can show me the way out of my nightmare.

"Your father and I are going to help you get your life back," she says, without perceiving the anguish that will not leave me. "When you are well, we'll spend time with you in Palm Beach and on the French Riviera. We'll ski in Lausanne and paraglide in Brazil. We're going to do everything we can to make you happy."

My father comes into it again.

"Put a smile on your face," he tells me. "Even if you are feeling miserable and convinced that you've reached the lowest point in your life, don't let anyone else know. A true Hayworth never apologizes and never asks for pity. Apologies are signs of weakness. So are appeals for pity. Both are forms of begging."

"You needn't worry," I fire back at him, insolent even in my despair and defeat. "I won't disgrace the Hayworth name. I'll be as hardhearted and as calculating as the most rotten of the Hayworths."

My father glares at me in the same moment that he notices the flares of rebellion that have pushed my words forward. Then, because possibly he recognizes in my angry words a measure of his own capacity for insolence and rebellion, he breaks into harsh and grating laughter. His laugh has no merriment or affection. It is simply his wary appreciation of my self-possession, my aptitude for fighting back at my adversaries, my inclination for using words as if they were sharp blades.

"Whatever you do," he says, "make certain you win. Everything else is unimportant."

"A very wise policy, Rachel," my mother tells me. "Apply it to your life and you'll always find a reason to be happy."

"What happens if you lose someone that you love? How do you find a reason to be happy then?"

My mother does not like my questions. She does not like any sign of my anguish. Always, she grows impatient with what she has called my "emotional neediness." She is impatient now and hurries to set me straight.

"You move on to the next chapter," she says. "You don't look back. What's done is finished. What's happened cannot be called back. You have to accept the way things are. You can't let your feelings get in the way of your moving forward."

My brow creases. My anger rises. I cannot accept my mother's words.

"Do you really believe what you are saying? Do you actually think that an uncaring disregard of the past can make you happy? Do you always find it easy to forget the persons who have brought something special into your life, the ones who have died or who have gone far away?"

"Of course I do," my mother answers me. "I trust my instincts. I'm a survivor. I always find my way out of the darkness."

"Then you have never really loved."

All this while, my father has stood still, calibrating the emotional charge of my heated exchange with my mother. Now, my accusing my mother of never having loved anyone intensifies his interest.

"Of course I have loved," my mother exclaims. "But in my own way. Not in your way. Not with neurotic dependency or with the subtly tyrannical obsession that makes a prisoner of the beloved."

"I've never made a prisoner of Tyler!" I shout at her. "I've never prevented him from living the life that he wants."

My father comes back into it.

"If that's true," he says, "then you must know that it is time to let him go. It's time to move on without him to a new chapter in your life."

"With him!" I say. "Only with him. As long as he is alive, and forever after that."

Displeased by my stubbornness and my misplaced loyalty, my mother has more to say.

"Your Tyler is not coming back," she says. "He's been in a coma for three months. You know what the doctors have told his parents. He has made very little progress in these many weeks. They are doing all that they can to bring him back. But the odds are against him."

That my mother is unfeeling does not surprise me. That she taunts me with her negative thoughts while I am trapped here in a hospital makes her dislike of me even more hurtful.

"Tyler *will* come back to me," I say as tears fill my eyes. "I know he will. I know it."

"Maybe he will," my father says. "Maybe he won't. But don't depend on it. Don't make him the only measure of your future happiness. Don't lean on anybody. Be tough. Be like your brothers. Don't let your emotions mess you up."

"I am not my brothers," I tell him, "and I have no plans of becoming like them."

"You could do worse, honey," he says. "There's no woman better than the one who thinks like a man."

My father's words do not surprise me. For a long time, his contempt of me and his blunt dismissal of my thoughts and my actions have shown me that he never wanted a daughter. He has reveled in the rearing of his sons—my two brothers who are several years older than I. They have not been able to escape his influence even though they are living away from him. On most days, they are pleased to be anchored to that influence. Kendall, an honor student at Yale University Law School, is preparing to join our father's corporation. John, who is also aiming for a top spot in the corporation, is studying international law at The University of London. His future also belongs to our father. While they were living at home, our father treated my brothers as though they were recruits in an officer-training program and he was their drill instructor. They recognized no option except to become like him.

Now, a few years older and far more cynical, they are intolerant of any signs of weakness in the people around them. They are particularly hard on their male peers, befriending only men who are as strong and as confident as they are. Their interest in women is only sensual. They prefer nightclub girls who are used to being manhandled and are willing to trade their self-respect for diamonds, a fashionable wardrobe, and an upscale apartment. Eventually, when they marry, my brothers may choose career women who are like our mother—tough-minded, unsentimental, and ambitious. The wives they choose will know how to help them increase the fortunes they have inherited from our father and our mother.

Brainwashed, my brothers actually enjoy being our father's protégés. They even resemble him—tall, dark-haired, and good-looking. Some journalists, aware of my brothers' success on hockey rinks and in boxing rings and informed about their high academic rank, have predicted that they will equal and even exceed our father's success in the global business scene. These same journalists, ignoring our father's toxic masculinity, have called him a brilliant dealmaker in corporate boardrooms around the globe. With goals acquired from our father's instruction and with the same driving courage, my brothers have often joined him in his adventurous lifestyle. With him, they have hunted lions in the jungles of Africa. They have battled whales in the Galapagos Islands. They have raced Toyota Hybrids with other big leaguers in Le Mans Endurance Championships. They have piloted his Cessna Skycatcher across the skies of New York, Boston, Chicago, Los Angeles, and Montreal. In so many important ways, my brothers have become fully indoctrinated sons of our father.

In years to come, after their university days, they will always be seeking ruthless victories over business rivals, new and ingenious deals that spawn bigger profits, and exciting, global adventures that might dispel their occasional doubts about the lives they have made for themselves.

Whether flashes of truth subvert the lies that they now tell themselves about our father, I cannot say. I perceive, though, that they refuse to regard him as a man corrupted by false values. Most of the time, they tell themselves that he is the prototype of the man that they want to become.

Only one journalist wrote an accurate news article about my father. In that honest appraisal, this journalist spoke of the privileged life into which my father was born. He mentioned the wealth that my father, Randolph Hayworth, had inherited from the immense fortunes of other Hayworths. He evaluated the success that he had achieved because of his education at the best private schools and universities and because of his first-hand knowledge of the business world. This journalist severely criticized my father's lack of empathy toward most of his employees and his failure to pay them substantial wages and benefits. He analyzed some possible causes of my father's greed and his self-centeredness. With specific details drawn from my father's history, this journalist suggested that Randolph Hayworth always wanted more of everything. He was used to riding roughshod over his competitors. He was known to bully his adversaries. On several occasions, he expressed his displeasure with those indigent citizens who couldn't find a way to move up the ladder or discover an escape hatch from poverty and malnutrition or reinvent themselves by acquiring marketable skills. Yet his corporation was doing very little to improve the lot of the average worker.

Having noted all these shortcomings, this award-winning journalist called my father a sleeping prince—an entitled man who, despite having been born into one of the wealthiest families in the United States, has not yet wakened to the higher morality that makes an individual truly human. Randolph Hayworth is, this famous journalist asserted, a selfish man who disdains the disenfranchised poor and struggling middle-class workers. He is an arrogant leader who denies his hard-working employees first-rate health benefits and adequate pensions. He is a tyrant of industry whose immense power reflects the wide division that exists between the haves and the have-nots.

This stern journalist, judgmental yet fair, predicted that my brothers —"Randolph Hayworth's ambitious sons who have been ruthlessly programmed by their father"— will in time become his richly rewarded henchmen, glorified wingmen, duplicate versions of his sleeping prince status.

Now, in this moment here in my hospital room when I confront my heartless parents, there flashes through my troubled mind all these scenes from the past. I know my parents well. They want me to be like them. They prefer that

I enter each day searching for the newest, glamorous thrills; discovering the latest fashions; preparing for a top-flight career in banking or law or real estate; and learning the wiliest strategies for making hundreds of millions of dollars. They are planning to do everything they can to dissuade me from my loyalty to Tyler, whom they regard as a dying boy with no future at all. It is this disturbing thought which rouses my anger to a new pitch of fury. My parents' belief that I could ever abandon Tyler or even forget him tells me everything that I need to know about them. My father's assertion that I should think like a man, and my mother's silent acquiescence to that assertion, goad my fury to an even higher pitch. Tense and bitter and sorrowful—and all at the same time—I lash out at them.

"You've never loved anyone the way that I love Tyler," I say, my voice at first tremulous with anger and low-pitched. "You couldn't have loved like that, or you wouldn't be telling me to forget the only boy that I will ever love."

With an uncaring shrug and matter-of-fact words, my father dismisses my angry remarks.

"You're too young to know what real love is," he says. "Maybe a boy your age knows. Most savvy boys are tuned in to the hard facts of life. They know that adolescent love is temporary. It never lasts and it's not worth much."

"It's not that way at all," I insist. "Not for everyone my age. Some of us do know what real love is. Some of us are even willing to die for it."

"Nonsense," he says. "Anybody willing to die for love is really screwed up. Your mother and I know that. We live on the realistic level. Too bad you're not like us. You're just a fantasist who acts like a silly girl hampered by wishful thinking."

Now my mother joins in, her arched eyebrows signifying her displeasure and her ingrained *hauteur*—her overbearing pride and her sense of herself as belonging to a social class higher and more important than nearly everyone else's.

"Don't ruin things for yourself, my girl," she tells me. "Do not make yourself a prisoner of your feelings. Your father is setting you straight. You need to be tough with yourself. You need to think the way a successful man thinks. That's the only way you will count for something. That's the only way a woman can move up to the top. That's the best way a woman can beat down any man who wants to deprive her of her rightful place or who wants to steal her chances to make a fortune. Think the way a man does. Forget these sentimental notions. Romance is a temporary illusion. When the first thrills wear away, you always have to deal with the harshness of the world. There will always be lovers who betray you, friends who disappoint you, and adversaries who use every low trick they can to ruin you. Think like a man and climb to the top like a woman who has claimed her fair share of the world."

With no hesitation at all, I fire abrasive words back at her.

"I'll think like myself," I say, my voice still firmly controlled yet seething with hatred of all that she and my father are saying. "I'll do things my way and win everything that's important to me."

"Do things your way?" my father scoffs. "What has that ever got you except a bad reputation and a mess of trouble? You got yourself expelled from Brooks School, one of the best private schools in this country, because you did things your way. Now you have to settle for a run-of-the-mill public school."

"Blue Ridge High School is not run-of-the-mill," I answer him. "It's one of the best public schools in this country. It's on every list of the ten best public high schools."

My father hurries past my remark, intent on reviewing for my discomfort all my past offenses.

"You guzzled *your way* through bourbon, vodka, and whiskey at all your wild parties. You experimented with marijuana and cocaine, and you would have moved on to heroin if the police hadn't stopped you. You and your hoodlum boyfriends were crazy rebels and a disgrace to your families. Even in this period when you've tried to turn things around for yourself, you got yourself into a nearly fatal car crash. You've always been trouble for your mother and me. I suppose it's too late now to expect anything else from you."

My temper flares out of control. I raise my voice now in protest.

"Tyler did not cause that car crash," I say, quick to defend the boy that I love. "I didn't do anything wrong by attending the dance with him. He didn't do anything wrong. Besides, he's a better person than I am. He's helped me to change my life. He's shown me how to make amends for my past wrongdoing. He's brought me hope. He's convinced me that, if I try really hard, I can make the world a little better."

"He's brought you bad luck," my father says.

"Tyler Danforth is finished," my mother declares. "Only a miracle could bring him back. Don't be the fool who thinks that you are that miracle. You're in this thing way over your head. You always have been. Be sensible for a change. Do the smart thing. Turn away from Tyler and move on."

Now I lose control. I begin screaming as I jump out of my bed—stumble more than jump. Fury has overtaken me, scattering my frayed patience and smashing apart the promise I made to myself to remain docile and subdued.

"I've already told you how I feel! Over and over, at every one of your visits here, I've told you! Tyler is the only person who makes this world real to me. I'll never move away from him. Never! Never!"

I rush toward my father and begin punching his strong right arm and shoulder. Still weak from my many surgeries and the aftermath of pneumonia, I make an ineffectual opponent. My punches are more like closed-fist slaps. Their impact upon my father is far more psychological than physical. This is the first time that I have raised my hand against him. I go on screaming and crying at the same time, astonished by my act of rebellion and instantly fearful that, after this show of defiance, this blunt assault, I may never repair my broken bond with my father. I am only vaguely aware that, without much effort, my father has pinioned my arms and hands to my sides and, with my mother's assistance, brought me back to my sick bed.

"You've never loved me," I say to him and to my mother as my head sinks into the soft folds of my pillow. "You've never been on my side."

Miss Pearson, an efficient and kindhearted nurse, rushes into the room. Apparently, she has heard the screaming commotion. I notice the purity of her white hair, the wrinkled traceries of age upon her calm features, and the nearly concealed look of concern upon those same features. I imagine that she is dismayed because I am upset. She is well aware of the long, painful journey I have made toward recovery. But my journey is not over. My recovery is tenuous and ongoing. With gentle efficiency, she coaxes me to accept a sleeping pill.

"There, there, Rachel" she says with her quiet tone of encouragement. "You've pushed yourself too hard. You'll feel better after you've had a nap."

The pill quickly takes effect, but not before I see my father and my mother observing me with ambivalent interest.

My father stares at me with tightlipped disdain. Anger and bitterness take hold of his sullen features and, almost imperceptibly, merge with the newborn regret and sadness that he tries hard to suppress. He turns away from my bed now, as though he cannot bear to look upon me. I am, after all, a conspicuous disappointment that calls into question his belief that he is an ideal father. He moves toward my mother and gently places his big hand upon her right shoulder. They are in collusion with each other. He whispers words to her that I cannot hear. Whatever those words mean, they bring to the blue eyes within her sculpted features an approving glance upon him and upon her lips the hint of a consenting smile. For an instant, she looks back at me with pity rather than love. I am the burden from whom she intends to escape. Then, as though she is trying to determine how far away I have traveled from being an acceptable daughter, she gazes upon me with piercing inquiry. How long she gazes upon me, I cannot say. The sleeping pill takes complete possession of my senses. Weariness draws me into its folds. Only vaguely am I aware that my father and my mother are no longer standing there. It is as if Miss Pearson or the sleeping pill or my own secret wish has, with magical powers, made them disappear.

CHAPTER THREE
A VISITOR FROM THE PAST

The days are swiftly passing, their precise similarity and their methodical schedules blurring the subtle differences that keep them separate and distinctive. My parents are once again in New York, busy with their thriving careers and with the glamorous parties that they host in their penthouse on Sutton Place. They have left me in the care of the team of doctors and nurses who have been guiding me back to good health, here at Blue Ridge Medical Center. Doctor Andrew Bronson, with snow-white hair, cragged features, and a reserved yet paternal manner, continues to offer me his expert care, and Miss Janet Pearson, my first-rate nurse, goes on comforting me through my blue spells. Mrs. Emily Hathaway, who is my physical therapist, and Doctor Hannah Morrison, who is my clinical psychologist, have also been my essential caregivers. All these wonderful, hospital people want me to get well. They want me to recover the self that I have lost, if that is possible.

Please do not imagine that I am locked into a prison here at Blue Ridge Medical Center, or that my private rooms condemn me to solitary confinement. True, I cannot altogether escape the claustrophobic feeling that the cream-white walls and laminate sliding doors are closing in upon me, sealing me inside a tomb-like existence. Not even my beige, tufted sleigh bed with its scrolled headboard and footboard and its walnut solidity appeases my melancholy. Nor do the other carefully appointed furnishings convince me that I am living in a home-like setting: not the gleaming floors and oriental throw rugs; not the warm walnut-finished dresser with its twelve drawers and scrolling pulls; not the tall, beige wood wardrobe armoire with my pretty dresses and casual slacks; not the night tables flanking my bed and containing a pitcher of spring water and a book of Emily Dickinson's poems; not the two wingback chairs with saturated peacock color and tapered almond-finished, Brazilian parawood legs; not the vivid canvases adorning the walls with images of a calm sea at sunrise, a summer forest filled with noonday light and lush greenery, and the delighted face of a teenage girl—titian-haired and willowy—standing on a walker's path within a flower park, surrounded by rows upon rows of wind-caressed yellow, red, pink, lavender, and cream-white tulips. Not any of these luxurious possessions solace me.

This glamorous hospital suite may satisfy my parents' insistence that their daughter must live in a grand style even when she is confined to a hospital. Always conscious of their upper-class status and of the favorable impression they leave with their equally wealthy friends, my parents regard this luxury hospital suite as an emblem of their immense success and a public statement of their privileged rank. But the suite, even with its plush amenities, does not satisfy me. I am not at home. I am not at rest. I am cast adrift, unmoored from the girl that I used to know—confident and vibrant and life-loving Rachel Hayworth. Weary of my hospital confinement and yearning to be home, I bristle at the day-to-day sight of this room and at the familiar sight of the discreetly plush adjoining room in which my parents usually visit me.

But I am for the most part acutely aware that my hospital team is doing all that it can to rescue me not only from my serious injuries, but also from my home problems and from my mind-battering depression. My team helps me to regain the full strength of my young body. Each member of the team works to allay my fear that I have lost my true bearings, the inner compass that could help me to chart a successful life journey. My primary care physician and my tried-and-true psychologist monitor my physical and emotional wellbeing. A social worker and a registered nurse are part of a therapeutic community presence.

Now that I have made some progress in my recovery, my team allows me to interrelate with other patients, both young and old. I know only their first names. I also know some of the happy sparks and a few of the dark passages of their lives. I can tell you about fragments of their stories, the shards and broken pieces of their troubled histories. There is Abigail, the fifteen-year-old, red-haired girl whose boyfriend eloped with her older sister. There is Craig, the rugged, seventeen-year-old athlete whose father, a prominent lawyer, beat him up and turned him out of the house when he found out that he was gay. There is Myra, the thirty-five-year-old champagne blonde who lost her modeling career and her philandering husband in the same month. There is Gordon, the fifty-four-year-old commercial airline pilot whose trouble-haunted face and ashen complexion suggest that in a special way the life force within him—the will to live and be happy—has died. He is traumatized and guilt-ridden because the plane that he was piloting two years ago crashed and killed forty-nine passengers. There is Brian, the seventy-two-year-old oncologist, as tall as he is gaunt, whose medical expertise saved many patients grievously ill with cancer, though he could not save his dying wife from the pancreatic cancer that consumed her life.

Sometimes, I share with these troubled residents of Blue Ridge Medical Center my memories of the happy experiences and the mind-bruising disappointments that have made me the person that I am right now. Gradually, I have become genuinely interested in what they have to say. On some days, we believe that we have sighted a light flaring its signal from out of the maelstrom of darkness within ourselves, a luminous promise that we might one day find our way out of our nightmares. In those hours, we share—breezily or haltingly or remorsefully—the tentative meanings of our lives, or at least the complicated messages that our actions have often conveyed to the most important people in our lives and sometimes to passing acquaintances. We chat in the comforting expanse of the medical center's community living room, its cream-white walls instantly brightening the atmosphere, and its bucolic canvases and richly upholstered furniture bringing further solace to our senses.

We are not allowed to use any phones or even desktop computers. Nor are we permitted to write letters or send cards to our relatives and friends. But the Blue Ridge medical staff welcomes our befriending the patients whose mutual suffering may invite our pity and our empathy. Most of all, we need to befriend ourselves even as we admit the errors that we have made, the opportunities that we have missed, and the negative, self-defeating attitudes that hamper our progress.

"You need to build from within yourself," Doctor Bronson explains to me in one of our private meetings.

I regard him as a substitute father as well as my primary care physician.

"You need to examine who you have been and who you want to be," he says. "Learn to be self-aware and independent. Rely upon yourself first of all even when you invite the influences of other people."

In her counseling sessions with me, my other essential doctor—Doctor Morrison, my life-affirming psychologist—has echoed those words.

I know why Doctor Bronson and Doctor Morrison have used those rescuing words. I understand that those words are also a warning. They carry signals or alarms the way that a meteorologist sends predictions of storm dangers and trouble. Doctor Bronson and Doctor Morrison know about my love for Tyler. They regard the intensity of that love as both admirable and troublesome. They perceive it as an obsession that may heave up my life and rob me of my sanity, if I allow that love to make me its prisoner.

They want to protect me, but they cannot do so. I can never abandon or forget the boy I love—his larger-than-life presence, the magnificent physicality that defines his every move, and the authentic promise of his extraordinary life.

They have not yet allowed me to see Tyler, trapped inside a deep sleep from which he may never awaken. He lies sleeping here in Blue Ridge Medical Center, but not in the east wing where I am assigned. He lies in the secluded west wing of the hospital. When I will be allowed to see him, I cannot say.

I wait, searching for the miracle that will save him. I search my own capacity for bringing good fortune to the unlucky and for breathing new life into an athlete's body that lies very still and that, I imagine, appears ghostlike and otherworldly.

Today, a week after my unhappy meeting with my parents, the morning hours are testing my stamina. Though I struggle to hide it, weariness is overtaking me. Mrs.

Hathaway is pushing me harder than usual on this sun-radiant morning. Because I am no longer wearing a leg cast or a boot, she expects more of me. She wants me to achieve a stronger control of my mobility. In these early hours when she is challenging me to do the exercises that she believes I can do if I really push myself, the mid-January sun keeps spreading its glow upon the floor-to-ceiling panoramic, tempered glass window inside the hospital wing that contains the gym. The sunglow sharpens my senses. It quickens my confidence. It feeds my assurance that I can do all that Mrs. Hathaway requires of me. Twenty-four years old, she is an emblem of excellent health and physical prowess. Her pixie, titian haircut; turned-up nose; and smooth complexion enhance her self-possession and her natural congeniality. Her well-honed skills and her long, lithe body make her a proficient teacher and trainer. Her protective manner makes her an encouraging therapist.

At times, whenever I need to confide in someone because I cannot hold back my anxiety about the bad things that have happened to Tyler and to me, Mrs. Hathaway approaches me as if she were my older sister. She is a good listener. Sometimes I regard her as my second counselor, even though she is more easy-going than Doctor Morrison and more outwardly nurturing. Mrs. Hathaway is sensitive without being sentimental. She is matter of fact without being blunt. She is knowledgeable without acting superior. On those occasions when I have told her my fears, expressed my doubts about my future, and lamented my wrongdoing, she has listened to me with genuine concern. Yet the brightness of her studious glance tells me that she believes in my best capacities. She is rooting for me.

"You can do it, Rachel," she tells me whenever my hope or my energy seems to flag. "You have it in you to get back what you've lost."

How? I ask myself when, alone in my hospital room, I struggle to devise a rescue plan. How do I find my way back now that I am lost?

Earlier today, I asked Mrs. Hathaway this same question: "How do I find my way back?"

"You keep moving on," she answered me. "You keep moving forward."

So, here I am, caught inside a wilderness not entirely of my own making, trapped inside a nightmare that with spiraling velocity sometimes rises out of my memory, rendering vivid and alive the surly faces from my past and the unhappy, destructive scenes. Nor does my recurring nightmare belong only to my past. It has overtaken this present time as well. My parents and my brothers have become strangers, and the boy I love is slowly vanishing. Though doctors, nurses, and therapists are offering me their expert care through many hours of the day, there are the hours of sleepless nights that I have to endure alone. I am a sixteen-year-old girl who is trying to learn all over again how to be brave. Tight-lipped and determined, I am beginning once more to summon the wilder courage that has often acted as my sentry whenever I confront tense situations or unrelenting adversaries. Slowly, with cautious maneuvering of willful choices and chance happenings, I move forward into the unknown, into the darkness, into my private nightmare.

Through most of today's morning hours, Mrs. Hathaway guides me through walking and knee-bending exercises that strengthen my left leg and through swimming sessions that revive the ease of my swift movements in the moderately heated hospital pool. Not only on this morning, but also on so many other mornings, I have been striving more than ever before to regain my agility. I am almost there. I have nearly attained my goal. Now I do walk with a natural gait. I swim with long and supple strokes, my feet and legs accepting the pressure of the pool waters that are constantly in swirling motion. I have made such progress that my daily sessions with Mrs. Hathaway will be coming to an end. For the time being, I will be seeing her twice a month. I shall miss our exercise sessions and her wise counsel.

I have also freed myself from my throbbing headaches. I have gone past the painful aftermath of my concussion.

The progress I have made is reason enough to be cheerful, at least most of the time. Yet the news that Doctor Andrew Bronson, my primary physician, and Doctor Hannah Morrison, my equally helpful counselor, are allowing a friend from my past to visit me today here in this pristine hospital setting gives me an even greater reason to be cheerful. The visitor is unexpected and seems like a special gift. Until today, my doctors have not allowed anyone except my parents to visit me. Both Doctor Bronson and Doctor Morrison suggest that I receive my guest in the comfortable visitors' room that adjoins the secluded room to which only my parents as well as my doctors and the staff that assists them have been allowed to confer with me.

My visitor, a lean male with rugged shoulders and soldierly gait, enters the room covered by sunlight. So bright is the afternoon sun as its rays come streaming through the panoramic window, that I do not at first recognize his identity. He stands at five foot, eleven inches, the full height of him suffused by an eerie radiance that instantly makes mystery his accidental ally. But only for a moment does he conceal himself inside this winter light. As he walks forward with precisely measured steps that emphasize his strong will and self-command, he moves apart from the sunlight. I see his oblong, ashen face with its rounded corners and a broad forehead that is similar in size to its cheekbones and jawline. I notice, too, his sandy-colored hair and his brown-eyed, inquiring gaze. Now I recognize him. Now, in this very instant when my heart leaps with surprise and apprehension, I know that he is Theo Ryan, a boy who not so long ago played at being in love with me and joined me in a few misbegotten adventures that eventually landed him in a rehabilitation center.

I suppress my surprise. I tamp down my ambivalence, my confusion, and—yes—my bitter sorrow. I focus, instead, upon the minor and transparent details that suggest but do not reveal Theo's mind and soul.

On this New England, January afternoon, Theo is wearing a navy-blue parka in a rugged mountaineering design. I see the rubberized buttons and guess at the hidden zipper that also fastens the jacket. I glance at the faux fur-trimmed hood, the inset ribbed cuffs, and the drawstring attached to the waist. At Theo's neck, a cobalt-blue flannel shirt shows some of its color, because Theo has not zipped the top part of his jacket. I glimpse, too, the navy jeans and the mid-cut, ginger-brown leather hiking boots with their water-and-stain-resistant suede trim and their metal, D-ring lace-up closure.

Only after I have studied the surface emblems of Theo's appearance am I aware that a tall red-haired man with broad shoulders, burly physique, and large hands is hovering behind him. Even in the sun-misted hallway, he appears to be an assured, thirty-five-year-old man and a formidable presence. Beneath his open black trench coat, he is wearing black hospital scrubs. His shirt has a classic high-neck collar, and his form-fitting trousers are made of the same stain-resistant, twill fabric. In his black athletic shoes, he stands as a soldierly presence—a reliable guardian figure. I guess at once that he is a male nurse. Later, I will learn that his name is Connor Adams. Seeing him there with Theo, I tell myself that Theo has never left the rehab center. But I have no time to imagine a more complicated scenario, because Miss Pearson comes into my view. Apparently, she has guided this male nurse and Theo toward this visitors' room in which I sit waiting. She is too surprised by Theo to take note of my wary regard of Connor or of my nervous anticipation. Also apparently and with a graceful signal of her hand beyond my seeing, she invited Theo to enter the room. Only then did Connor, the conscientious male nurse, step away from Theo and wait like a disciplined sentry in the private hallway that overlooks this artfully decorated room.

With its soft blue walls and sunlit, panoramic window, the room serves as a place for greeting friends and family while we sit in richly upholstered wing chairs with their Honduran mahogany stability and with their beige velvet upholstery, tufted backrest, and padded armrests. On some occasions, though not today, my visitors and I may sit at the long, mahogany table behind the Louis XV sofa that shares the center of the room with an Aubusson carpet and with the primary light blueness of the carpet and its ancillary colors: cream, brown, green, red, and tan. There, at the table, we may confer about cautiously pleasant subjects while a tuxedoed wait staff serves us imported teas, angel food cupcakes, scones, bread pudding, and fresh fruit.

I notice all the details of this private visitors' room as my stay against confusion. At the same time, I finger the gold Rolex on my wrist. I adjust the pleats in my slacks. I touch the gold, heart-shaped pin upon the lapel of my jacket. I wait until my fast-beating heart finds its ordinary rhythms. Only then am I ready to receive this unexpected visitor whose presence intrigues and alarms me.

Kindhearted Miss Pearson walks behind Theo. Always my nurse-efficient protector, she is observing my reaction to the surprise and the tension that Theo's appearance has brought to this room. She does not want this visit to upset me. She is, I imagine, skeptical about my doctors' allowing Theo Ryan, a problematic friend from my past, to come back into my life in this desolate period when everything has gone wrong for me.

"I've brought a friend to see you," she says as she approaches the sofa in which I am seated, with its turquoise abundance of a down comforter and the galaxy of quilted, poly-filled shams—a medley of red, russet, forest green, silver, teal, and porcelain blue.

She searches my face to calculate the degree of my tension while, pensive and withdrawn, I lean against the colorful pillows as though they are my ballast against confusion, the anchor that moors me to a safe harbor.

Theo waits, while the stillness in the room hovers around us—a studious calm insinuating its influence upon this awkward and disconcerting moment.

This stillness quickly works its powers. I break free of my reluctance. I toss aside my resentment. I discard my hesitation. I find the words that it is necessary for me to speak.

"It's all right, Miss Pearson," I say, choosing the words that signal my acceptance of this moment that is unfolding about me and enfolding my guest, as well. "Theo is a friend. I'm eager to hear what he has to say."

Miss Pearson smiles. She is pleased that I welcome this visitor.

"Good," she says. "Then I'll leave you two to catch up on things."

She guides Theo to a chair a few feet across from me. Then she leaves quickly, the sheen of her white hair glowing in the sunlight that fills the room and her upright posture and brisk pace aligning themselves with practical goals and effective skills.

Alone with Theo now, I take a moment to contemplate the words that I want to say to him. Weeks before the car crash that skewered my hope and my happiness, Theo was struggling through his own hard journey. Because my doctors would not allow any of my school friends or even my relatives to visit me here in Blue Ridge Medical Center, I had lost track of Theo. Whatever was happening to him in these three months of my hospital seclusion, I had no way of knowing. Now, with quickened interest and inside the flash and sting of familiar unease, my memory scans the days and weeks and months of our impulsive and exciting friendship—its liberating adventures, its furious rebellions, and its self-defeating aftermath. But my thoughts scatter amidst my nervousness. I cannot discover quickly enough the specific and bracing words that will tell Theo exactly how I feel about his walking back into my life.

So Theo is the first to speak.

"I've been worried about you," he begins, his voice husky with genuine feeling. "Ever since I heard about the car crash, I've wanted to come to you. But your doctors kept me away."

"You are here now," I tell him, "and that's what matters."

"I wanted to see you so that I could be certain that you really are getting well. But I need to see you for so many other reasons."

He pauses, studying anew my reaction to this promise of an explanation for his being here.

Pensive and interested, I coax him to say more.

"Well, don't keep me in suspense," I say, careful to bring a lighthearted lift to my words. "Tell me why you've come to see me."

The words hurry out of him now. His searching eyes and forthright manner grant him a newly born maturity, an earned gravity that makes him appear older than his sixteen years.

"I've come to ask you to forgive me," he says. "I'm sorry for last year, when I made a mess of your life. I'm sorry for pulling you down with me. I'm sorry about the drugs and about the trouble with the police."

"That's all in the past," I answer him. "Leave it back there. Just forget it."

He frowns, his furrowed brow a sign of his anxiety and of the sadness that will not leave him.

"Some things should never be forgotten," he says. "That messy year is one of them."

"Not all of it was messy. There were many days when we did everything right."

"You are kind to say so," he says, while the sadness of a suddenly grownup male still holds his features taut. "You were always the kind one."

"Don't give me too much credit," I tell him, resisting his praise as too generous, and resisting, too, his willingness to carry the full load of mistakes that we made.

Perverse and impulsive in spite of my own anguish, I send my bitterness scattering, at least for the moment.

"I was as wild and as self-concerned as you were," I insist. "I have plenty of regrets about last year. But in that same year I learned a lot about life, and I had a terrific time."

He falls silent again while with his searching gaze he tries to fathom my acceptance of everything that happened to us during a time that seems so far away and yet, even now in my lonely hours, feels mind-bruising and disturbing.

His quickened gaze still upon me, he once again breaks away from his silence and asks the questions that are goading his curiosity and his disbelief.

"Did you really have a good time?" he asks me, a familiar cynical grin touching his lips for a moment or two. "Or are you saying so just to make me feel good?"

"We had a good time," I say. "You and I. Together. And more often than you care to remember."

A grin takes hold of him again, though not emphatic enough to dispel the sorrow and regret that he wears with a disciplined bearing, as if he were a seasoned cadet. Misfortune has pummeled his brashness and his arrogance. I see it in his haunted eyes. I notice it in the militant and wary posture and the clenched fists that keep at bay whatever imaginary adversaries might try to thwart his stern efforts to make amends for his past mistakes. This is a different Theo Ryan from the wild adolescent whose presence seemed absolutely charismatic—a force field of daring adventures, a magnetic human being drawing to himself impressionable followers. This Theo who is seated opposite me in my secluded visitors' room, is very different, indeed. He is navigating his own personal hell. I try to recall the news that I had heard about his misfortune and the reason that he spent time in a hospital. Before I can retrieve that memory, though, Theo offers me that saddened grin and a tentative willingness to perceive truth in my remark that he and I did share many enjoyable days in that year of self-punishing mistakes.

"I guess you're right," he says. "We did make an exciting time of it. We had terrific days together. Some of the time."

Then, as though his new perception of things is urging him to resist this easy praise of our year of adventures and misadventures, Theo qualifies his remarks.

"But there were so many things that were wrong about last year. *I* was wrong. I was wrong for you and for so many other friends."

No sooner has Theo spoken these words, than the memory of that year comes swiftly back to me.

I recall some of the reasons why Theo and I were drawn to each other as friends. We come from similar, privileged backgrounds. Our home lives are troubled and make us feel abandoned. Our parents are far more interested in advancing their careers and in maintaining their celebrity status than they are in guiding us through the rough patches of our adolescence. At least my parents have stayed married, even though the love that they once felt for each other has bonded with frayed emotions, tattered responses, and superficial gestures.

Theo's story is similar to mine, yet different. Before our troubled year together, he had been an honor roll student at Blue Ridge High School. He was one of our school's top-notch swimmers, as well as an accomplished defensive player for our hockey team. Among Blue Ridge's many affluent sons, he was regarded as the boy who had everything. He rode a swift, chestnut-coated Arabian horse; he piloted a Blanik L-23 Glider; and he drove an Outerlimits SL 41 Speedboat. There was also the promise that, when he turned seventeen, he would be driving a sleek Porsche Taycan, and with a cousin named Derek who was an experienced aviator he was going to co-pilot a Cessna 206. By the time Theo was fourteen, his father owned four upscale apartment buildings, two shopping malls that include a total of forty-six stores, and five-star restaurants located within the mall. More recently, his father has expanded his real estate holdings and has increased his fortune.

Theo's home life was another adrenalin rush. Under his father's tutelage, he built a mid-size sailboat. This same, dynamic father persuaded a retired boxer to give him lessons that sharpened his self-assurance, toughened his already resilient body, and qualified him for a place on our school's boxing team. During the winter break from school and always with his thrill-seeking father, he hunted red-tail deer in Patagonia. In the spring, they fished for giant marlin in the Florida Everglades.

Then, suddenly in the middle of his freshman year and without any clues to help him prepare for the upheaval, his mother—a hedge fund manager based in New York—and his father got a divorce. After that, he rarely saw either of them. He lived in the care of his maternal grandparents, who also were absent from his life much of the time. Their travels to South America, Australia, and Europe kept them away for months at a time. During their absences, they left Theo in the care of a retired Army sergeant and his wife, who became his rigid and repressive guardians. Whenever Theo missed a curfew or protested the militant regimen enforced upon him or explored the wild side of things with rich school friends, this sergeant, whose name was Rory Cooper, revealed his savage nature. Each time that Theo committed what the sergeant perceived as an infraction of the rules he demanded that Theo follow, he challenged him to a boxing match in the gym that was located in the west wing of Theo's grandparents' fourteen-room home. At first, Theo was reluctant to use his boxing skills on a man who was twenty-five years older than he was. But Sergeant Cooper called him a coward, a spoiled Mister Somebody who wasn't a real man, a good-for-nothing who didn't know the first thing about self-defense.

"Try me," Theo snarled in the same moment that he delivered his own challenge to the sergeant.

In the gym, isolated from the housekeeper, the groundskeeper, and the cook who maintained the care of his grandparents' home even when they were away, Theo and the sergeant battled one another. Theo fought very hard. He landed solid punches on the sergeant's face, chin, and chest.

When he landed a punishing blow at the side of Sergeant Cooper's neck, the sergeant fell upon his knees, dizzy from the impact of Theo's powerful glove. But the fight wasn't over. The sergeant pushed himself out of his dizziness, pushed himself up, and landed fierce punches upon Theo's stomach, throat, and kidneys. Three rapid punches upon his jaw were enough to knock Theo out.

That was the first of the six boxing matches between them. Though these fights left Theo's face and body with purple welts, swollen lips and bleeding mouth, and bruised chest and chin, he refused to phone his parents and grandparents so that he could tell them about the sergeant's beating of him. Nor would he go to the police. To his friends, he attributed his bruises to a skiing accident, a motorcycle mishap, a fall from his bicycle, and a brutal turn as a winger in a hockey game. His tough-minded understanding of the way the world works enabled him to accept the painful aftermath of these bouts and endure his humiliation. Each time that the sergeant fought him in the boxing ring within the privacy of his grandparents' gym, Theo unleashed all of his battling powers and all of the hatred that he felt not only for the sergeant, but also for his own unhappy life. The sergeant never left the ring unscathed. He, too, carried the bruises and the bleeding that Theo's punches inflicted upon him.

For many months of his freshman year at Blue Ridge High School, Theo tolerated these brute-force encounters with Sergeant Cooper.

It was in this period that he befriended me. He often opened himself to me whenever I was on a break from Brooks School, the private school in North Andover, Massachusetts, where I had made a few loyal friends and always met the academic challenges. Sometimes, Theo told me his problems when he was driving me home from an auto race in which he had participated. More frequently, he revealed his troubles to me when we were sharing a secluded corner in a restaurant that looked out at the ocean.

One afternoon in the summer of that year, when we were having lunch at our favorite restaurant that looked out at chalk-white cliffs; blue-gray, soaring gulls; a man and a woman surfboarding the waves; and a boat whose sails were billowing in the wind—on *that* specific summer afternoon, Theo expressed in a new way some of the anger and sadness that were destroying his life.

"Bear with me," he said as he sat opposite me and, with his penetrating brown eyes, studied my reaction to his words. "Every time that we are alone together, I tell myself that I won't mention my problems to you. Yet I can't help myself. I always tell you everything. You are my lifeline. You are the girl who gives me a boost. You are the one friend who may save me."

He paused, still observing my response to his handsome, brooding face and to his earned, rugged manliness that was struggling to suppress his fury. There were no tears in the flash of his eyes or even a muffled sob at the cusp of his deep voice. In those days, tears and sobs were not Theo's style. Usually, he fought his inner furies with tight-lipped aloneness. He waged battle with his fears and his discouragement by working out at the gym or in the boxing ring. Revealing his uncertainty and his unhappiness so openly and with raw, accurate words showed me how much he respected and trusted me. Had we been lovers, he would probably have closed himself off from me. He would not have allowed himself to reveal any weakness. But on this afternoon, a few weeks before he began to fall in love with me, he regarded me as a loyal friend that he promised himself he was going to treat as a sister. He would keep his distance even when the sight of me in a swimsuit or a party dress or form-fitting denims roused him. My troubled life at home intensified his trust in me. He could talk openly to me and know that I would understand everything that he was telling me. I knew what he was going through. I was experiencing similar disappointments, doubts, and conflicts.

"My parents don't really care what happens to me," he said while distant, merry voices and the clink of martini glasses echoed in the capacious main room of that summer restaurant and while our scanning glances showed us well-groomed patrons and meticulous servers moving briskly to various booths and tables. "They've made my life a prison. They've foisted this madman sergeant upon me. If I don't get away from him, he'll end by killing me."

He stopped himself from saying other words that were stoking his anger. But only for a moment did he hold himself to that silence. Only for a moment did he resist blurting out the words that carried with them a heavy burden of imminent violence.

"Maybe, if I stay in that house, I'll kill him."

"Don't talk that way," I told him. "You have a wonderful life ahead of you. You have been doing all the right things. Stay cool. Stay levelheaded. Maybe it will help if you imagine that when you are at home you are in an Army camp. Pretend that you are in officer-training school and that you can succeed at any challenge that Sergeant Cooper throws out at you."

For a few moments, Theo pondered my words. He was about to summon new words that would tell me what he thought about my advice. But our server, a good-natured, middle-aged woman with a motherly manner and a gentle voice, was bringing our food to the table. So Theo retreated to the silence that harbors pent-up anguish and a bruised spirit. For a few minutes we ate our lunch without saying anything at all. In fact, we ate without enthusiasm, though the food was delicious. Theo merely picked at his steak and salad, and I ate only a portion of my soufflé.

Then, as though the thought had come to him in that very moment, Theo told me what he planned to do.

"Maybe you're right," he said. "I'll go a few more rounds with the sergeant. I'll pretend I'm in boot camp. I'll keep telling myself that I have a lot to lose if I do the wrong thing. There won't be any life for me if I kill him."

"I'm glad to hear you say these words," I told him, relieved that he was going to do the right thing. "I'm glad that you won't allow this mad sergeant to beat you down."

Hearing my words, he smiled at me. He appreciated my cheering him on. He recognized my empathy. He raised his glass of milk and signaled me to raise mine. We clicked our glasses as a pledge of loyalty to one another. As we drank the milk, we made a show of exuberance. We managed to laugh, and I became happy enough to make a lighthearted remark.

"We'll make the drinking of milk a sophisticated habit," I said. "We'll serve it at all of our parties."

"That's a promise," Theo said. "I'll persuade all my friends to take up the habit."

He was still smiling when he made another pledge.

"If things with the sergeant get too bad, I'm running away."

His words thrilled me even as they wakened new fears in me.

"Maybe you *will* run away," I said. "Maybe that's the best way to save yourself."

For a few more weeks, he did stay. Then, in October, when he had just begun his sophomore year at Blue Ridge High School and while I was continuing my studies at Brooks School, a hundred seventy-five miles away, Theo made a life-changing decision. Suddenly on a cloud-filled morning that seemed like all the other somber mornings that called him out of his uneasy sleep, so suddenly that months later in retrospect he wondered whether the suddenness was merely his consciousness wakening to a deeper awareness of what was happening on that morning, he ran away from the makeshift home that his self-centered parents and his equally selfish grandparents had devised for him.

I ran away with him.

Weary of his parents' self-centered indifference, his grandparents' self-deluded attempts to revive their lost youth, and the sergeant's sadistic treatment of him, Theo rebelled against all of these people who were thwarting his happiness. Together, with fake glee that masked our misery and our suicidal inclinations, we avenged ourselves against our parents and our guardians by breaking as many rules as possible. Heedless of the consequences that would eventually fall upon us, he took flight from Blue Ridge and I ran away from North Andover. Before the police began their search for us, we boarded the plane that brought us to Aruba. Theo had taken thirty thousand dollars from a biometric safe located behind a bookshelf in his bedroom.

His parents had allowed him to keep sixty thousand dollars inside his personal safe. They advised him to draw upon the money whenever he needed it. At the beginning of each month, they opened the safe to find out the amount of money he had spent. He had to account for every dollar that was missing. In this way, his parents closely monitored his use of the money and every investment he made with the advice of their broker. Each month became a test of his financial acumen and a proof of his responsibility or lack of it. Theo was also carrying a few of the more prestigious credit cards.

I had a similar safe in my bedroom. I withdrew twenty thousand dollars from the thirty thousand dollars my two sets of grandparents had given me for my fifteenth birthday. Our parents had their reasons for allowing us access to so much money. Conscious of their status within their competitive and mercenary social group, they wanted Theo and me to enter the wider world in style. They did not yet belong to the top one percent of the nation's wealthy, but they were paving a path in that direction.

"Ironic, isn't it," Theo remarked. "We have plenty of money, yet we are not happy. I suppose the money is good for something, though. With fistfuls of hundred-dollar bills, we can run away in style."

"Money will open doors for us," I said. "We both know that people with money always have an edge up."

"That, we do have," he said, while managing a smile that nearly concealed his bitterness. "Let's use it well."

Theo and I planned on putting our troubles behind us. We were determined to have a good time.

We did have a good time. There were days and days when happiness became our constant friend, our loyal advocate, and our soul-reviving champion. Freed of all the traps that our home life had set for us, Theo and I came alive again, for the first time in years. Every waking minute of every day filled us with a joy that quickened our senses even as it intensified our awareness during those moments when we were alone on a beach or in a gym or in our separate hotel rooms that the happiness we were experiencing was merely transitory. Our renovated lives gave us many gifts and granted us numerous pleasures. But these same lives had imprisoned us, had blocked our freedom, and had left us with ambivalent feelings about the luck that we had stolen when we escaped from the indifference of our families. This knowledge that our escape was temporary clouded our joy. Even when exhilaration nearly dispelled our uncertainty about the future, there lurked in the hidden corners of our awareness the blunt truth of our situation. One day very soon, we would have to go back to the hardened ambivalence of our families. Not yet legal adults, we were not free to choose the way we lived.

But we could choose the way we died. With that thought calling to us from way back inside the deepest corners of our mind, we navigated the temporary thrills of happiness and embraced all of its fervency without ever believing that happiness was our lasting friend. Happiness was a nebulous experience. It was as evanescent as a ghost and as wily in its promises as the most jaded, streetwise hucksters. There were times when happiness came to us as a gentle visitor, a circumspect acquaintance, and a secret ally inviting nobody's envy or malice. Those were times to cherish. There were the other times, though, when happiness wore a disguise to trick us into believing that our alliance with joy and laughter and solace would last forever. Those were times that crushed our spirit. Betrayed by our belief in a lasting happiness, Theo and I were ready to make a pact with Death.

But not yet. Not in those first days of our escape from the prison to which our parents had condemned us. Instead, we savored the temporary joys that happiness brought to us. Only in pensive and solitary moments did Theo and I remember that Death was waiting for us in a dark and invisible corner. One day not so far away, Death was going to call us to him.

In Aruba, we jet skied on mountainous waves that propelled us across new rims of peril, and in Acapulco we leaped from forty-five-foot cliffs into rugged, windswept ocean waters. Navigating still another danger while whitewater kayaking, we rode the unforgiving rapids of the James River in Virginia.

Later, in the sixth week of our escape from Blue Ridge and shortly after we got hooked on cocaine (and Theo on heroin) in England, we decided to throw ourselves out of existence. At a skydiving center in Reading, a university town about forty miles west of London, we carried out our suicide pact. We went skydiving from a Cessna 206 that was flying fourteen thousand feet at a speed of one hundred twenty miles per hour. After a sixty-second free fall, we did not deploy our parachutes and waited instead for the swift plummeting to earth through a five-minute drop that would bring us instant death. But we did not die that day. To our surprise and dismay, a computerized automatic device called a cybernetic parachute release system activated the parachute. On that afternoon, neither Theo nor I was relieved that Fate had spared our lives. We felt numb. We felt detached. We felt altogether alienated from the troubled home lives that we could escape only temporarily, unless we died. There was a part of us that loved life. There was a part of us that wanted to die. Willful and reckless, we were playing with Death, whether we were jet skiing, whitewater kayaking, cliff diving, or skydiving. We were gambling with Fate, goading Blind Chance. Yet in spite of the enormous risks we were taking during our escape from our families, we kept Death at bay.

Theo and I did not sleep together. Before we made our escape, I had set rules for our friendship. I did not care to have sex with any of the boys that I liked. I wasn't ready. There were too many complications in my life. Theo was disappointed, but he accepted my terms. There was, he believed, a chance that I might change my mind. Besides, without the complication of sex, we could focus on our adventures and on playing our game with Fate and Danger and Death.

We stayed away from Blue Ridge for nine weeks. In all that time, we ran free of the police and of detectives. Only later did we learn that our parents refused to cancel our credit cards or our access to our personal bank accounts, even though their lawyers and the chief of police believed that cutting off our funds would bring us home more quickly. On the contrary, our parents believed that we might fall into harm if we had no money to keep us in the safe places where people of our class vacationed. Instead, they decided to wait for our return. They were not especially alarmed by our rebellious absence. In fact, they were not particularly interested in the reasons that had compelled us to run away. They had their own, even more exciting lives to live. They had little time to notice our awkward and sometimes perilous passage into adulthood.

Only at the end of our sixth week away from home did we fall into trouble. It was in that sixth week, while we were in London, that Theo began hanging out with a group of university students who came from backgrounds as wealthy as our own and who were addicted to cocaine and heroin. Eager for their acceptance and angry because his parents were uninterested in his wellbeing, he joined these dissolute rebels in their bad habits. At first, he was drinking whiskey, bourbon, and scotch with them. Later, he turned to cocaine and cannabis and, at the end of his wild run, began mixing whiskey with heroin.

I, too, began experimenting with cocaine. For the twenty times I used it, I was glad to experience happiness that was so intense it seemed otherworldly. I went outside myself. I met my *doppelgänger* in every one of my drug-induced confrontations with my imagined self. The identities of my imagined self multiplied over and over again, whirling around me, spinning past me, gyrating and wheeling and coiling. They were my ghostly counterparts, my carbon copies, my look-alikes, and my mirror images. As if I were awake in a dream, I came face to face with my ideal self—a girl who was fifteen years old and who appeared to be radiantly happy. To make certain that I would continue to sight her Spirit-driven reality, I doubled my intake of cocaine. Twice a day, I eagerly snorted the white powder into my nose. Sometimes, I rubbed it onto my gums. Occasionally, Theo and I heated up the rock crystal and breathed the smoke into our lungs.

"I might go a few more rounds with Life if I have cocaine as my backup," Theo said, nearly delirious with the pleasure of hurrying out of ordinary experience. "I might almost find my life acceptable."

"We'll be fantasists together," I told him. "We'll be escape artists. We'll hang out and still find our way to a new beginning, as temporary as that may be."

Theo laughed a hollow laugh. It was a laugh that strained for boisterous delight. Its sound was guttural, gravelly, raspy, and finally despairing. It was a harsh laugh that edged its way to a muffled sob. The sob made me pause. Theo had never before given in to sobbing. Sobbing was not supposed to be in his DNA.

But apparently it was. Apparently, Theo's pent-up suffering was becoming too much for him to bear.

Once again, I tried to cheer him up, promising him escape and a new start.

"Don't you doubt it," I said, encouraging his hope without believing that hope would ever again visit us. "You'll get to that new beginning, and I'll be with you."

To my disingenuous remark, Theo said nothing. A familiar tension took hold of him. His entire body became very still, like the body of an imprisoned man who has accepted the inevitability of his imminent death. Though he was not yet sixteen, Theo no longer believed that he could save himself or that anyone else could save him.

That was the night the police raided the private club where Theo and I were drinking and drugging and dancing. The club, which was all Art Deco and upscale, catered to a moneyed clientele. The business corporation that ran the club did not mind looking the other way when rich, underage teens spent their money there. That was the night that we pledged to be each other's friend forever and, if the Fates allowed, to become each other's lover. We were sitting with three university couples that sent up a cheer for us because of our pledges of fidelity. They toasted us with Champagne. Some of them spiked theirs with heroin. Theo did. I spiked my drink with cocaine. We were feeling very happy.

That night, the police caught up with us.

My Aunt Deborah sent a team of detectives in search of me. She was my favorite relative, sensitive to my needs, aware of my disappointments, generous in her gifts, and helpful in every way that she could be. Even at the age of thirty-eight, she was the essence of beauty both natural and serene. Her auburn-red hair, coiled neatly at the nape of her neck; her friendly blue eyes; her bee-stung lips; and her smooth and youthful skin made her an ideal aunt. Happily married to a New York corporate lawyer, she was the loving mother of a ten-year old boy and a seven-year-old girl. Aunt Deborah had never approved of my parents' indifference toward me, but their lawyers prevented her from interfering with their rearing of me. Now, worried beyond measure because I had gone missing for so many weeks and even more alarmed when her friends told her that magazine and internet postings showed Theo and me caught up in the wilder night life in various locales, she commissioned a group of four detectives to search for Theo and me in the United States and in Europe.

The detective based in Europe spotted us as the rich, young Americans whose life-loving spirit and luxurious lifestyle had begun attracting the attention of fashion magazines and the interest of journalists who wrote about the young and privileged set. Theo and I had not objected to the photo shoots or the newspaper interviews that asked us about the clothes and shoes we enjoyed wearing, the foreign countries we had visited, and the activities that quickened our lives. Though we never spoke of it, there was, I think, a part of us that wanted to attract the attention of our parents and, at the same time, reinforce the message that we were quite capable of living enjoyably apart from them.

"What fun!" we exclaimed when, sitting in the hotel dining room and musing over the day's activities, we found reasons to laugh and to feel delighted by all that was happening around us and all that we were making happen.

"What a lark! What luck!" I told Theo, while my voice sounded as lighthearted as if I were singing the words.

"Enjoy it while you can," Theo said, already uneasy because our parents had allowed so many weeks to pass without sending their paid henchmen to pursue us.

At the start of our escape from our parents and from our Blue Ridge imprisonment, Theo and I understood that whatever solace we discovered in our run-away adventures would be merely temporary. Eventually, some adversary would appear to thwart our freedom.

When the adversary did show up, the scene played out differently from what we were anticipating. An American detective proved to be our adversary. He was a tall, muscular fellow in his mid-forties whose good looks were marred by a thick, red-tinged scar traveling a jagged line across the left side of his face. His name was Darren Burns, a former Army colonel who had led a team of commandos in the war raging inside Afghanistan.

This American detective, working with the London police, arrested Theo at our favorite nightclub. Theo was carrying two grams of heroin inside the pocket of his jacket. I was carrying cocaine and a needle for injecting it into my left arm.

"Game's up," Detective Burns told Theo when he came to our table that was crowded with six of our friends—three young couples who were as rich and as spoiled as we were. "You and your girlfriend will have to come with us."

These friends looked startled and then resentful when they saw Burns and two London cops standing at our table. By the time they heard Burns issue his first directive to Theo and me, our friends' anger was flaring its danger not only with frowns and verbal protests, but also with their clenched fists and blunt objects such as ashtrays, dinner plates and glasses, and even a lamp. Only when Josh Burton, a brawny Cambridge student who was one of our wilder friends, pulled out a snub-nose revolver did the taller of the two policemen fire a stun gun at the would-be assailant. The million volts pushed Josh and his sleekly upholstered chair backward. His body dropped out of the chair and landed, pain-contorted and sprawling, upon the high-gloss, laminate oak floor. Panic and retaliation overtook our friends, as well as Theo and me. Drug-addled and furious, we rushed upon the two policemen and the detective. The policemen beat us back with their billy clubs and pepper spray, and Detective Burns fired his revolver in the air and sent us scattering into various corners of the restaurant.

Josh Burton spent a week in a hospital. The rest of us spent that night in solitary cells within the city jail.

Aunt Deborah paid Theo's fine and mine. Her lawyers negotiated the release of our university friends after she paid their fines. But the court would not permit her to pay Josh's fine. Instead, the Burton family lawyers paid a heavy fine for Josh's brandishing a weapon in public and using it to threaten police officers. In the court trial that occurred a few weeks later, the judge sent Josh to a Yorkshire work farm for ninety days, placed him on probation for two years after he completed his sentence, arranged psychiatric and drug counseling for him, and revoked his gun license.

The consequences of that rancorous night did not end there. American authorities, including social workers, clinical psychologists, and substance abuse counselors, closed in on Theo and me. By this time, Theo was so heavily addicted to cocaine and heroin that he had to spend months in a Blue Ridge rehabilitation facility. I was expelled from Brooks School. After six weeks in a rehab facility different from the one where Theo was struggling through his recovery, I enrolled as a sophomore in Blue Ridge High School.

Right after we were arrested in London, I lost contact with Theo. I heard that, confined as he was to the rehab facility for four months, he had appeared to be making a solid recovery from his addiction. He returned home, but he did not return to Blue Ridge High School. Instead, his parents arranged for him to be home schooled. A month later, he ran away from home and fell once more into his heroin addiction. In that period, he nearly died from an overdose. When he returned to rehab, he was making an even stronger effort to conquer his addiction.

Now, in this visitors' room within my hospital suite nearly a year after our adventuring together, Theo is seated opposite me with straight-back posture and a military cadet's bearing. He has changed. No longer is he the free-spirited adolescent with a spark of danger in his eyes and in his athletic movements. He has lost his ruddy complexion and his carefree manner. Up close, he looks pale, gaunt, and sickly. He appears to be someone else, someone that only vaguely resembles the youth with the ruddy complexion and the assured manner. Nevertheless, there is new strength in his gauntness. There is in his steady gaze the pride and the resilience of a true fighter. He may be a ghost of the Theo Ryan whom I once knew well and who imagined he was in love with me. He may be a soul-scarred replica of the once-healthy athlete that I met not so long ago. But there is, I sense, something tremendous in the battle he is waging against all the inner demons that have been afflicting him.

For most of our time together, I had regarded him as a platonic friend whose life had fallen away from him. At the beginning of our friendship, I treated him as if he were the loyal brother I never had, a favorable contrast to the two brothers who have always worked against my best interests. Later, in the last weeks that Theo and I spent together, I began to regard him with more knowing eyes. I was beginning to fall in love with him. But something held me back from loving him completely. It was my pity for him. I pitied him for the hard life he was experiencing with the sadistic sergeant and with selfish and indifferent parents and grandparents. I connected to him because our troubled lives were so similar. Yet even at so inexperienced an age as fifteen, I understood that romantic love requires more than pity.

I loved Theo because, in spite of his self-defeating life choices, he was basically a decent human being. In fact, he was an extraordinary human being. He excelled not only in science and mathematics, but also in the humanities. He was a self-reliant athlete who brought excitement and expertise to hockey, baseball, and boxing. He was an outdoorsman, too. With his woodworking class at Blue Ridge High School, he had built log cabins in a picturesque, wooded area and in the strange and remote wilderness. With those same classmates, he built a boat that would enable them to fish for bass or trout in nearby lakes and streams. It was, I remember, the second boat that he built. In happier times, he'd built a sailboat with his father.

With his school friends, he hunted deer, turkeys, and rabbits that they donated to a community center that fed orphaned children. In a state-owned farm field and with other athletic friends, he planted corn, wheat, and potatoes that his school gave to the families that were working hard in low-paying jobs. He proved to himself and to his team that he was a first-rate farmer. He carried within himself a pioneer spirit. One day he might become a research scientist or a corporate executive or an Air Force pilot. No matter what kind of life he chose to live, Theo would always be witty and passionate and honest. He possessed all of those qualities then. He was a prince among his peers.

But I was not in love with him.

Now, as he sits by me, I see that he is the prince that I could not save. Nor could he save me then. The thought saddens me. Yet only for a moment does this thought hold me in its spell. Theo is speaking to me, and his new words quicken my attention. These words tell me that, even though many hard months have separated us, he has come here after all to save me now.

"I heard what happened to you and Tyler," he says, his voice matter-of-fact yet filled with compassion. "For what it's worth, I want to tell you not to despair. Don't give up. Find the courage to go on with your life. Find the courage to believe that Tyler will eventually be a part of that life."

The gravity of his words astonishes me. I am grateful and humbled because he believes in me.

"I'm trying," I tell him. "I'm trying to believe that some miracle will bring Tyler back to me. But, before he met me, I was self-centered and rebellious. I broke so many rules. I've made so many mistakes. Now I'm paying for them. I don't know whether I'm good enough to save Tyler. Maybe I'm the girl who brought him bad luck."

"Don't talk like that. Keep remembering that Tyler saw goodness in you. He believed in you."

His words amaze me. They prod me forward.

"Yes, he *did* believe in me. I'd nearly forgotten that."

"We all make mistakes," he tells me. "I've made many mistakes. Now I am paying for them. But I am not going to allow those mistakes to swallow me up. I'm fighting to stay alive. I'm fighting to change things for the better. You must fight, too. Don't give in. Don't give up. Work to make things better for yourself and for all the people you disappointed."

"*You* are brave," I tell him. "You have such courage. And you have goodness in you. I sense it. I know that it's there.

That's what you're all about. You've always had courage, even when you've made mistakes. You've always been fighting hard to win your battles."

Before Theo can respond to my words, Connor Adams steps into the room. As Theo's guardian and nurse, he imparts subdued yet firm authority.

"It's time for us to be heading back, Theo," he says. "You have a couple of doctors waiting to see you."

His words do not upset Theo. On the contrary, Theo accepts the words as appropriate and helpful. He turns to face Connor and addresses him in a courteous and concise manner.

"I need only a minute, Connor."

Connor observes him carefully, recognizes his courtesy, and nods his approval.

Theo turns back to me.

"You have courage, too," he says. "It's always been a part of you. Use it to your advantage. Use it to save your life. Use it to bring Tyler back."

Once again, I make a promise to myself and to Theo.

"I'll try," I say. "I'll try to be as brave as I can be."

Now Miss Pearson comes into the room. For the last minute or so, she had waited at the door with Connor as Theo concluded his visit with me. She heard the closing part of our conversation. She is pleased that Theo's visit has brought a smile to my lips and a new glow to my eyes.

"You must come again, Theo," she says. "You are good company for Rachel."

"I will come," Theo tells her. "That's a promise."

He and Connor leave quickly. Then Miss Pearson guides me away from my private visitors' room and back to the privacy of my more secluded room and the comfort of my bed. There, she takes my temperature and reads my pulse.

"Your pulse is racing," she says. "And why not? A good friend has been visiting you."

"Yes," I answer her, while my ambivalent feelings for Theo fall away from me. So does my bitterness. With new eyes, I see the bravery that is in him. I become acquainted once more with the honesty that has compelled him to confront all the wrong things he has done and to recognize some of the right things. "Theo is a very good friend."

Before she leaves my room, Miss Pearson rearranges my pillows and the down comforter covering my bed. But she does not, with the press of a wall switch, turn the laminated glass of my window from clear to frosted white. She knows that I savor every beam of sunlight that brightens my room. The light that radiates its glowing warmth solaces me as I begin the journey into my afternoon nap.

At the cusp of sleep, I recall the vivid reality of Theo's visit. I see his wary yet determined face. I hear his husky voice. I sense the wild courage that pushed him away from his hospital bed to deliver the message that might salvage my tattered hope and save my life. Whether Theo's message will help me to waken Tyler from the nightmare he has entered, I do not know. What I do know is this: I must find my way out of my own nightmare before I can bring Tyler back. Uncertain and remorseful, I have to do battle with my own demons before I try to save the only boy I can ever love.

CHAPTER FOUR
TYLER'S PARENTS

"You can do it, Rachel," Mrs. Danforth tells me. "You can call Tyler back. You can bring him into life again."

Amanda Danforth and her husband, Clive, are sitting opposite me in the visitors' room of my hospital suite. Their being here makes the day not only eventful, but also extraordinary. They are, after all, Tyler's parents. Their affection and their concern for me are genuine because of their innate goodness and because I love Tyler. He is not their only son, but he is the one who has chosen to remain with them in Blue Ridge while he completes his high school years. Their other son, Tristan, whom I have never met and whom they love as much as they love Tyler, attends a military cadet school in Texas. Before his accident, Tyler had always lived with his parents. His abrupt absence from their lives has become for them a grievous and unbearable loss.

Three days have passed since Theo's visit. In those three days, without anticipating this visit from Mr. and Mrs. Danforth, my troubled mind has been searching for a rescue plan through which I might guide Tyler into new days and months and years of happiness. But my memory of our time together gives back no clues for prodding him out of his sleep. I cannot find the precise words that will waken him.

Nor can I guess at the specific moment when, hearing my call, he opens his blue, haunted eyes and—while observing my beseeching face—answers me with husky, surprise-laden tones.

What will Tyler say?

"I'm here, Rachel. I've always been here. I've been waiting for you for such a long time."

I wonder.

No, it is better I do not guess at that specific moment. Yet I yearn to be inside such a moment, elated and buoyant once again because Tyler has come back to me. Right now, he is a sleeping prince who, paradoxically, has already wakened to a higher morality. In all that he has said and in everything that he has done, Tyler has offered the world his best capacities. To me and to those who know him well, he represents the ideal human being. He personifies the qualities about which Saint Thomas Aquinas, a thirteenth-century Italian philosopher and priest, wrote in his treatise about the virtues of charity and right-minded thinking. In that learned document, Aquinas explains the three things that are necessary if we are to liberate ourselves from the power of sin. We must know what we ought to believe. We must know what we ought to desire. We must know what we ought to do.

Even at the age of fifteen when I first met him, Tyler believed in all the right things. He desired to make achievements that would benefit other people. He did the things that needed to be done. The world is less bright because he is not awake in it. My world will always be dark until he returns to me, alert and buoyant and healthy.

But how—how can I bring Tyler back to me? The question goads my tension and my melancholy. Answerless and dismayed, I have been sinking deeper and deeper into my waking nightmare. Thirteen weeks have passed since the car crash—thirteen weeks of living without seeing Tyler and of enduring long hours and days and weeks without him. No longer have I with uncompromised assurance been telling myself that I am the special person whom the Fates or my compassionate and forgiving angels have chosen to bring Tyler back into life again. I am a blemished creature. I have not led a virtuous life.

Though Tyler Danforth lifted me out of the abyss into which I had fallen, I have never considered myself good enough to walk alongside him into the journey that looms unknown and mysterious before us. Yet I want so much to be his partner in that journey. I have been striving with every fiber of my being to become good enough for him. My good deeds and my quiet acts of charity and compassion toward others do not outweigh my past infractions, my willful flouting of decorum, and my rebellious betrayal of the loyal school friends and kindhearted relatives who had placed their trust in me.

Tough-minded and realistic, I have stopped believing that I am the girl who can bring Tyler into life again, as vigorous and self-possessed as he had always been before the car crash.

Then suddenly, here in this sun-blanched visitors' room within my hospital suite—right here this afternoon and quite suddenly—Tyler's mother is urging me forward. With words made plausible by her honest conviction, she guides me to the hope that I had nearly abandoned, despite my love for Tyler and despite Theo Ryan's wise, encouraging words. She reacquaints me with the possibility that lately I have been suppressing deep down in the secret corners of my mind. If I follow all the rules, if—without hesitating or flinching—I leap into the unknown, I may after all be able to rescue Tyler.

"You must do it," Mrs. Danforth says. "You must do everything you can to save Tyler. You owe it to him and to yourself."

She sits opposite me at the long, mahogany table behind the Louis XV sofa that shares the center of the room with an Aubusson carpet while she observes me with gentle, brown-eyed gaze and motherly concern. Her brown hair, fair-skinned oval face, full lips, and slim figure grant her a natural beauty even at the age of forty-one. With her elegant self-possession, she is wearing a double-breasted camel coat with an A-line silhouette, notched lapels, long sleeves, a six-button front, and side flap pockets. No sooner had she entered the room and begun speaking to me, than she removed her coat and placed it with casual flair upon the nearby sofa. Today, she brings a well-modulated sophistication to her casual style: long-sleeve black silk blouse, gray cashmere slacks, and black suede pumps. She wears her clothes with a natural authority. I admire her look. I admire even more her warmhearted and compassionate nature.

She is waiting for my response. She wants to hear the impassioned words that tell her I will do all that I can to bring Tyler back to us, conscious and dynamic and prevailing. But I can't find those words. I can make no claim to the heroism that she expects of me. I hesitate. I falter. I fumble for words that might satisfy her expectation that I am that special person who can rouse Tyler from his sleep.

"I'll try," I tell her. "I'll do anything I can to bring Tyler back to us."

Now Tyler's father, Clive Danforth, comes into it. He has been standing at the threshold of the room, quietly studying my response to the request that his wife has made of me. He steps forward to greet me, his manly gait brushing past the radiant sunlight that until this moment has suffused his tall and lean presence. After he greets me with a friendly "hello," he takes a seat beside his wife, comfortably mated with her and sharing in this moment her expectation that I am the girl who is going to rescue his son. Mr. Danforth's prematurely white hair makes a fitting crown for a face with strong, rugged features: blue-eyed, honest glance; straight-edged nose; full, symmetrical lips. He is an older version of

Tyler. His aging handsomeness is a prediction of Tyler's future, middle-aged appearance if Tyler wakens and lives once again the happy life that he began sixteen years ago.

For this visit, Mr. Danforth matches his wife's casual style. He is wearing a gray cashmere coat that, upon entering the room, he quickly removes and then places next to his wife's coat on the sofa. He brings a comfortable ease to his navy cashmere jacket; cobalt blue, tieless shirt; and gray trousers. When he hears me promise to do anything I can to bring Tyler back to all of us, he smiles with an honest appreciation.

"Of course, you will try," he says while echoing my remark. "Of course you will do anything you can to bring Tyler back to us. My wife and I know that. We also know how much you and Tyler mean to each other."

"That's why we've come to you today," Mrs. Danforth explains. "We have reason to believe that you will bring Tyler back to us."

"We have a very strong reason to believe that you will be Tyler's rescuer," Mr. Danforth says.

"Why?" I ask them. "Why do you imagine that I can save Tyler? I wouldn't know where to begin. I have no special powers."

"Oh, but you do, Rachel," Mrs. Danforth says. "You most certainly do. Tyler was profoundly in love with you. My husband and I know that as a certainty that no one can deny. After his accident, after he went away from us deep inside the sleep that locks him inside a coma, we read his journal. It told us so much about him—all the things that we already knew and all the wonderful things that we had not even imagined."

"We hesitated before reading his journal," Mr. Danforth says. "We felt we were intruding upon his privacy. Our only excuse is that we were thinking that we'd lost him forever. Two months had passed, and he was still trapped inside his sleep. We wanted him back. His journal was a way to be with him again. As we read his words, we could hear him speaking to us. Everything about him came swiftly back to us—his compassion toward others, his loyalty to his teammates, his defense of the meek and the different, and his determination to surmount whatever obstacles that life placed in his way."

"He wrote so many lovely things about you," Mrs. Danforth says, her voice softer now, almost a whisper, as though she is confiding a secret to me. Her eyes become misty, and her lips tremble while she suppresses the cry of grief and longing for her son that sticks in her throat.

Noticing what I imagine to be a returning expression of her anguish, Mr. Danforth moves closer to his wife and with his big, protective hand gently pats her shoulder.

"Take it easy, honey," he says. "Just take it slow and easy."

"I'll do that," she answers him, her voice jagged now yet straining still to suppress the sadness that has come into her life as an unwanted and surprising visitor. "I'll take a deep breath, and I'll be myself again."

I wait, while silently observing the two of them. Too awed by Mrs. Danforth's sorrow and by Mr. Danforth's concern for her wellbeing, I lean into the soft velvet of the richly upholstered chair that in this moment brings me no comfort. The touch of the velvet upon my back is, nevertheless, my ballast against confusion, my stay against the return of my own despair.

Mrs. Danforth takes only a moment to modulate her emotions and to activate the confidence and the self-possession that are inscribed into her DNA. Now, as she speaks, she sounds forthright and hopeful.

"I'm so happy that Tyler met you and that he fell in love with you," she says. "In his journal, he calls you his soul mate, his inspiration, the love of his life, and the girl who makes him feel that he is being reborn every day that he is in your company."

Mr. Danforth tells me even more.

"In one of his journal entries, he calls you his lifeline. He writes that, whenever people or situations disappoint him, some of the spark that drives him to his success dies a little. His determination, energy, ambition, and optimism glow less brightly. Then he remembers you. He recalls the happiness you bring him simply by walking beside him in your day-to-day experiences and by sharing your dreams of a happy future together. You bring him joy. You revive his love of life."

Hearing her husband's words, Mrs. Danforth smiles once again. She is eager to draw me into their plan for saving Tyler. Her next words become a careful declaration as well as a warmhearted invitation.

"You are the one person who can bring Tyler back to us."

Their matter-of-fact words, uttered with a calm that suppresses the excitement they are feeling, mystify and then startle me. I measure the folly of their trust in me and plumb the depths of their wishful thinking. I hurry to defuse their expectations or, at least, to resist their optimism.

"I wouldn't know where to begin," I tell them. "I've never saved anyone's life before. Besides, I think that you are overestimating my influence upon Tyler."

"You can save someone now. You can save Tyler," Mr. Danforth says, while urging me forward. "Listen to what my wife has to say. She has more to tell you."

Mrs. Danforth extends her arms across the table. She takes my hands into her hands, her motherly disposition offering me genuine solace and a precise explanation of why she regards me as the girl who can save her son. She begins by asking me a question without requiring me to answer it, at least not right away.

"Do you believe that dreams can tell you what you must do if you want to make things better for yourself and for others? I'd never really thought about it until three weeks ago. That's when I first had the dream about you and Tyler. At the beginning, the message that it brought me seemed too mixed up with my wishful thinking and my unanswered prayers to warrant further contemplation or more serious reflection. But the dream keeps recurring. Night after night for three weeks, the same dream has come back to stir my curiosity and to excite my conviction that the dream is bringing me a message about you. The dream keeps telling me that you are the special girl who can save Tyler."

"I wish that were so," I say. "I wish that I could be that special girl who rescues Tyler. But I'm not certain that I can save even myself. I make no claim to having extraordinary powers."

"You'll never know unless you enter the adventure," Mr. Danforth says. "You owe it to yourself and to Tyler to find out whether you can save him."

The Danforths' belief in my influence over Tyler amazes me. They have always been kind to me, even during the hard six months in which Tyler was guiding me to a life-affirming path. But I never imagined that they saw me as a girl who belonged in Tyler's future. In this moment, when they are connecting me with their son's once-promising future, I do not want to cloud their hope or disappoint their expectations or undervalue their affection. Nor do I want to pretend that the scenario they have envisioned or the message that Mrs. Danforth's dream has brought them is plausible or realistic.

I make my way carefully.

"What did you see in your dream?" I ask Mrs. Danforth. "How am I a part if it?"

"I saw you standing by Tyler's hospital bed," she tells me. "You placed a kiss upon his lips. His eyelids fluttered, and then his eyes opened. His breathing became easy and natural. He caught sight of you and smiled. He held out his hands to touch you.

"'I heard you calling my name,' he said. 'I felt your kiss, and I heard your voice. I've come back because you called me to you.'"

I resist the promise of her words. I resent her too-easy encouragement. I push away the prediction that is bonded with foolish imagining and well-meaning prayers.

"That never happened," I say. "You know that I was never in that room with Tyler. I never kissed him. I never called to him."

"But you will be there," Mrs. Danforth says. "You will be in Tyler's room within this hour. You will call to him today and for many days afterwards, if necessary. You will kiss him. If you do the right things, he will answer you on one of those days. He will answer your call and your kiss."

Suddenly, Miss Pearson has taken a seat at the table. Mr. Danforth has courteously made a place for her so that this nurse who has been so nurturing and helpful can invite me to enter the plan that the Danforths have created for me. Just as suddenly, I imagine that Doctor Bronson and Doctor Morrison, the physician and the psychologist who with guardian care have been bringing me back to healthy days and new-born hope, have granted the Danforths' request that I visit their son in his room within the west wing of this hospital.

"You will have your wish come true today, Rachel," Miss Pearson says, her voice both mild and motherly. "You are at last going to visit Tyler."

My heart beats faster. My pulse quickens. My face blushes because of my excited anticipation.

"Is it really true?" I ask Miss Pearson. "Am I being allowed to see Tyler because all of you believe that my visit will make a difference?"

Cautious in her reply and humble, Miss Pearson sets me straight.

"We are not certain about what will happen during your first visit to Tyler," she says. "We are hoping for the best. Maybe the miracle that we've been praying for will happen right away. Maybe it will happen after you have made many visits to Tyler. Whatever the case, we want to believe that the miracle will happen."

"What if I don't believe in miracles? What happens then?"

For the fraction of a minute, Miss Pearson ponders my questions and, after that pausing, answers them with her inherent honesty and with her bracing moral authority.

"You will want to visit Tyler anyway," she says, "even without the expectation of miracles. And if the miracle does happen, if Tyler does waken to your call and your kiss, the miracle will seem that much more wonderful."

Hearing her words, Mr. and Mrs. Danforth smile in easy and grateful accord.

"There, Rachel," Mrs. Danforth says. "You have the plan set out before you. It won't be difficult to carry forward. Nor is it merely a madcap fantasy. Your doctors and your nurse approve of it. And my husband and I are also rooting for you to make the plan work. Rescuing Tyler is a real possibility."

I am still not ready to agree to her plan. I cling to my realistic view of things. I find new words to express my doubts.

"Tyler has been in a coma for thirteen weeks," I say. "It's unlikely that he will come back to us. Usually, if a comatose person doesn't revive after four weeks, the prognosis for his recovery is negative. I know. I've been reading about comas in medical journals. There *have* been times when a comatose person has emerged from a coma after many years. But, by then, many of them have lost their intellectual sharpness, and none of them has ever lived very long afterwards. Only a miracle could bring Tyler back as keen-minded and healthy as he was before the accident."

Mr. Danforth has more to say.

"My wife and I have read those medical journals, too. We know about everything that you have been telling us. We have also conferred with all the top brain surgeons. They have not been optimistic. As we go forward, we are going to be traveling in the dark. But miracles do happen."

Mrs. Danforth comes into it again.

"Because of Tyler's love, you are the one person who can call him into life again. You can be an essential part of that miracle."

Despite my promise to myself to stay bound to realistic expectations, I find my resolve shaken. The Danforths' absolute belief in the power of Tyler's love for me points me toward the path that I was ready to forsake. They are convinced that this path might lead me to Tyler. It might draw me into a miracle. I try to fight my doubts. I try to renegotiate with my willfulness. I wish I could believe as strongly as the Danforths and Theo believe. I wish I had their unconditional faith. I wish that I could greet each day with the hope that Tyler might very well come back to me during the late morning or in the middle of that afternoon. I used to greet the morning in that way. But lately I do not. Nevertheless, the steadfastness of the Danforths' belief during this visit has shaken my certainty that miracles do not exist.

"Maybe," I answer Mrs. Danforth without yielding my doubt. "Maybe miracles do occur sometimes. Let's see what happens."

With no further hesitation, we make our way to the lonely room in the west wing where Tyler goes on sleeping the long, relentless sleep that has overtaken him. Now I am especially pleased that early this morning, because I was expecting a visit from Tyler's parents, I took special care of my appearance. Miss Pearson helped me to dress in a gray tweed herringbone jacket, white silk blouse, navy skirt, and navy platform loafers, with their animal-print calf hair finish and leather lining. If in my visit to him I call Tyler awake, he will open his blue eyes and see me first of all. Despite my tension and the dismay that derives from my lack of strong faith in this plan to call Tyler out of his sleep, I feel a momentary exhilaration. Today I will see Tyler, even if my call does not awaken him. It is also one more day that I am free of my hospital rooms and grateful that I am walking with steady gait and regained assurance. I am ready to return to the unpredictable and hectic world outside this large and imposing medical center, even if my journey begins with this visit to Tyler's room within an adjoining wing of this hospital inside the same medical center that I shall soon be leaving.

Miss Pearson walks briskly beside me, confident that I can make this journey without her help, yet reluctant to withdraw her guardian care of me.

Mr. and Mrs. Danforth walk behind us, silent within what I imagine is their own exhilaration and eager to traverse the halls that will bring us to the wing where their son Tyler is sleeping the deep sleep of a youth who waits to be freed from his death-in-life trance.

We pass through the long, gleaming hall that leads us out of the privacy of my secluded rooms. Still in the east wing, we enter an adjoining hall that draws us into an array of rooms with laminated sliding doors that, having been opened, show us senior citizens—men as well as women—busy at their water-color canvases or immersed in the afternoon newscast of a cable television channel or enthralled by a game of chess with a neighboring patient or solaced by an afternoon nap.

A white-haired, loose-limbed physician peering at a clipboard of information looks up to observe us, waves a greeting, and passes by. Two young, female nurses carrying trays of prescribed capsules, packets of needles, and pitchers of spring water also pass by and offer us their friendly smiles.

We make a right turn onto another long, gleaming hall and quickly pass room after room with teenagers, each of them propped against colorful galaxies of pillows while they lie, solitary and logy, attached to leg or arm casts or while layers of thick bandages serve as helmets that protect their heads, healing from intricate surgeries. The stillness in these rooms makes this kaleidoscope of scenes eerie and melancholic.

Then, without a pause to consider these fleet impressions, we move—as if with sudden and extemporaneous passage—into the long, polished corridor that serves as a bridge between the east and west wings. We pass two rooms that show us tow-headed young men in their twenties learning to walk again, guided as they are by physical therapists who sport crew cuts and have big-boned, muscular physiques. I hear the husky chuckle of one of the tow-headed men, alert and lean and rangy, as he succeeds in maintaining his balance and his steady, forward motion.

We quicken our pace. We move as though we are gliding toward our destination. We see room after room hurrying by us. Middle-school boys and girls, healing from surgeries to their skulls, shoulders, arms, and legs, lie bedridden and medicated while male and female nurses check their pulses or hand them silver-tipped pills or observe them sipping refreshing spring water from paper cups with hospital straws. We pass five of these rooms, bonded as they are with the quiet of convalescence and the discipline of a hospital regimen.

Now, as quickly as we entered, we move out of this long, undulating corridor that serves as a bridge between two wings. Without a word to declare our exhilaration or our tension, we arrive inside the west wing.

Suddenly, this journey to the west wing becomes for me both surreal and otherworldly. I seem to leave my body behind or apart from me. I feel displaced from the ordinary implications of my life. I am dislocated from familiar meanings and from too-casual interpretations of the reality that is unfolding around me. I do not forget that I am traversing this experience with Mr. and Mrs. Danforth and with Miss Pearson. Yet I feel completely alone and strangely abandoned. Despite their company, I am on my own. Whatever happens when I enter Room 1W depends on the words that I, and I alone, speak to Tyler. Though my love for him is true, though it is yoked to the most authentic emotions that I have ever felt for any human being, I am not worthy of him. My blemished past hovers about me. Saint Paul once wrote that our past is the body of death that we carry on our backs all through the days that are allotted to us, until we reach the grave. He spoke the truth. My young experience of life has already proven the accuracy of his words. My past is part of a personal history that I cannot in good conscience deny. It is a record of wrongful deeds and selfish motives. It is a burden that robs me of most of my hope.

Yet, even though my misbegotten deeds have confiscated most of my right to hope, I go on hoping. Tyler guided me back to hope. Unobtrusive in his helpfulness and inspired by an inner glow, he showed me how to earn back my right to hope. Even during these weeks when my world has turned into a wilderness of loss and dismay, I try to cling to my hope. I do not want to let Tyler down. I want his influence always to guide me. I need him more than ever, because my hope is wavering.

We reach Room 1 W.

Miss Pearson never leaves my side. She studies my every move, deciphering as much as she can the sudden hesitation in my gait, the straight-back tension of my posture, and my tight-lipped concentration upon the twenty-or-so footsteps that separate me from the immaculate hospital bed and from the youth who lies in that bed, sleeping a deep, deep sleep, locked as he is inside the sleep of the lost.

Mr. and Mrs. Danforth walk behind us. Without peering back at them, I sense that they, too, have cast their watchful eyes upon me. Silence holds us tightly to its mandates, while we make our way across the threshold of the room. Not even a whisper from any one of us disturbs the stillness. Even when Miss Pearson gently takes hold of my right hand and guides me toward the bed, there are no words that pass between us. Nor do the Danforths give voice to their fervent wish that I hurry to Tyler's side and call him awake. They are waiting for me to speak. I know. I guess at their anticipation. They are hoping that, when I speak, Tyler will hear me. Slowly, as though he is emerging from a faraway dream, he will open his eyes and notice me first of all, standing at the side of his bed. He will smile a beaming smile and, pleased beyond measure, he will laugh a happy laugh.

Elated as well as astonished, I will call his name again.

"Tyler," I will say. "You've come back. You've really come back."

"Yes," he will answer. "I am back, and I promise that I will never go away again."

So, as I move toward the bed, I imagine this wished-for scene that the Danforths are anchoring to their anticipation.

But neither they, nor I can escape this specific moment that draws us into its here-and-now reality.

Whether Tyler will answer my call, I dare not guess. Uncertain of my influence upon him, I move closer to the bed until I find myself standing by his pillowed head and by his long athletic body that wears a light-blue hospital coat that opens at the sides to accommodate his physician's examinations. His body is leaner than I remember and is partly concealed beneath a cobalt-blue blanket that matches the color of the sheets and the pillow coverings. On the opposite side of the bed, intravenous tubes extend from a chrome-plated stand with four prongs holding the bags that feed fluids and medicine into Tyler' body. EKG electrodes are taped to his chest to monitor the rhythms of his heart. These electrodes or conductive pads are, in turn, connected to an electrocardiograph with integrated display and keyboard that sit on a wheeled cart only a few feet from where I am standing. Hooked up as he is to these life-monitoring tubes, bags, and electrodes, Tyler seems mysterious and even mystical, perhaps a young god from some ancient myth being prepared for rebirth or a sleeping prince upon whom some sinister Fate has cast a spell.

Standing near him, I notice first the glow of sunlight streaming across Tyler's pale yet still-handsome face. I notice, too, his muscular arms and his big hands, their powers dormant now and waiting to be called into new, prodigious living and tremendous, everyday adventures. Vivid light and more intense light after that radiate from the panoramic window and imbue Tyler's entire body with a heavenly glow. His very essence, his specific presence as Tyler Danforth, merges with the light and twines itself around saintly implications.

Enthralled and uncertain, I stand in silence before him. Then, pushing myself past my apprehension, I try to speak his name. But the sound of my voice, imprisoned as it is by my fear and my inadequacy, stays trapped in my throat.

Now good Miss Pearson coaxes me forward.

"It's time, Rachel," she whispers to me. "Do the thing that you were meant to do. Do the thing that you were born for."

I turn and see and hear Mr. and Mrs. Danforth with tense and supplicating voices also urging me to do this thing that I was born for.

"Do it," Mrs. Danforth says. "Call him back to us."

"Don't hold it in," Mr. Danforth tells me. "Give it all you've got."

Now, with no further hesitation, I gaze upon Tyler's perfect face and call out the words that may save him.

"Tyler, it's me. It's Rachel. I miss you so much. I love you and need you. Please come back to me. Please wake up. Be the person you have always been. Be well again."

But Tyler does not stir. Nor does he open his eyes or offer me a smile. He does not assure me that he has come back for good. Instead, he remains enclosed within his eerie stillness—a haunted youth, a prisoner of Random Chance, and the pawn of a malevolent destiny.

The stillness in the room envelops all of us, cryptic and ominous. I falter beneath its weight, trapped firmly inside its tentacles. I am aware that I have failed. My voice is not pure enough to waken Tyler. My imperfections corrupt the sound of my speech and even the timbre or resonance of each word.

I hesitate once more. I want to call to Tyler again, yet I do not want to fail. I say no more.

Gentle yet firm, Miss Pearson urges me forward.

"Call him again," she says. "Let Tyler know that you are waiting for him to come back to you."

Mrs. Danforth, as gentle as Miss Pearson, entreats me as well.

"Tyler has journeyed far away from us," she says. "Keep that in mind. You may have to call him many times and for many days or weeks. But call him you must. One day he may hear you. One day he may come back to us."

I try again. I push away my hesitation and my prideful self-awareness. I think only of Tyler.

"Please come back to us, Tyler. Come back to everyone here who loves you. Come back to me, who loves you in a very special way. We are rooting for you, Tyler. We are waiting to greet you. We are praying for you to be the Tyler Danforth that we have always known and respected and loved."

My words leave echoes inside the otherwise silent room that like us—like Mr. and Mrs. Danforth and Miss Pearson and me—waits for the miracle to happen. But even now, even after my second calling to him, Tyler does not come back to us.

I stand forlorn and defeated once more by the harsh fate that keeps Tyler a prisoner.

Miss Pearson, no less sorrow-laden than I, pats my shoulder and offers encouraging words as she guides me away from Tyler's bed.

"You must not lose hope, Rachel," she says. "Maybe next time Tyler will come back to all of us."

The Danforths, too, with heads bowed low, also move apart from Tyler as he goes on sleeping the long, long sleep that keeps him from returning to us.

Mr. Danforth, harnessing tightly the grief that might throw him off his proper path, finds other words to comfort me.

"You did a good job," he tells me. "You did your best. You did everything that you could do."

Mrs. Danforth holds back her tears. Her voice trembles now as she, too, offers words meant to solace me.

"If anyone can bring him back to us, you are that person," she says. "Tyler loves you very much."

Her kind words, and those of Mr. Danforth and Miss Pearson, subdue the sting of my failure. But, as well meant as they are, those words cannot revive my self-assurance or my belief that the same Fate that holds Tyler its prisoner will hear my words and, with pity roused and with haphazard decisiveness, will send Tyler back to me.

Days pass after that visit and after many other visits to Tyler. But, whether I am there in his room with the Danforths and Miss Pearson or only with Miss Pearson or with his surgeon, my calling to Tyler does not bring him back. The stillness that seems so eerie to my senses is the only answer that the room with its immaculate neatness grants me.

Now, in the middle of the restless nights that draw me uneasily inside my own sleep, something extraordinary happens—something astonishing and supernatural and vividly present. Something—a faraway sound; a husky, familiar voice; an elated calling to me—wakens me. A gleaming light as intense as summer sunshine or Heaven-sent radiance touches my eyelids, saturates my sleeping senses, and draws me into a startled awakening.

Tyler is in the room with me.

There, by the panoramic window—right *there*, standing within the sheen of his own brightness, Tyler waves to me. He is wearing the same navy suit that had enhanced his romantic appearance on the night of our school's autumn dance. His tall ruggedness, his soldierly posture, his sparkling eyes and gleaming smile—all these signs of his confident identity show me that he has returned to me. Tyler Danforth is *there*, standing by the panoramic window alive and well and beckoning to me.

He calls to me. He urges me forward.

"I'm right here, Rachel," he says, his words a gravelly, intimate sound that is meant for me alone. "All you have to do is to reach out to me. Stretch your right arm outward. Reach. Take hold of my hand. I'm here, not more than twenty feet from where you are, there in your hospital bed. But *you* must come to me. You must reach out and try your luck. Reach out and you may draw me back to you."

"I *will* reach out," I tell him, my voice clear and emphatic. "I will. I will."

I hurry from my bed and run across the room to the place where Tyler is standing by the window. Excited and overjoyed and a little apprehensive—and all at the same time, I reach out not with one arm but with two and with hands eager and open, intending to take hold of his hands, to embrace his ruggedness, and then to kiss him again and again.

But the moment that I find myself standing at the panoramic window, this very moment when my extended arms and reaching hands should be touching his warm arms and hands and when my lips should be caressing and kissing his lips, Tyler disappears. The dazzling light that suffused his body vanishes as quickly. Only the light of the moon streams inward, covering as it does my dejected face and my motionless body. For a long time, I stand by the window, alone and dismayed and helpless.

Was Tyler ever really there? Or was the whole form of him, the face and body that was so palpable and intense—was that form merely a hallucination, a mirage or apparition springing from my troubled mind? I wonder, searching for clues that might yield an answer and struggling with doubts that assail me.

Whether my sighting of Tyler was an apparition spawned from a dream or a phantom foretelling his eventual return or a specter, a ghost, a fully embodied Spirit calling me to rescue him from the long, long sleep that is sometimes an ally of Death, I do not know.

What I do know is this: Tyler reappears for the next six nights. Always, he calls me out of my troubled sleep. Always, I hurry out of my bed. Always, with an encouraging smile and his beckoning hand, he draws me to him, standing as though he is really there by the moonlit window, vital and confident and thrilling.

"Keep me in your memory," he tells me. "Keep me alive in your thoughts. Reach out to me now. Always keep reaching out until I find my way to you."

Though I do reach out, though on every sighting of him I nearly touch him, he always vanishes from me.

I go on wondering whether my mind is playing tricks on me. On some mornings, right after dawn while I lie in my bed recollecting my sighting of Tyler on the preceding night, I tell myself that it is my yearning for him, my intense desire to be with him again, that has called forth his apparition, the mystic shadow and embodied spirit of him that waits for a call from me that he can hear and, hearing, recognize as the call of an honest and authentic rescuer. Always, he prods my belief in myself. Always, he expresses just as firmly his belief in me.

"I see goodness in you, Rachel," he tells me. "Go on perfecting your goodness. It is your goodness that will bring me back to you."

"I am not very good," I confess to him. "But I will try to be better. I will try hard. I want to be worthy of the word *goodness*. I want to be good enough to rescue you."

I speak these words on the last night that Tyler appears to me while I am here in the hospital.

I tell no one about Tyler's reappearing to me because I am not certain that he has really been here in my hospital room and because I do not want to alarm my doctors or my nurse or my therapists. I do not want to forfeit my imminent release from this hospital setting.

On the following morning, I am discharged from Blue Ridge Medical Center. I return to my parents' country home that overlooks a quiet lake and provides a nurturing and healthy environment. My parents stay away, busy with their thriving careers. But good Miss Pearson accompanies me to my home and expects to stay with me for several weeks. Mr. and Mrs. Collins will also be sharing the house with me. They are the well-qualified teachers who will be guiding me through a college-preparatory home schooling. From time to time, I expect to visit Doctor Bronson, Doctor Morrison, and Mrs. Hathaway in their offices so that they can go on monitoring my physical and emotional health. I long to see some of my school friends, too—the ones who are sensitive enough not to mention Tyler or the night of the car crash. But those visits will come later, after my parents have given their approval.

Twice a week, I visit Tyler at Blue Ridge Medical center. Always, his parents are there as well as Miss Pearson. During each of these visits, with a voice that is clear and precise and friendly, I call to Tyler.

"Come back, Tyler," I say. "Please try very hard to come back. Come back to me and to everyone else who loves you."

But never does Tyler stir. Never do his eyelids flicker or his arms and hands move. Never does he raise his head from the colorful pillows or lift his body from his bed.

At home, I move as though I am living in a dream that is chained to the inside of a nightmare. Clever at disguise, I smile when I am expected to do so. I even laugh a laugh that hides its melancholy. I wonder when Tyler will next appear to me as a living apparition or whether he will never again appear.

February and March arrive with the oppressive steadiness of hours and days and weeks of wild snowstorms, turbulent winds, near-freezing temperatures, and punishing loneliness. No longer does Tyler visit me. Instead, when the storms and the wind abate, I visit him in his hospital room. I call to him. I touch his warm hands. I kiss his warmer lips. But never do his eyes open to observe me. Never does his husky voice call out a greeting. He goes on sleeping his long, long, death-like sleep. Always, the stillness in the room binds itself to melancholy and to the grief that Mr. and Mrs. Danforth and I carefully suppress, so chary are we of disconcerting or alarming Tyler, who may hear every word that we speak and intuit every emotion that we are feeling.

I fall into a depression that with wily skillfulness I conceal from my caregivers.

I go on waiting.

Chapter Five

THE REAPPEARING

Breathless while striving always to maintain the stillness within my catlike agility, I make my way down the carpeted stairs, open the front door, and hurry from my home in the Alpine Hills section of Blue Ridge, Connecticut, with its white clapboard solidity and its twelve-room capaciousness.

I run across the green lawn that expands and slopes five hundred feet ahead of me and, guided by the modulated sheen of path lighting, look for the twelve red brick steps that will bring me down to the path at the edge of the private lake that borders the property. I run faster and faster, eager to reach my destination. Around my hastening motion swirl the momentary sight of evergreen hedges wearing red-leafed foliage; dainty shrubs of lantern blooms spring-wakening with large, bell-shaped flowers, their papery texture fiery-red, orange, yellow, and white; lilac trees alive with purple-blue, breeze-tossed colors; and golden robinia trees, their pendant sprays of white perfumed blossoms and fern-like leaves iridescent beneath the sheen of the moon that is lightly touching them. With kaleidoscopic swiftness, all of these colorful forms pass by me.

Or, rather, I pass them as I run my race across the lawn in search of the twelve brick steps.

Never, not even once, do I look back at my house, fearful that the watchers within it have detected my flight and are even now rushing to overtake me. Perhaps, it is not my fear of them that disquiets my senses. Perhaps, it is the fear that even as I run I am dreaming and that my desire to reach the edge of the lake will bring me only dismay. Quickly, I tell myself that I am not dreaming. The scene that is unfolding around me is real and happening in this very instant. I notice the specific height of the bushes, hedges, and trees as they fly past my seeing. I confirm the colors of the flowers and the caress of the breeze upon my face. This night is really unfolding around me. My race will bring me the reward that I seek. It will give me back the happiness that some misbegotten nightmare has stolen from me.

I run and run and run. I yearn with new, compelling intensity, to lose the grieving and bewildered girl that I have become.

Then, as abruptly as I began, I stop. I find the twelve brick steps and hurry downward.

I have run my race. I have reached my destination. I pause by the lake behind my home, parentless because my mother and father stay based in New York, busy with their famous careers. Then I make my way onto the jetty, the pier that stretches its thick, polymer-coated pinewood over the dark waters that glisten with sunset influences.

THE REAPPEARING

I have eluded the watchful gaze of Matt and Sandra Collins and their too solicitous monitoring of me during this rough patch in my life. I try not to resent them or to regard them as intruders. Their instruction, their companionship, and their guardian care are exemplary. Matt has earned a doctorate in English Literature from Johns Hopkins University. Sandra is a graduate of Yale University, with a double major that includes mathematics and science. In their late twenties, they treat me with genuine affection. In a few months, they will launch their careers in North Carolina. Matt will teach in the English Department within the University of North Carolina, and Sandra will be working in a biotechnology lab. Ecumenical Catholics, they respect all worthwhile religions. In this season, they are bringing their proficient life skills to their care of me.

At the beginning of their university studies several years ago, they made a pact, a serious promise to the God in Whom they believe—with, I think, a rare humility—that they would devote the first year after they completed what Sandra has referred to as the first cycle of their ongoing studies to the rescue of troubled teenagers. I am the second teen to whom they have brought their guardian care—what Matt has sometimes called their "tough love." I do not know the identity of the first teen. The Collinses respect the privacy of every individual. Close friends of the Danforths, they became involved with my life when they learned that

Tyler and I are the ill-fated victims of a car crash and that I have been grieving for Tyler ever since that terrible night.

I like the Collinses very much, indeed. But tonight I need breathing space away from them. I have left them sitting at their desks on comfortably upholstered chairs inside the wood-paneled study in the east wing, where canvases by Winslow Homer and Mary Cassatt bring blue, green, and gold nautical colors into the quiet of that room. Working from their laptops, Matt and Sandra pore over the most recent essays that I have written, the intricate problems in calculus and trigonometry that I have solved, and the poems by Goethe and Rilke that I have translated from German and French into English. They are also reviewing the weekly reports they have written about my academic progress and my day-to-day behavior. They are secure in their belief that I have retired early and have already found some refuge in the frayed solace of medicated sleep.

But I cannot sleep, not on this evening when I am expecting Tyler to return. My intuition tells me that he is coming back as he promised, punctual and life-loving. It is not conscious reasoning that governs my thought. It is a second sight that tells me Tyler is coming back to me. It is a Spirit link that fuses my mind with his. It is some kind of telepathy that marries my anticipation to his promise.

It is all these things. Yet it is more than all these things, more than my intuition or conscious reasoning or second sight or the Spirit link that has made Tyler the one individual who completes my existence, the only boy who makes my life fortunate and whole. It is a presentiment that stirs my most trusted feelings. It is a premonition that tells me he is coming to my home within the next hour or two. It is a warning that, if I do not stand here as though I am a sentry of our happiness, a steadfast guard ready to protect the grand luck that could be stolen from us, he might not return within the hours that he had promised.

I am wearing casual-seeming black. Tyler Danforth, my loyal friend and the love of my life, has sometimes seen me wearing similar clothes in this halcyon setting that has so often served our happiness with discreet, exclusionary airs. His blue eyes have with a sensual glance always approved of my choice of a high-necked black top, slim black Capri pants, black ballet shoes, and a black wool coat as I stand waiting at the edge of the lake for his return. Surely, from his place at the helm of his boat, he will instantly recognize me. The lights emanating from my parents' home and from the park-like grounds are making my willowy form luminous and vivid.

I go on waiting, even after half an hour has passed. Excited and, yes, a bit tense, I keep searching for the sight of my lifeline, the extraordinary boyfriend that the Fates or God or some lesser eternal Spirit has meant for me alone.

The late April sunset disguises the funereal darkness of the waters with gold-yellow and blood red hues. The chill in the air intensifies my alertness. At every moment, I expect

Tyler to appear in his bass boat, beams of red, white, and green light rising from the masthead, sides, and stern. My intuition, leagued as it is with my anticipation, tells me that the boat is hurrying to me from inside the darkness. Not yet sighting him, I imagine how he will appear, precise and reliable at the helm while he notices me from afar. His laughing, handsome face tells me without any words that his night fishing has gone well, and that he is bringing home a fine catch of largemouth bass, chain pickerel, and bluegill.

Tonight, Tyler has not gone fishing with his buddies—Devon, Keith, and Ricardo, friends from Blue Ridge High School who have participated with him in many adventuring episodes, including skiing, mountain climbing, ice hockey, and sailing. Spurred on by the tremendous joy of being so vigorously alive in the awakening surrounds of spring, he decided to fish alone across this private lake. His enthusiasm quickened the spontaneous lift of his decision. So it seemed to my approving regard of him when, alone in my study, I saw his apparition a few hours earlier, right after the Collinses and I arrived home from an especially successful day at a science museum in Boston. There were other times before our car crash when he had not invited his fishing buddies to join him in an early evening expedition across the lake behind my home. On those occasions, I was pleased to accompany him as a skillful fisher of bass, bluegill, and pickerel.

"I'm a lucky fellow," he told me more than a few times when I had hauled in three or four largemouth bass and half-a-dozen bluegills. "You are not only my beautiful girlfriend. You are also a terrific fishing pal."

"Oh, come on," I had exclaimed in a mock show of disappointment. "Admit it. I am just as brilliant in a science class as I am in a fishing boat."

Even now, a year after that moment, I smile at the smoothness of his rejoinder.

"On that point, Rachel, my memory is too excited to be reliable," he had said. "But tonight I'm willing to test your fishing further."

I had accepted his words with an exuberant laugh that without the least artifice or hesitation made a sudden bond with silence and with the impassioned kiss that he planted upon my lips. I had met that kiss with a passion that equaled the intensity of his kiss. Even after the passage of a year and more, our kiss lives vital and revealing in my memory. The mutual impetus of that kiss was proof of the love that we had enjoyed for six months in that magical year. It was also a promise of days and days of new and splendid moments together.

On this April night, when clouds of mist are beginning to rise from the lake and to overtake the light of the moon that with slowly vanishing nuances is still lending a glow to the breeze-rippling waters, I once more yearn for Tyler's kiss. My body aches for his touch. My mind is unwilling to dispel the memory of his husky, articulate voice and his long, athletic body. I want him to hurry back to me. I no longer want to regret not having accompanied him on his journey across the lake. I had, of course, a perfectly valid reason for not joining him. On this evening I needed to prime myself for new tests in trigonometry, American history, and biology.

I go on waiting, here at the edge of the lake that so suddenly holds the image of the moon in ghostly alliance with the tenacious mist that with wily tentacles is concealing almost everything.

Now I watch the moon, vague and insubstantial, peering from behind clouds of mist. At any moment, surely, Tyler will appear, not vague or insubstantial, but vivid and palpable. He will guide his boat safely to the dock and, after with ropes and cable securing it there, he will hurry to meet me, here on the same jetty where he has during other visits so often come back to me, tremendously alive and well and always in search of new adventure and remarkable encounters.

"I've come back, Rachel," he will exclaim as he draws me into his caress and kisses me. "I've come back exactly as I said I would, right after the sun goes down. And I've brought you a nice haul of fish, too."

Lighthearted because he is standing beside me once more, I am going to tell him that I never doubted his return.

"I knew that you'd come back to me," I will say, "and that you'd bring me a nice haul of fish."

We will laugh together, our happiness in this casual-seeming moment alive and vital and already beginning its journey across the invisible paths of my memory.

For a quarter of an hour more, I wait, eager and patient and absolutely believing that my Tyler will return.

But a few minutes later something rankles my certainty—some thought sparking my awareness of how I had spent the day that in this very hour has vanished away from me. Today, I spent the day in Boston with the Collinses and with Miss Pearson. Nor can I remember being with Tyler at any time during this morning before I left for Boston or late in the afternoon, when he arrived at my home and found himself alone after a busy day at school and at soccer practice. I was not there when he hurried to pack his fishing gear and head for his boat that he often leaves moored to the dock rather than inside the boathouse nearby. I try to call back the last time that I was with him. My mind searches for the most recent hour that was ours to possess together, assured and predominant and successful. I close my eyes and hurry into the hidden recesses of my memory. I search for him in every conscious thought. I plunge through the darkness assailing my mind and heart, without the light of certainty to guide me and with tension that leaves me breathless. I have lost my way. I cannot find the path or the memory that will tell me when I last saw Tyler, my beloved friend and the only human being Spirit-appointed to complete my existence.

A frightened cry hurries out of me. Screams of anguish and rage overtake the sounds of my fearful weeping. I leave the pier and, blinded by my tears, stumble along the meandering path at the edge of the lake. My assurance dashed and my spirit bereft, I allow my eyes to glance at the capacious house in the distance that waits for me atop the hill above me, its whiteness shadowed now by the rising mist and by the night darkness that is enclosing it. Disappointed because Tyler has not returned, I hang my head in defeat. I begin to take the first steps back to the house.

Then my mind teaches me once again to remember. Tyler has always been true to me. He has always made it part of his integrity to honor a pledge, to fulfill a promise, and to remain true to his word. He promised me that he was going to come back to me. Whether he made that promise this morning or yesterday or the day before does not seem very important. Nor can I with certainty tell myself on this evening that seems suddenly strange to me. But that he made that promise is of the utmost importance. It prods my hope. It renews my conviction that he will indeed return on this very evening.

I turn my glance away from the house now. Instead, with searching eyes and renewed confidence, I look out at the lake. The mist like a shroud is concealing everything.

Yet glimmers of moonlight float through the mist. A ghostly radiance rises out of the darkness, revealing nothing more than whorls upon whorls of more darkness.

I stand there, at the edge of the lake, waiting once more for Tyler to come back to me.

Then I see the lights from his boat and, right after that, the boat itself or at least Tyler at the helm. He is not heading toward the pier. Instead, he is guiding his boat toward the place where I stand.

Overcome by surprise and joy, I rush into the April-cold waters of the lake, wading with vigorous strides and then swimming with front crawl strokes toward the lights that beam from Tyler's boat. I hear myself calling out to him.

"You've come back!" I shout to him, exhilarated beyond all measure. "You've come back to me!"

Heavy with water now, my clothes impede the swiftness of my strokes. Only vaguely sensing the coldness upon my body, I throw off my coat and watch it floating upon the dark ripples of lake waters and then disappearing.

I swim into deeper waters. Yet the boat seems no nearer.

Still, the lights from the boat beam their welcome. Still, Tyler waves his right hand, beckoning me to hurry to him.

I go on swimming, struggling through my stroking motions as the weight of the water upon my clothes hinders my speed.

I hear myself crying out my joy and my anticipation. Tyler is so near me now. In a few minutes, we will once again be together.

The lights of his boat seem closer. I swim faster and faster.

Then, from inside the murky darkness, a man's rugged arms take hold of me and draw me away from my race. I hear myself screaming, frightened at first because of his powerful grip and because the darkness conceals who he is. With flailing motion, I struggle against his grip. He holds me more tightly as he swims back to the shore, his rescuing gait confident and unyielding.

He begins speaking to me.

"It's all right, Rachel," he says. "It's all right. I'm here to help you."

The voice belongs to Matt Collins—my teacher, my caregiver, and my unofficial guardian.

"He's there, I tell you!" I scream to him. "Tyler's in his boat. He's waiting for me!"

Matt doesn't answer me. Heedless of the cold waters, he keeps on swimming, with hastening movements bringing us back to the banks of the lake.

Confused and despairing, I begin crying.

"I want Tyler," I say, all the while sobbing uncontrollably. "He's in his boat. I don't want to leave him."

We reach the banks of the lake. Matt lifts me out of the water and, with his strong right arm enfolding me, leads me toward the house.

I go on sobbing. Ashamed, I feel as helpless as if I were a child. I feel lost, too, because I have not brought Tyler back with me.

This time, I plead even more urgently as my sorrow pushes out each word.

"I tell you he's there, Matt," I say. "Tyler's in his boat, and he is waiting for me."

We have reached the steps that will bring us into the house.

His arms with guardian care still restricting my movement, Matt chooses quiet words to tell me what deep down and way, way back in the hidden corners of my mind I already know.

"The boat is where it should be, Rachel," he says. "It's stored in the boathouse."

Still I resist him.

"Tyler's waiting for me," I insist. "I saw him. He was waving to me. He's out on the lake, and he's trying to come back to me."

Now, just before we reach the door where Sandra Collins is waiting to help me, Matt tells me what I need to know, yet do not want to hear.

"Tyler's in the hospital," he says. "He's been in a coma for six months."

A scream leaps out of me. The wild sound of my anguish cuts across the cool night air. Its echoing lament scatters its grief into the darkness.

Matt's words astonish and then anger me. In an instant, I am once more struggling against his hold upon me. I twist my body and, with a force that surprises both of us, I begin pummeling his chest and even his face. I separate my body from his and, at the same time that his big hands reach out to grab me, I lurch and then spring forward. I begin running toward the lake, toward the light of the moon that peers through shrouds of mist, as though it is watching me.

In that very moment, I see Tyler. I fill my eyes with the sight of him, there at the helm on the dark waters that reflect the lights from his boat.

"He's there, I tell you! He's there!" I shout with new joy that his handsome, beaming face is bringing to me.

I run as fast as my long, lithe body and my willful tenacity allow. Once more, I am racing to meet him. I see him docking his boat. He is jumping onto the jetty and running his own race to me.

"I'm here, Tyler!" I hear myself screaming, my raspy, nearly breathless voice rising out of my wild happiness that is so like hysteria. "I'm here! I'm right here! I've been waiting for you for such a long time!"

Matt Collins is running right behind me. Without turning to him, I sense that his powerful hands are getting ready to grab me.

With quick, zigzag movements, I elude his grasp and without a pause push myself forward.

Ahead, there on the jetty in the moon-spotted darkness, I once again see Tyler. He is still running toward me. For just one thrilling moment, when the inconstant moon emerges from behind the cloud where it has been hiding, I see—luminous and emphatic—Tyler's rugged face and his tall, muscular body.

So alive does he appear to me, so vital and sensate and kinetic, that I stop in my tracks. He is my god. He is the one boy whose very being breathes life into me. He is the mate to my soul, without whom my soul could never be whole or happy.

"I'm here, Tyler!" I scream once again. I wave to him, so that he can more easily keep sight of me.

By this time, Matt has grabbed me in one of his shoulder locks, and Sandra is by my side trying to comfort me with the soft words of her genuine kindness.

"Take hold, Rachel. Take hold," she says.

Then, as though my sighting of Tyler may have been a *trompe-l'oeil*—some deception or trick of the eye, a will-o'-the wisp imagining, a wishful thinking run amok and scattering my proper bearings—Tyler disappears.

"He's there!" I scream, this time with unabated rage. "He's there in the darkness. He's waiting for me to come to him!"

I try to pummel Matt. I struggle to wrench free of him. Twisting my body, I manage only to slip between his grasp and fall to my knees. Swiftly, Matt lifts my body from the lawn, once again pinions it, and carries me while racing toward the house. His hold upon me now is so firm that I can no longer initiate my movements.

Surrounded by his massive arms, I become imprisoned and helpless. My hands are not free to pummel his chest and to scratch his face. Nor can I look back in search of a new glimpse of Tyler, out there in the moon-shrouded darkness as he keeps running toward me.

Even my voice has lost its power, wavering and raspy now as it breaches the night's ghostly stillness.

"He's there!" I insist once again.

But I do not scream now. I cry and wail and whimper as Matt presses his arms more firmly around me and carries me into the house and up the long staircase that leads to my bedroom. Sandra and now Miss Pearson are following behind us, offering promises that things will get better for me.

"Just hang on, Rachel," Sandra murmurs. "Hang on as long as you need to. Hang on for dear life."

By this time, with the skill of a meticulous nurse, Miss Pearson is injecting me with the medicine that will draw me into the deep sleep where I will not have to worry about finding Tyler.

THE REAPPEARING

When I awake in the morning, I will once more go in search of Tyler. This time I will run even more swiftly. I, running as swiftly, will fall into his arms. He will take gentle hold of me. He will kiss me again and again and, afterwards, tell me why it took him so long to find his way back to me. Even now, while sleep slowly overtakes me, I see his honest, grinning face and his blue eyes that gleam with love for me. I hear myself whimpering and am surprised that sorrow could have any reason for visiting me.

Chapter Six
TWO COUNSELORS

"What do you think that these imaginary meetings with Tyler will bring you?"

Doctor Morrison is asking me the question two weeks after my breakdown. I am sitting before her desk in the pristine orderliness of her office within the Blue Ridge Medical Center. I have returned to the Medical Center not as a resident, but as a patient who is conferring with this esteemed psychiatrist who is working to bring me back to good health and to a willingness to negotiate with the reality that is unfolding around me. Doctor Morrison's voice is crisp, her inquiry matter of fact, and her manner helpful without being cloying or sentimental.

Her question unsettles me. I need time to discover an answer that reveals the truth of my feelings and the fears that lurk within the most secret recesses of my mind. My gaze upon this good doctor remains direct and honest. My straight-back posture and folded hands enable me to summon an outward calm that with my hard-earned discipline suppresses my inner furies.

Before I can find my way to a proper answer, though, I draw my attention to the impressive desk behind which Doctor Morrison is seated as she contemplates my hesitation and my careful pondering of her question. An admirer of handcrafted furniture, I notice first of all the rectangular shape, the solid cherry wood, the intricate hand carvings, and the ebony and gold leaf accents. All these perfect elements I perceive with keen-sighted awareness as I study the finished back of the desk that faces me. In a woodworking course at the private school that I attended before the car crash, my peers and I had studied the craftsmanship of such a desk before we made a respectable facsimile. Without seeing the front of Doctor Morrison's desk, I can easily guess at the seven drawers, the drawer glide mechanisms, and the Italian artistry.

I notice, too, the impressive chair in which Doctor Morrison is sitting. It is an executive swivel chair, upholstered in an elegant indigo blue with a tufted back, a poly-fiber seat cushion, and a knee-tilt mechanism.

In the seconds that pass after Doctor Morrison has asked me such a troubling question, I regard just as pensively the Impressionist canvas that fills the wall behind and above her desk. Within that canvas, a Native Indian youth wearing a red calico shirt, navy denims, and dark brown leather riding boots is standing by a paddock that is resplendent with a dozen spotted horses that are frisky and agile while circling the wide span of the enclosure, their mottled coats vivid with a leopard pattern—white coloring over the loins and hips with dark, round, or egg-shaped spots. A beautiful red-haired girl with Irish features is standing next to the tall youth who carries his rugged muscularity with easy self-possession. The girl wears an emerald-green blouse, tan slacks, and waxy, red-brown leather boots. Her blue eyes gleam with happiness as she looks upon the youth who has learned to bank his fires and to modulate his heartfelt glance at her.

Beyond them and the paddock of spotted horses, beyond even the capacious surround of golden-hued wheat and corn fields that fan out to still other unfolding fields, a noonday sun—a giant disc of radiant whiteness—rises over a distant array of verdant hills. Above the hills, an azure, cloud-flecked sky, predominant and apparently omnipotent, observes the life below—the flourishing green of the hills, the nimbleness of the horses, and the joy of the red-haired girl as she stands with subdued intimacy next to her prince, whose love of her has wakened him to the tremendousness of being alive and well.

All these images on the canvas, life-like and palpable, take hold of my attention for less than a minute while I search for an answer to Doctor Morrison's question.

Noticing my furrowed brow as I struggle to explain my need of the Spirit-fused meetings with Tyler, Doctor Morrison offers a variation of her question.

"Why do you need these meetings?" she asks me. "Why has it become necessary for you to imagine that Tyler is there, speaking to you?"

Now her words quicken my own thoughts. Now, in this very instant, I find the answer to her questions.

"I need to know that Tyler is with me," I tell her. "I need to bring him back so that I can get through these terrible days. I need him so much. He is an essential part of my existence. He completes me. He is my male counterpart, just as I am the female who completes him. Without him, I am only a tormented version of myself, a pale replica of the fulfilled and happy girl that I was becoming with him beside me. Without him standing beside me, alive and well, my entire being becomes a prolonged dying, a death in life. I am a ghost of that happy girl he helped me to become. I am as pale and as ghostly as he is while he lies sleeping in his hospital bed or when he appears to me."

"Do you really believe that Tyler is there when you imagine that you are seeing him?"

"I do believe it, and that surprises me. Ever since I was a child, I have experienced a connection to the Spirit world, but only intermittently. I sometimes witnessed events before they occurred. I found that during every day in February, May, July, and October I could predict the future. In those months, I could save my friends and my relatives from harm. I could foresee the happy and sad events that were going to occur in my life as well as in their lives."

Doctor Morrison wants to know more.

"Who were these people that you believe your visions saved and what were the circumstances?"

"My vision saved a five-year-old boy from drowning in the lake behind his family's summer home. My ability to see into the future also saved my ten-year-old cousin who had foolishly set herself on fire when she was working on a science experiment as part of a school homework assignment. My gift of foresight prevented a sixteen-year-old boy from dying in a car crash. My second sight stopped a war veteran, traumatized by his battle years in Iraq, from killing himself.

"There was no black magic in what I accomplished. Call my gift a sixth sense or second sight or extrasensory perception or clairvoyance, if you wish. Whatever it was—and is, even now—gave me the power to see and to know about things that are not present to ordinary awareness. All those persons—the drowning boy, the burning girl, the imperiled teen driver, and the war-scarred veteran—escaped death because of my gift. Seeing what was going to happen to them, I alerted the right people, the savvy adults who moved fast to rescue them. I was not their physical, up-close rescuer. But I was a rescuing agent, nevertheless. I was essential to the saving of their lives."

Doctor Morrison listens quietly as I explain my sixth sense to her. A thorough realist and a well-trained pragmatist, she is reluctant to accept as valid so unlikely a concept as sixth sense or second sight. Her mind tells her that a formal scientific study of my rescuing powers might reveal more ordinary, earthbound explanations. When she does find words to push our conference forward, she asks a new, probing question.

"Do you often have experiences that involve your sixth sense?"

"Not anymore. Not that I couldn't have them. I close my visions down now when they rise up before me. I turn my attention to other matters. I do not allow the visions to take over my life."

"Why is that so?"

"After my elementary school classmates and their parents as well as my parents and my friends discovered the gift that some blessed angel or some kind Fate had granted me, they pressed me to predict their futures. When I explained that I could not always see into the future, all of them, including my parents, accused me of being an eccentric girl who had no special powers. I merely craved attention. My parents scoffed at me. But they did not become angry. Nor did their friends become angry, at least not outwardly. I am, after all, the daughter of Randolph Hayworth, whose prestige influences what is happening in the global economy. Yet in subtle ways they and their children kept their distance from me. I was very unhappy until my parents allowed me to attend a different private school, one located in North Andover rather than in New York.

"From that time forward, I ignored my dreams and my apparitions. I wanted to be like every other person. 'Let come what may,' I told myself. 'I'd rather not pay attention to my dreams. I choose not to communicate with apparitions.'"

"Maybe you grew up a little," Doctor Morrison says. "Maybe you grew more knowing. You chose not to carry the burden of the paranormal. You felt more comfortable with ordinary reality."

"Yes," I answer her. "But I always believed in my apparitions. I never doubted the truth of them. Nevertheless, my childhood experience showed me that my predictions could be dangerous. They could rouse the envy or anger or malice of the people around me."

"What about now? Why are you depending upon your dreams to solve your problems? Why, all of a sudden, have you reactivated what you believe is your ability to predict the future and to converse with apparitions?"

"Tyler," I answer her. "Tyler has everything to do with it."

"You have a need to talk with him. You need to see him, even if he isn't really there."

"He may be there," I tell her. "His reappearing, his being there with me as he used to be, may be the most real part of my life right now."

"You once told me that you were a realist. You weren't interested in what-ifs or make-believes or fairy tales or imaginary sightings."

"It is true that for most of my life I've always lived on the realistic level. I've preferred to know the truth of things, no matter how bruising the truth might be. But now I want to use this gift of foresight that I've been given. I need to believe that my dreams can come true. Whenever he appears to me, as though he is stepping out of a dream or journeying to me from a Spirit world, Tyler seems so real. The entire reality of him—his athletic presence, his steady gaze, his assured manner, and his husky voice—is so absolutely *there*, right there by the lake that borders my family's home. He is *there* in our library or the study or my bedroom or the especially large room in the east wing that has become my school at home, the place where Mr. and Mrs. Collins teach me languages, mathematics, literature, and science. He is always *there*. He never abandons me. He is faithful and true and constant."

Pensive and concerned while maintaining her serene disposition, Doctor Morrison quietly reflects upon my words. She is, I think, parsing my thoughts—dividing them into logical units and identifying their relation to each other. Later, when she is alone, she will replay the digital voice recorder that fills a prominent place in the right corner of her desk and, hearing a playback of our conversation, will try to decipher not only the surface meanings, but also the intricate subtexts.

But in this hour of our conference, while our words spark the atmosphere for the first time and while our questions and our answers aim to find a circuitous pathway to the truth, Doctor Morrison wants to know more about my meetings with the fully embodied ghost of Tyler Danforth.

"When did you first experience these meetings with Tyler's Spirit?"

"A few days after I returned home from my long stay at the medical center."

"You missed Tyler. Several days passed after your return home without your seeing Tyler. You hadn't visited him because of the heavy rainstorms that overtook Blue Ridge and because Mr. and Mrs. Collins and Miss Pearson, as well as I, feared that you might imperil your health if you traveled during those rainstorms. You might even have caught pneumonia again."

"The rainstorms didn't frighten me. I'm sixteen years old, and I don't need coddling. I felt that I was letting Tyler down. Even though he could not waken from his sleep, I believe that he'd grown used to my calling to him. I believe that he'd heard every word that I spoke to him in all my visits to him. Even in the first hour after I returned home from all those weeks in the hospital, I missed Tyler. I couldn't enjoy anything. I couldn't sleep. I kept thinking about him. I began to wish that, since I could not go to him, he would come to me. I prayed for him to visit me. I prayed for the miracle that would allow me to see him again."

"So you used your imagination. You dreamed. Possibly, you were awake while you were dreaming. You made the miracle happen."

"Tyler was there, I tell you. He was really there every time that I saw him. He was in my room with me, sequestered as it is in the east wing of my home. He was with me again and again, every time that he appeared to me. He was hurrying toward me on the dock by the lake. He was sitting with me under our favorite tree in the meadow behind my home. Lately, in all of our meetings, he has spoken to me. He tells me to be brave. He tells me to have hope."

"Could I see him if I were in the room when he appeared to you? Could Miss Pearson see him or Mr. and Mrs. Collins?"

"I don't think so."

"What makes you think that?"

"One time, Tyler appeared to me while I was sitting beneath the lavender blue flowers of a lilac tree in a meadow behind my family's home. The meadow brimmed with colorful, early-blooming wildflowers—the dark pink of red clover, the whiteness of Queen Anne's lace, the deep purple of New England asters, and the burnished yellow of goldenrod. I'd been reading Emily Brontë's novel *Wuthering Heights*. In that hour when I had turned away from the book to talk with Tyler about our love for each other and about my fear that I could not go on living without him, Miss

Pearson approached the tree where I was sitting with Tyler. Because I had stayed away from the house longer than she expected, she came looking for me. She was afraid that I might have fallen or that I had run away. I did not see her when she came near the tree, so immersed was I in my conversation with Tyler.

"'I heard your voice just before I approached you. To whom were you speaking?' Miss Pearson asked me the moment that she arrived to stand before me, peering and quizzical. 'There's nobody here.'"

"'I was reading aloud,' I answered her. 'I was reading the passage where Heathcliff, the lover tormented by his loss, has a vision of Cathy, the love of his life who died young.'"

"'That sounds very tragic,' she said."

"'It *is* tragic. It is always tragic when two people who love each other are separated forever.'"

"My words made Miss Pearson pause. She saw the connection between Heathcliff's grief and my own."

Doctor Morrison asks another question.

"Did Miss Pearson see Tyler while you sat with him beneath that tree?"

"No, she did not. The moment that Miss Pearson approached the tree, Tyler took leave of me, though not before withdrawing from our meeting with a beaming smile and while saluting me with a wave of his hand."

"Do you think that your reading the passage in which Heathcliff has a vision of Cathy may have influenced you to imagine that Tyler was really there with you?"

"I can't say. I do know that Tyler appeared to me during other days and nights before I began reading *Wuthering Heights*."

For a moment or two, Doctor Morrison muses upon my remark. Then, with ingrained composure and an inquiring disposition, she proceeds to ask more of me.

"Are your meetings with Tyler your only recent, otherworldly experience?"

"Yes. There have been no others. There has never been anyone except Tyler who has meant so much to me."

With penetrating eyes that are both searching and judgmental, Doctor Morrison studies once again my upright posture and my nearly invisible tension.

"You're making trouble for yourself, Rachel," she says. "You are weaving a web around yourself that has already begun to trap you. You are seeing Tyler's ghost even though he is not there. You are trying to convince yourself that you absolutely need him if you are to get on with your life. You are chaining yourself to illusion and pretending. You are making a pact with an apparition, a shadow, a phantom, or a specter—call these visions what you will. None of these are Tyler. They exist only in your mind. You must let them go. You must release yourself from the prison that you have made for yourself."

"I can't," I tell her. "I can't let them go. Tyler is in every one of my visions."

"You must let them go. That's the only way you can save yourself."

"I won't let them go. I won't let *him* go. He's there, I tell you. He's really there in every one of his appearances to me. I need him to be there. I need him the way I need air to breathe, eyes to see, water to quench my thirst, and hope to get me through each day."

"You are leaning on a Tyler who does not exist except in your clouded visions. All those visions are part of your private fictions, your makeshift reality. Let them go, I say. Let them go."

"Never!" I tell her, my voice turbulent with a tremulous scream and my body—the tall and slender form of me—rising from the chair. "Never!"

Doctor Morrison rises from her chair, too. Our counseling session is over. She presses a button on the speakerphone in the right corner of her desk that buzzes an alert to her secretary who is busy at her desk in the doctor's reception room. The secretary will send in Miss Pearson, who accompanied me to this visit and who will accompany me home.

Before Miss Pearson enters and before I turn my glance away from Doctor Morrison, I leave her with polite, remorseful words.

"I'm sorry," I tell her. "I'm sorry."

Doctor Morrison takes my outburst in her stride.

"Apology accepted," she says. "Believe me, I understand how you are feeling. You're excited. You're upset. You need to rest. We'll talk later. But I want to leave you with this thought. Tyler is a leader. He won't want a leaner as his partner."

A few hours later, as the day sheds its waning light and as if to validate Doctor Morrison's closing remark, Tyler appears to me once again. I am standing a hundred yards or so beyond my home at the rim of the darkening waters of the wide lake that gleams beneath a magenta sky. I am searching with yearning eyes for the boy I love whose vital, quickened presence is already lost to me and who may vanish from my life forever. In this hour that is electric with anticipation, I am especially meticulous in my grooming because I am hoping that Tyler will appear to me once again. I am wearing knitted slacks and a boat neck, long sleeve jersey, their burgundy color intensified by my white, mid-length trench coat that has a drawstring hood, snaps at the cuffs, a zipper at the front, and flap front pockets. Burgundy round-toed ballet flats, with their white crisscross strap detailing, complete my casual appearance. But there is nothing casual or inadvertent or unpremeditated about my anticipation, anchored as it is to apprehension, longing, and sorrow.

Uneasy, I watch the sun and the wavering shimmer of its light vanish beneath the horizon. I witness the night slowly descending, eerie and predominant. I observe the gold blaze of the moon rising through the darkness and competing with the glow of the stars that peer from the unfurling surround of the night. I wait. I search. I gaze into the moonlit blackness in the distance. I wonder whether Tyler will appear to me while standing at the wheel of one of his boats. I look for Tyler's favorite boat, the twenty-nine-foot open-cockpit Cape Cod with its elegant, overhanging stern and bluff bow. I recall the comfortable U-shaped bench seat that accommodated eight persons. I remember, too, the clever popup cockpit lunch table, and I visualize just as clearly the stowable ladder that Tyler and I and two other couples climbed a year earlier as we returned to the boat, agile and exuberant, after we'd gone swimming. But tonight no boat is navigating these lake waters.

Dismayed and heavy-hearted, I turn away from the fathomless mystery of the dark lake and enter the long path, undulating and lighted, that will guide me back to my house at the top of the hill. Apparently, my intuition and my foresight have failed me. Tonight, Tyler will not be reappearing.

Then suddenly, as I move quickly along the path—quite suddenly and now unexpectedly, Tyler is walking beside me.

"You are here," I exclaim. "You heard my call. You were aware of my private weeping. You listened to the uneasy beating of my heart. You understood my need to see you."

"I *am* here," Tyler answers me. His voice is husky with its understated emotion, and his blue-eyed glance is warm with his love for me. "I understand everything. That is why I've come to talk with you. I want to help you if I can."

His tall, lithe body glows with an otherworldly radiance. Yet in this spectral moment he appears to belong to the here-and-now, earthbound world. He is wearing the uniform of a prince, the role he personified so well in our high school play only a few months before the car crash. In his navy jacket, with its gold fringe and chain details, and his navy trousers and well-polished black shoes, he appears every inch a handsome prince. Overcome with my love for him and with the sublime happiness of walking beside him, I pause on the pathway and lean forward to kiss his cheek. But, though my body stands very close to him, I cannot make contact with his body. Nor does he attempt to kiss me.

"Why?" I ask him. "Why can't I kiss your face or touch your hands?"

"We are not ready for that," he says, with melancholy tones deepening his gravelly voice. "There are tests that we need to pass."

"Tests? What kind of tests? Why, of all people, do *you* need to pass any tests?"

"I have to remain strong. I have to maintain my desire to go on living. I have to stay alive. I have to wait until you or someone else draws me out of my deep sleep."

"You're here now. You've been released from your sleep."

"I'm here temporarily. I'm here as an apparition. I can stay for only a few minutes."

"I've been calling you back," I tell him. "I've visited you at the hospital. I've touched your hands. I've kissed your lips. But you never awakened."

"I did not hear you. I did not feel your touch upon my hands or my lips. That will happen only when you have passed the tests that the blessed angel who watches over you or possibly one of the sterner Fates has planned for you."

"I have to pass tests?"

"You have to learn how to be braver than you have ever been. You have to discover how to make your own way without me."

"How do I do that?"

"You have to swing free of your dependency upon me."

"I love you, Tyler. I love you with all my heart. I can't stop loving you. I can't."

"You need to walk free of me without losing your authentic love of me."

"I need you. I can't live happily without you."

"Don't let your love of me steal away your self-determination and your self-knowledge. Work to make yourself count for something. You were already doing that before the car crash. You were learning many new things about yourself, including the self-centeredness that sometimes closes you off from your school friends and the generosity that has always lived within the truest part of your nature, suppressed and unused. In those months before the car crash, you were learning to redefine yourself. You were paying attention to other people's problems. You were teaching your school friends and some new acquaintances how to rescue themselves, and you were rescuing those especially troubled persons who had given up on themselves and believed they were not worth saving. You were helping all these people, both young and elderly, who are victims of racism, poverty, domestic brutality, and their self-destructive tendencies.

"In those days and weeks and months before the accident, you were learning that the definition of who you are is always being revised. You revise it every time that you take action to make yourself better and to help others, as well. You are, after all, the only Rachel Hayworth who exists in the world exactly as you are now and as you are always becoming."

"What if I'm not good enough or strong enough? What if I can't count for anything special?"

"Keep believing in yourself. Work to make this world better."

"If I learn to do that, if I pass all the tests, will you be there at the end of my journey, alive and awake and waiting for me?"

"If your good angel or the sterner Fate permits, I'll be there. But that will not be the end of your journey. That will be a new beginning, with me walking beside you without dispossessing you or robbing you of your individuality. Nor will you be leaning on me. On your own terms, you will walk tall and make your way in the world, and you will make a life with me."

"I'll do everything that my good angel or the sterner Fate asks of me. I'll strive to be braver than I have ever been. I will. I will, I tell you. That's a promise."

"That's all that I or anyone else can ask of you."

Suddenly, the wind with spiraling velocity rises around me. I grow dizzy and lose sight of Tyler. My body weaves and sways and totters. The stars and the moon and the night sky itself seem to hasten away, as if they were mere chaff being tossed into the wind's whirling and spinning motions. For two swift and spectral minutes, my body goes on wavering and wobbling, and the night scene at the lake rushes by me—an oscillating profusion of images, a montage of moon-glistening objects, a kaleidoscope of dark and eerie hiddenness.

Then, just as suddenly, the spinning stops, and the lake scene around me becomes once again a sensate and palpable reality. No longer does my body reel. No longer is my vision blurred and confused by the heaved-up, fantastical moon and the swirling waters of the lake and the ever-mysterious darkness. The night readjusts itself to my ordinary seeing. The moon returns to its proprietary ascendance in the sky. The waters of the lake in front of me accept the moonlit cover that is the darkness. The jetty extending from the bank of the lake, steadfast and useful, waits once again for the arrival of a morning yacht or the departure of one of my family's boats. The boathouse near the jetty goes on sheltering and protecting my family's cabin cruiser, sailboat, yacht, and catamaran. In the distance behind me, our home on the hill, the expansive and flourishing gardens, and the lighted pathway that will eventually guide me to rooms that no longer bring me solace—all of these familiar things reassemble themselves from the fragmented forms of themselves that were only a moment ago rushing by me. A haunted stillness like the quiet after the heaves of storm takes possession of this night scene.

Because the confusion and the spinning have stopped, I am myself once again. I turn to ask Tyler whether he is all right. But he is not standing beside me. Nor is he standing on the jetty or waiting on the path near the garden abundant with tulips, lilacs, and daffodils or climbing the hill toward my home. He is nowhere in sight. He has vanished. He has disappeared.

"Where are you, Tyler?" I call out to him. "Where are you? I need you to tell me more. I need to know with certainty all the things I must do if I am to save you and save myself."

But Tyler does not answer me. Only the night listens to me, and the waning wind, and the golden moon that to my eyes appears to be a sky god's amulet or talisman, a giant disc powerful enough to ward off every evil. With tough-minded clarity that, these days, works for me only intermittently, I understand that a talisman as powerful as a moon is unavailable to me. I will have to make my own luck. I will have to keep in mind the counsel that Tyler has given me, as though he is a young and brave navy cadet or an adventuring prince lost in a story from long ago.

Suddenly, as I turn onto the path that will guide me home—quite suddenly, with heavy heart and troubling uncertainty, I recall the sight of Tyler in his princely uniform. I remember when he first wore it, and I revisit the story that he and I entered for a brief while as though it were our own. Our classmates David Turner and Mariel Whitman wrote the play, drawing upon Jacob and Wilhelm Grimm's *Story of Briar Rose*. In David and Mariel's version of the fairy tale, the prince falls into a deep sleep, not the princess.

"The role of the princess is too passive," Mariel said of the Grimm brothers' narrative as she and David were outlining their new version of the story. "She does not really represent the independent and complicated nature of modern girls."

David, who is Mariel's boyfriend and a star goalie on our school's hockey team, agreed.

"Let's change it," he said. "Let's give the character of the princess a modern spin."

And so they did. The two of them, collaborative and quick-witted, worked swiftly and ingeniously as they created a compelling variant of the Grimm brothers' tale. David and Mariel gave their play a title as long as it is revealing: *The Prince Who Falls into a Deep Sleep and the Princess Who Tries to Rescue Him.*

In the play, I became Princess Elsa, the selfish and devious daughter of a king. Elsa falls in love with heroic Prince Erik, the part played by Tyler. But Erik's parents and Five Heavenly Spirits will not allow Elsa to marry Erik because of her selfish behavior. The Five Spirits, who are the angels of justice, place Erik in a deep sleep to protect him from a bad marriage. Then they challenge Elsa to pass three tests to prove that she is worthy of becoming the prince's bride.

First of all, she must plunge her way through a dangerous nightmare. In the depths of that nightmare, she has to pass the first two tests. She has to confront and do battle against two monster vices named Self-Centeredness and Deceit. If she wins those battles, she will then have to win the approval of one of the strongest virtues of all, Self-Sacrifice. During her battles, she learns that the two vices and the virtue are extensions of her own nature. Because the play is an allegory, the vices are symbols of Elsa's narcissism and her deviousness. The virtue represents her willingness to sacrifice her comfort and her safety so that she can awaken the prince to a new, happy life. There is virtue, too, in her victories over her wiliness and her selfishness.

The story within the play comes swiftly back to me. Is it Tyler's reappearing in his uniform as the prince that revives my memory of that allegorical play? Is Tyler's decision to wear that uniform meant as a secret message between us, an urgent prod to my sleeping memory, a prescription for saving myself from myself and doing good for others? Is it his way of showing me what I must do, the kind of life I must lead, if I am to awaken him from his fast sleep, the death-in-life to which Blind Chance or a rigorous Fate has condemned him? I wonder. I am determined to accept the mission that Tyler has assigned me. I tell myself that I must strive to be braver and more generous than I have ever been. I speak the words aloud, reciting them with a show of confidence and determination.

"I *will* be brave and generous," I tell the gleaming moon and the glittering stars, the quiet lake and the nearly invisible garden.

Once more, I make my pledge to Tyler, who has disappeared from my seeing and who has hurried back to the private and otherworldly realm that I cannot enter. "I will do everything that you ask of me, Tyler. I will be the best person that I can be for you, for all the other people in my life, and—yes—for myself."

With these words riding across night silences and moon glow, I make my way back to the house that stands, protective and waiting, at the top of the hill. Mr. and Mrs. Collins and Miss Pearson are expecting me. I know. Ever watchful and genuinely caring, they have stood at the top of the hill just beyond my home observing my every move. Each one of them is peering at me through Nikon binoculars that are waterproof and fog-proof and that have Eco-glass lenses, turn-and-slide eyecups, and rubber-armored coating. They will be pleased to see that I have returned of my own volition. This time, and many times before tonight, I have not jumped into the lake while searching for Tyler. I have not run into the dark woods behind our home, frantic and screaming and seeking the full-bodied reality of Tyler.

I have, in some important ways, learned to accept my loneliness without Tyler and to accept, as well, my isolation from my classmates, whom the doctors have not permitted to visit me while I am struggling toward a recovery from my breakdown. Caught inside the throes of my private anguish, I understand—a little—that my heart is slow to learn that Blind Chance or stern Fate or random tragedies—call them what you will—strew fresh wreckage upon our lives with careless detachment.

The next weeks pass with a swifter momentum. Though I strive to conceal my sorrow, Mr. and Mrs. Collins and Miss Pearson notice the suppressed signs of my tension and my grief. There is no real joy in my face or in my voice. There is no uninhibited energy in my walk, no natural ring to my laughter, no happy gleam in my blue-eyed gaze. Noticing these signs, my three protectors draw me to activities beyond the spacious room that serves as my home school. With them, I visit art galleries in New Haven, Boston, and New York. I observe the remarkable art of Monet, Renoir, Gauguin, Homer Winslow, Edvard Munch, and Mary Cassatt. At times, I see myself in the canvases—the exuberant girl I used to be and the pensive, forlorn girl that I have become. The joyful faces please me most of all. Yet the sorrow-laden faces also bring me relief. They show me that many girls my age have endured and even weathered disappointment and loss.

During other excursions, we fish for trout in Maine, kayak in New Hampshire, ride Arab bays on a horse farm in Connecticut, and climb a mountain in Vermont. Each one of these excursions becomes a test that I pass with natural enthusiasm and reclaimed exhilaration. The joy that I discover through each of these experiences validates new chapters in my recovery. Hearing of my success while they remain in New York, my parents agree that some of my classmates should be allowed to visit me. But they also assert that I will be returning to Blue Ridge High School only after I have been beaming with good health for several months.

More good news quickly follows. Tyler's parents phone to tell me that Tyler's brother, Tristan, is coming home at the end of May. After his parents conferred with him, Tristan agreed to withdraw from the military academy he is attending in Texas and return to his parents' home here in Blue Ridge. Hearing about this conference from Mrs. Danforth, I imagine that Tyler's parents need Tristan to fill the void, the dark empty space into which Tyler's accident has thrown them. Though I have never met him, I perceive the news of Tristan's imminent arrival as a favorable omen. According to the words that Tyler has spoken to me in our supernatural meetings, only a girl who truly loves Tyler will call him out of his long, long sleep. Tristan's presence will not stir Tyler awake. But Tristan may boost my confidence. If he is as kind as Tyler, he will persuade me to believe in myself and to trust my capacity for bravery and self-sacrifice.

I wait for his arrival. I look forward to the visits of my classmates. I have valid reasons to be hopeful once again.

Yet, only hours after I have received the good news, hesitation and doubt overtake my will. I cannot be braver or better without Tyler standing next to me, right now and here, while the uncertain present keeps unfolding its surprises and disappointments. My fallible nature hampers my acceptance of the ordeal assigned me, the ambiguous trials awaiting me, and the perilous unknown looming before me.

Even while my hope falters, though, I begin to believe that some extraordinary things are about to happen.

Whether they involve Tyler's brother, I cannot with certainty tell. But my intuition tells me that the arrival of Tristan Danforth is about to change my life in extraordinary ways.

Chapter Seven
TWO PRINCES DIFFERENT AND THE SAME

As their way of introducing me to their son Tristan, Mr. and Mrs. Danforth invite me, as well as my guardian teachers, Matt and Sandra Collins, to a small dinner party that they are hosting at Blue Ridge Country Club. Located five miles from my parents' home and overlooking a lake, the club with its upscale membership and exclusionary airs has often provided a solacing atmosphere for me. My parents are members of long and honorable standing here. For more than a decade and sometimes from his Sutton Place residence fifty miles away, my father has brought his crafty and ambitious drive to his place on the board of directors. Reined in though he is by the conservative rules of the club, he manages to push forward all the changes that give the club a modern ambience even while he protects the high standards that maintain the club's inherent excellence and award-winning reputation.

"You've never mentioned Tristan before," Sandra remarks right after Mrs. Danforth phones to invite the Collinses and me to the dinner party. "Until two weeks ago, when you told us that Tristan was returning home, Matt and I were not aware that Tyler had a brother."

"I haven't met Tristan yet," I tell her. "He's been away at a military academy in Texas. The few times that his schedule has allowed him to break away from the academy, he has linked up with his parents and his brother in some faraway vacation spot."

"Well, then," Matt says, "this should be a very interesting dinner party. We are about to meet a mysterious brother."

I laugh a lighthearted laugh as a way of easing the tension that already hovers by me, an ambivalent Spirit observing my every move.

"Yes," I agree. "Mysterious people can spark a party."

On the following Saturday, the Collinses and I arrive at Blue Ridge Country Club in a timely manner. We make an impressive arrival in Matt's Mercedes Benz, a wedding gift from his parents. The valet, an aged and dignified man with a mane of thick white hair and a face that wears his cragged features with humble assurance, courteously greets us. His rheumy, brown eyes light up with muted recognition of me, but he carefully abstains from any words that might reveal his pleasure in my arriving here on this crisp and unusually cool evening in the third week of May. Rather, it is I who cross that invisible and sometimes uncomfortable barrier called protocol and, with quietly calibrated decorum, offer him a greeting that is both friendly and natural.

"It's good to see you, Mr. Johnson," I tell him. "I hope the evening finds you well."

He beams with appreciation and quietly answers me.

"It does, indeed, Miss Hayworth. It does, indeed. Thank you for asking."

We make our way into the club with a nearly lighthearted anticipation of the rewards that the evening may dispense to us. Two women, pretty with titian hair, hazel eyes, and hour-glass figures and in their twenties, welcome us with proficient courtesies and help us to remove our coats—Matt's beige cashmere topcoat with its oversized notched collar and double-breasted button front; Sandra's elegant shamrock-green coat, with its crew neck, long, ruffled sleeves, six large black front buttons, and paneled styling; and my azure blue sheath coat, with its shirt collar, long sleeves, and cobalt blue piping.

Right after that, a *maître d'* warmly receives us and guides us up the long, wine-colored carpeted staircase to a dining room on the second floor, where the preferred placement enhances the privacy and the pleasures of the evening. Once inside its guarded serenity, I move with familiar ease through the capacious room, noticing without acknowledging them my parents' business acquaintances and loyal friends and a few Blue Ridge teens that have remained my steadfast advocates despite my troubled past. In the southwest corner of the room, a young, sandy-haired pianist, sitting with relaxed poise at a satin walnut Steinway, plays the romantic melodies of George Gershwin, Jerome Kern, Stephen Sondheim, John Lennon, and Franz

Lehar. As I have done in so many previous visits here, I scan the room's well-ordered design with attentive admiration and with a tinge of nostalgia, recalling as I do the evenings when Tyler escorted me here. With its beautiful antiques, burnished mahogany, rich fabrics, and dignified atmosphere, as well as original canvases by Grandma Moses, Andrew Wyeth, and Thomas Hart Benton, the room creates a setting that is both elegant and stately.

As this dining room and all its amenities unfold their influences around me, I guess with worldly awareness and well-honed cynicism that the Danforths have chosen so staid a setting for our dinner party because the refined atmosphere, the upright conduct of guests young and older at neighboring tables, and the disciplined cordiality of the servers might hold our senses still. The Danforths are eager to celebrate the return of their son Tristan. But a dark cloud hovers over them and over me as well. Tyler is not *here* in this grand dining room. Nor is he really *there*, keen-minded and alert, in that solitary hospital room, tethered as he is to a network of tubes. The vital part of him that thinks and feels and moves with well-earned agility has gone missing, even while his princely body appears vivid and constant as a still-living presence.

We arrive at a large, round table that appears to be waiting for us by the floor-to-ceiling window. The gold-hued velvet drapes are drawn so that the light of the moon that gleams upon the wide expanse of green lawn fanning out to the even more expansive greenery of a golf course also caresses the more private area where we will be seated. Moonlight touches, as well, the gold tablecloth with its delicately woven jacquard poinsettia design and the yellow, red, and white roses that are tucked into a crystal vase with ivy and ferns. I notice at once Mr. and Mrs. Danforth, patrician and sociable as they converse with the young couple sharing the table with them. I know the young couple well. They are Tyler's close friends, and they are my friends, too. I first knew them even before Tyler and I began dating one another. They brought Tyler into my life. They introduced me to the boy who rescued me from my wild and destructive self.

They are Kyle Holden and his girlfriend Li, whose surname is Zhang. I am pleased to see them at the same time that I am dismayed that no other guest is sitting at the table. Tristan is not here, and I wonder why he is missing.

I am careful not to mention his name or to express my disappointment because of his absence. Instead, I join Matt and Sandra in exchanging cordial greetings with Mr. and Mrs. Danforth and with Kyle and Li.

Attentive though I am to our conversation, I focus at the same time upon what everyone is wearing. It is a way to hold my senses still, so keen is my anticipation of the person that Tristan will prove to be and the influence that I may have upon his life.

We make a well-groomed party. Matt looks casually impressive in his gray suit, its slim, masculine lines made perfect because of the symmetry of its notch lapels, waist flap pockets, and dual back vents. His necktie in blue silk twill that matches the blue of his shirt is printed with a red polka dot pattern and a background of blue, red, and gray swirls.

Mr. Danforth's ingrained dignity enhances a double-breasted navy-blue suit, with its notch collar, double-breasted button front, and chest welt and front welt pockets. His tie, navy with light blue rhombi designs, nicely complements the suit and brings color to the whiteness of his shirt.

Kyle, brown-haired and wind-burned, brings a tall, rangy physique and a stylized teen vitality to a black suit in a check pattern with a peak lapel, a two-button front with horn buttons, front flap pockets, and a double vented back. His tie, a paisley print with gold, gray, cream white, and rose colors on a black wool base, lends a quickened vibrancy to his suit and to his gray shirt.

The well-groomed appearance of these men quickens my appreciation of fabrics and colors and their designers. I know very well the works of Calvin Klein, Ermengildo Zegna, Giorgio Armani, Salvatore Ferragamo, and Tom Ford. I studied them in a fashion design course at the private school from which I was eventually expelled.

We women look equally impressive. Sandra's tall, slender figure matches the beauty and elegance of her white sheath turtleneck evening dress.

Mrs. Danforth wears with understated authority her boat-neck, dark blue A-line party dress that has long sleeves and a floral embroidered skirt.

Li looks especially lovely in a sleeveless black A-line evening dress that has a crew neck and blue, green, and gold floral embellishments.

I am wearing a cobalt blue sweater dress that has a turtleneck collar, long sleeves, and gold abstract designs on its front and back, as well as on its shoulders.

I tell myself that I am in my glamour mode. I want this evening to work for me. I want Tristan to like me, though why his liking me is suddenly important I cannot say, so uneasy and disarranged are my feelings on this strange-seeming evening when I am anticipating a new turn on the dark path that I have been traveling. Secretly tense and excited, I am waiting for a different rescuer than the boy that I tell myself I still love despite his having traveled far away into an oblivion I cannot enter.

As soon as the *maître d'* has brought us to our table, a young, red-haired waiter—tall, lean, and immaculately groomed in a black tuxedo—brings us our drinks. Mr. Danforth and Matt enjoy scotch on the rocks, Mrs. Danforth and Sandra find pleasure in delicate stem glasses of *Veuve*

Clicquot, and the rest of us, who are teens and are therefore forbidden alcoholic beverages, settle for ginger ale.

Convivial within the boundaries of decorum, we talk about many things. We are, I think, playing a serious game, sharing stories that include Tyler and that make the memory of him palpable and real, an invisible presence alive and influential here with us at the dinner table.

Mr. and Mrs. Danforth reminisce about their river rafting adventure on the Kitka River in Finland. During those daredevil hours two years earlier, they as well as Tyler and Tristan and a professional skipper paddled through the heave and swirl of seven white water rapids along an eight-mile route.

"Our hearts were beating faster that day," Mr. Danforth says. "What an adrenalin rush that trip was!"

His face beams with the happy memory.

Mrs. Danforth has a different kind of recollection. She remembers the adventure with a tinge of melancholy.

"We were there with our two sons," she says. "That's what made the river rafting special."

"It *was* special," Mr. Danforth says. "Tyler and Tristan made it special. Navigating those white waters, they were agile, skillful, fearless, and adventurous. In my book, they are A+!"

Li smiles when she hears Mr. and Mrs. Danforth's remarks. She admires the Danforths because they are good parents and because they genuinely love their sons. With Li, what you see is what you get. Honest in her words and her responses, sensitive to other people's feelings, and helpful whenever she can be, Li inspires everyone's trust and respect. She is one of the most beautiful girls in Blue Ridge. Her dark hair, fair skin, oval face, and straight nose, as well as her tapered jaw, round chin, and full lips intensify her exotic Chinese beauty. With Kyle, Li will be entering the pre-med program within Brown University in a year or so, right after she completes her high school education. Both Kyle and she hope to achieve impressive careers in medicine. Their families have done so. Kyle's parents are neurosurgeons, and Li's parents are cardiologists.

Li and Kyle are among my most reliable friends. Even when I was doing everything wrong in my life more than a year ago—even then, when my life had fallen apart, smashed up and apparently beyond repair, Li and Kyle stood by me. They reminded my adversaries, Blue Ridge conservatives and self-righteous busybodies who were condemning me and wanted me severely punished, that I was capable of doing wonderful things with my life if I were given a second chance.

With her soft voice and precise diction, Li shares with us the elation that she felt when she and Kyle, as well as Tyler and I, went scuba diving in the Andaman Sea, within the Beacon Reef of Thailand. We had traveled there with Kyle's and Li's parents. The Holdens and the Zhangs have been friends of long duration. But on that memorable day, Kyle, Li, Tyler, and I went scuba diving without parents.

"I never imagined that scuba diving could be so astonishing," Li tells us. Her blue eyes sparkle with elation as she calls back to her conscious awareness the lift and surprise of that time. "Under water, I saw mountains and coral gardens sparkle like indigo jewels. I saw each of us with masks, snorkels, and fins and head-mounted dive lights flashing red, yellow, and green. We looked otherworldly and supernatural. I saw Kyle next to me and, farther away, Tyler and Rachel swimming as though we were magical creatures of the sea. I felt that I'd been allowed to enter a fairy tale and that I was being turned into a princess."

As a way of deflecting my tension because Tristan has not yet arrived, I make a lighthearted remark. I draw Kyle into its orbit.

"If the reef turned Li into a princess, did it make you a prince?"

Kyle gets a kick out of my question. He laughs a hearty laugh and smoothly lobs a quick-witted retort my way.

"Li gives the reef too much credit," he says. "She was always a princess. The reef understood that. It simply spruced itself up and invited her into its color and glitter."

I decide to tease Kyle, good-naturedly.

"You haven't answered my question. Did the reef make you a prince?"

For just a moment, Kyle ponders my question. Then, with a husky energy that anchors itself to the lightheartedness, he carries our banter forward.

"Well, in that reef, batfish, lionfish, and moray eels were swimming around us. They didn't look like princes to me."

"You still haven't answered my question. Did the reef make *you* a prince?"

Kyle pauses once again. Then, when he is ready to answer me, his voice becomes low-key and serious.

"Li made me a prince," he says. "She made me a prince the first time she kissed me."

"What a wonderful thing to say," Mrs. Danforth exclaims. "And how brave of you. You *are* a romantic. These days, that makes you a very special young man."

Everyone laughs. Everyone is having a good time— everyone except me. I am waiting for Tristan. I want him to change my life for the better. I tell myself that I want him to help me bring Tyler back. But way back in the hidden corners of my awareness—way, way back within a darkness that I can rarely fathom—a thought lives, furtive and dangerous. If Tristan cannot bring Tyler back to me, if he cannot help me rescue the boy that I have learned to love so completely, perhaps he can replace him.

Faithless and rebellious, the thought at first repels me. But I do not let go of it.

As though he is testing my fidelity to Tyler, Mr. Danforth draws me into this game that we are adroitly playing—this verbal sleight, this stratagem of words we are performing, this series of narrative tricks that keep at bay our grief at having lost Tyler even temporarily and that keep back as well our punishing doubts that we may have lost him forever.

"What about you and Tyler?" he asks. "What stands out among all the adventurous times you shared together?"

I do not hesitate when Mr. Danforth reaches out to me. I know what I am going to say. The memory validates the rightness of Tyler and me as a team. It subdues, at least in part, my belief that I am not worthy of him. At the same time, I resist the mind-bruising tension that has been assailing me during this evening. I avoid any show of sentimentality. I tell my story with matter-of-fact understatement.

"Of all the auspicious occasions that I have shared with Tyler, I choose to call back through my telling not our sailing across Penobscot Bay with Mr. and Mrs. Danforth on a Fourth-of-July afternoon last year or our riding Arab bays on a horse farm in Connecticut in early September or sharing the Blue Ridge High School stage with Tyler in our play about the sleeping prince. Instead, I select from my store of memories the hours that Tyler and I spent as teen volunteers in the children's cancer ward within Blue Ridge Hospital. There, only a few months before the car crash, Tyler and I were teaching Gareth, an eight-year-old African American boy suffering from leukemia, to play a Yamaha

Three Quarter Size Classical Acoustic Guitar. Gareth had lost his curly, jet-black hair to radiation treatments. But he had not lost his brave spirit and his belief that he would recover from his illness. His father was the oncologist guiding him through his radiation therapy. That was a big plus for the boy. Tyler and I served as a kind of footnote in his hospital treatment. Nevertheless, his father regarded us as a welcome addition to the medical staff that was working to save Gareth."

"That guitar was better than a magic wand," Sandra says.

"Yes," I agree. "The guitar was an exciting thing for Gareth. With its solid spruce top, its redwood sides and back, its rosewood fingerboard and bridge, and its compliant nylon strings, the guitar delighted Gareth. Eager to learn and to discover the melodies rising out of it, he looked forward to the lessons that Tyler and I, together and sometimes alone, gave him three summer afternoons a week, precisely at two o'clock. Quick-witted and musically inclined, Gareth was soon playing many of the songs that children love: 'You Are My Sunshine,' 'Puff the Magic Dragon,' 'The Wheels on the Bus Go Round and Round,' 'You've Got a Friend,' and 'He's Got the Whole World in His Hands.' Privately, one time after I heard this boy playing especially well and when Tyler and I were driving home together, I called Gareth a prodigy. My praise of the boy pleased Tyler. I remember the special light that shone through his eyes and the smile that beamed with his pleasure upon hearing my words.

"'I'm glad we have been helping him enjoy at least a part of his day,' Tyler said. 'It's great that we have played even a small part in his journey toward recovery. But the praise belongs to him first of all. He's a very brave kid. He's winning his battle against leukemia.'"

The Danforths and the Collinses, as well as Li and Kyle, like what they hear. Their smile carries forth the admiration and respect they feel for Tyler and—yes—for me.

But Mrs. Danforth wants to know more.

"Why did you choose to tell us this particular memory of the times that you shared with Tyler? Why didn't you choose your sailing adventure across Penobscot Bay or your horse riding on that farm in Connecticut or your acting together in your high school play?"

Without a pause, I tell her and the group exactly what I feel.

"Helping Gareth take control of at least a portion of his life, teaching him how to make music through his guitar, influencing him to bring his talent to the mini-concerts he gave to the other children in the oncology wing of the hospital—all these things also helped Tyler and me. We were not only strengthening Gareth's belief in himself. While we were teaching him how to play the guitar, we were also discovering that we make a good team."

My remark, reflective and forthright, pleases everyone at the table, especially Mr. and Mrs. Danforth.

"Of course you make a good team, my dear," Mrs. Danforth tells me. "You two are meant for each other. I have known it from the beginning."

Her words thrill me. But my conscience is not clean. These months without Tyler are testing my fidelity. Feeling abandoned by him and cursed by some malevolent Fate, I—with my foolish impatience and my fear of a lonely and unhappy future—am already looking for another rescuer.

I thank Mrs. Danforth for her belief in me. Then I hurry to invite Sandra and Matt to tell us about a memorable time in their busy lives that they spent with Tyler.

Matt and Sandra tell us about one of their favorite afternoons out of all the afternoons that they spent with Tyler during the past year. On that summer day, they went skydiving with Tyler in Danielson, Connecticut, about eighty miles from their home in Blue Ridge. Licensed after months of training from a school of skydiving experts, they hurried into the adventure.

Matt is the first to tell us about that special day.

"From a Cessna 206 that was flying at fourteen thousand feet at a speed of one hundred twenty miles per hour, Sandra, Tyler, and I jumped into am amazing experience," he says. "We were not flying in tandem. We were on our own, individual and sparked up. We couldn't lean on each other. We had to jump alone. That's what made the thing scary. That's what made it amazing."

He pauses. He studies our responses to the words that he is using to tell us about this more-than-ordinary experience. As listeners, each of us is held rapt by the implicated thrills and dangers of those jumps. He notices, and he is pleased. Now he tells us more.

"After a sixty-second free fall, Sandra, Tyler, and I parachuted for five minutes into the vastness of space that received us as temporary floating specimens. After we made soft landings in a meadow of wild grasses not far from the airfield, Sandra and Tyler looked elated. Their eyes gleamed, and their laughing words floated on the sunshine stillness in the air.

"'What a lark! What tremendous fun!' Sandra called out to me.

"'A glimpse of Heaven!' Tyler exclaimed. 'I'm going to tell all my friends that I've been to Heaven and that I've found a good way to fly back.'"

Stillness takes hold of us just for a moment. Our memory of Tyler's good humor and his jaunty appreciation of life brushes against his comatose withdrawal from us. That loss makes our attempts at levity seem contrived and forced, an escape hatch from our unrelenting sorrow. Nevertheless, Mrs. Danforth maintains the tone of our meeting. She retrieves our lightheartedness before it can dissolve. She summons a light, decorous laugh that coaxes and revives our contrived exuberance.

"That's our Tyler to a T," she says. "He always knows how to enjoy every single moment that he is experiencing. He's always in it. He gives himself completely to the surprise and the wonder and the excitement of life. Bravo to him for loving life!"

She lifts her delicate stem glass that holds *Veuve Clicquot*, with its light golden color and its aromas of ripe apple and light cream. She raises her hand as she salutes her son.

"Bravo to you, Tyler! Bravo to you for loving life!"

All of us join her in this toast to Tyler. We teens raise, of course, our glasses of ginger ale. It is our way of keeping Tyler with us, even though he is not present. It is our way of dispelling the tension and the heartache that we are feeling.

"Bravo! Bravo to Tyler!"

Satisfied that we have found our proper bearings, that we know where we are in this moment unfolding itself around us, and that we understand what we might do in the next moment, Mrs. Danforth nudges us forward. She asks Matt a useful question.

"How did you feel on that skydiving day, Matt? You've told us how Tyler and Sandra felt. What about you?"

Matt ponders her question. Quiet now and soul-searching, he gives himself to further recollection. He finds the thought that will explain who he was on that day and hurries to tell us.

"I felt like someone other than myself. I felt newborn and reawakened. I felt that I was alive in a different and even more exciting way."

Now Sandra has something to say. Her eyes gleam with admiration for her husband's honesty and for his willingness to connect his experience of skydiving with spiritual transformation.

"That's what the extraordinary moments do," she says. "They change who we are, sometimes for the better. We do become new. After we have gone through the experience, after we allow it to change us, we come back to ourselves. We reappear. But not as the selves we have always lived with—at least not entirely. Our extraordinary experience, anchored as it is to our free fall into the daring and the original and the perilous, has made us someone in addition to ourselves. Our newness overtakes and replaces the selves we have left behind."

No sooner does Sandra speak about the experience of reappearing, than I look up and see Tyler walking toward our table. In the same instant, I cry out my astonishment.

"Tyler's *here*! He *is* here!"

Guided by the *maître d'*, he moves briskly toward me. He is real. He is not an apparition or a phantom or a specter. He is a flesh-and-blood reality, a here-and-now living presence. There is a swagger in his stride that is new to me. But everything else about him has not changed: the six foot-two-inch confident physicality, the dark hair, the strong cheekbones, and the long, tapering jaw line. Adhering to the formal dress code of this glamorous place, he is wearing a burgundy velvet dinner jacket, a white silk shirt, a jacquard silk tie with a paisley pattern of burgundy, gold, and black designs, and black cashmere trousers. The jacket has a notch lapel, two-button closure, four-button cuffs, and two front flap pockets. Even from a distance, I see that he wears his Ralph Lauren clothes with casual ease.

I rise from my place at the table and call out to him. I rush forward to meet him, all the while declaring my astonishment and my exhilaration. Only vaguely do I scan the surprise and perplexity of all the others at our table who have remained seated.

"Tyler! You are amazing. You've come back to us. Oh, you've really come back to us!"

Still at some distance from where I stand in this immaculately appointed room that overflows with guests who are as discreet as they are conservative, I feel my body swaying. For a moment, the room heaves up its imagery. Tables and chairs and convivial guests and renowned canvases pitch backward and slant and tilt and slope. Still my body sways and wavers and begins to fall into the darkness that begins to pull me inside its fathomless void until someone's large, strong hands take hold of my shoulders and hold me steady. Dizzy and breathless while the room goes on spinning, I allow those strong hands to guide me back to my chair. Only then does the spinning stop. Only now do I notice the surprised and quizzical faces of those conservative and senior guests who are nearest our table. Only in this instant, as my ragged breathing gradually becomes smoother, do I understand that Matt Collins has taken hold of me and has prevented me from falling upon the hand-knotted intricacies of an Aubusson carpet.

Sandra, seated next to me, coaxes me to drink some water. I am aware of the faster beating of my heart. I wonder whether I am dreaming because suddenly, here in this party atmosphere that is both regal and colorful, quite suddenly when I was not anticipating his arrival, Tyler has come back to me.

But only for the swift flash of these few minutes does my fate allow me to believe that Tyler is standing *there*, right there across the table, between Kyle and Li, who are still seated while they look toward him with surprise and elation. A young girl that I think I know but do not yet recognize is standing with Tyler. I grow uneasy. I become apprehensive. I begin to be angry. Why has Tyler brought this beautiful girl with him?

I notice Mr. Danforth and Kyle rising from their chairs to greet Tyler with a firm handshake. I hear them speaking his name, though I cannot decipher the exact sound of it. I notice Matt leaving his seat that flanks Sandra's chair and mine and hurrying around the table to welcome Tyler and the girl who has accompanied him to this special dinner party that the Danforths are hosting to celebrate Tristan's arrival and to pay tribute to Tyler, who cannot be present.

I watch the *maître d'* guide Tyler and the girl into the chairs that flank Kyle and Li.

I want to call out to him again. This time I want to ask why he does not come to sit next to me. Surely, Sandra—who has been sitting next to me and who knows how much Tyler means to me—will be willing to change her seat.

As though she has read my thoughts, Sandra whispers quick words into my ear.

"He is not Tyler," she tells me. "He is Tristan."

"Tristan?" I whisper back to her.

"I am as surprised as you are. I just heard Mr. Danforth speak his name."

Now Mrs. Danforth comes into it again.

"Here he is," she says, directing her words to me. "Here is Tristan. He's arriving late, but we are not surprised. Being late is his trademark. It doesn't matter. We are delighted that he is here. He is Tyler's twin brother. Now at last those of you who have never met him are meeting him here in this moment. Those of you who have already made a friend of him are meeting him once more. And he has brought his lovely young lady, Luna Cabello."

This girl named Luna is an extraordinary Latina. Her raven-black hair, her dark brown eyes and gleaming smile, her tan skin and her oblong face grant her a charismatic glow. Poised and assured, she radiates an ingrained decorum and an upright femininity. Because she is Tristan's girlfriend, she will be the competitor I need to surpass, the obstacle I have to overcome.

I am at once conflicted. I am disappointed that Tristan is not Tyler. I am dismayed that nobody, not even Tyler, mentioned that he had a twin. At the same time, I am devising a new plot, drawn as it is from my earlier fear-ridden schemes. I am imagining that, if Tyler never wakens, I may win his replacement—this mirror image of Tyler standing across from me, this *alter ego*, this mysterious double. But I will have to supplant Luna Cabello.

I tread cautiously. The path I am entering seems dark to me and dangerous.

"You are a tremendous surprise," I tell Tristan. "Nobody, not even Tyler, told me he had a twin."

Tristan doesn't hesitate to ease my confusion. His voice is as husky and as deep as Tyler's, but more gravelly. The outline of a sneer touches the right corner of his mouth even as he smiles through his too-smooth explanation.

"We Danforths like to believe that each of us is unique. Every one of us is different. We are Individuals, with a capital I. We move through this world on our own, distinctive and one-of-a-kind, even when we happen to be twins. In Tyler's and my case, the word *twin* was rarely mentioned. We are Tyler and Tristan, unique and separate."

"Your declaration of freedom."

"Absolutely," he says. "That's the way we put our own brand on our adventures."

"Sounds like a lot of fun."

"Sometimes it's fun. When people don't try to get in your way."

It is in this moment that I recall some news about Tristan that was being whispered in even the most conservative circles of my family's friends and acquaintances. He was involved in scandals that ricocheted their ruinous effects upon several lives. The lurid details of those scandals—the schemes, obsessions, and betrayals yoked to ill-fated consequences—I never discovered, so caught up was I in my own misadventures with Theo Ryan and his gang. But here and now at this grand party, as I push my way into Tristan's life, I remember angry and bitter words that referred to him as a scapegrace, a daredevil, a self-centered rebel who smashed other people's lives and never counted the cost.

Tristan is a troubled soul. I know. In that way, he and I share similar self-destructive urges. We scoff at tired conventions. We often break free of the rules that would rein in our wildness or subdue our adventurous impulses.

I detect a hardness concealed within the lightness of his remarks. I have met his kind before. I imagine that he has entered some dark corners of the world. Like Theo and his troubled friends and like me, Tristan is streetwise and cynical. He's gone a few rounds with the wrong people.

That explains why the Danforths sent him away to a military school. That also explains why, when he is drawing the attention of his father, Tristan grows cautious, just a little, the way a boxer keeps his eye on one of his wilier opponents. I merely conjecture, imagining continuing darkness where there may only be new light. Nevertheless, I begin probing.

"Why did you choose to study at a military academy?" I ask him, my voice gentle and my inquiry anchored to courtesy and affability. "Forgive me for saying so. You don't look the military type. You look too freewheeling."

He parries my remark with cool detachment. He does not return his father's studious gaze. He concentrates on me and on our brisk exchange of words. He's clever, and he is not giving away any of his secrets.

"Looks can be deceiving," he says. "Even freewheeling guys know how to follow strict rules when it's to their advantage to do so."

"Following military rules, striving to be a worthwhile cadet, must be one of the hardest challenges, especially when there is a wildness in you."

Mr. Danforth comes into it now. He is clearly proud of this son's recent accomplishments.

"Tristan has learned to be a first-rate cadet," he says. "The time that he's spent at Southwestern Texas Military Academy has made him a solid citizen. I must confess that I had my doubts about him. I wasn't certain that he was interested in changing his self-defeating habits. He's come through his year at the academy with an impressive record. He's left that formidable place with an honorable standing. His commanding officer has praised him for his tough-hearted confidence, his mental and physical agility, and his expert handling of rifles and revolvers."

"The real surprise and cause for wonderment is that the military suits his wildness," I answer him, calm and polite in my appraisal. I resist his belief in his son's ability to follow all the rules. Tristan is a renegade. I sense it. I see it in the sly curve of his mouth. I notice it in the role of the dutiful son that he subtly impersonates while he is in the company of his father. I perceive it in the quiet intimacy of the glance he furtively casts upon me.

Mr. Danforth notices my skepticism and finds other words to explain this son whose current reformation has revived his fatherly allegiance.

"There *is* wildness in Tristan," he says. "But there's more than that. There's new self-discipline. There's an ongoing discovery of his potential. His commanding officer at the academy told me that Tristan was defining himself in many exciting ways. Each day, every month, he was discovering new facets of the person named Tristan Danforth. He kept changing for the better. He kept reappearing to himself, coming back as someone more than the self he thought he knew well. Sometimes these transformations pleased his instructors, astonished his fellow cadets, and surprised even him. Amanda and I are very proud of him. It's great to have him back with us."

"Dad is too kind," Tristan says. "I'm not certain that I've changed that much. But I am learning to tame the wildness."

Now Luna comes into it.

"I'll tame the wildness with you," she says, her sweet-natured voice finding its rhythms inside the perimeters of decorum. "I'm good at that."

Mrs. Danforth has more to say.

"Separating Tyler and Tristan has turned out to be a good thing," she says. "They were never leaners. They were never excessively dependent upon each other. They had their own sets of friends. They often traveled on their own, without one another. Nevertheless, their being twins did make a difference. It did influence who they believed they were. It spurred them on to behavior that might prove to themselves and to their friends that they were two distinct human beings. Tristan especially wanted his friends to understand that he was his own man—the same as Tyler in his looks and in his mannerisms, but also different because of the paths he chose to travel as he explored the mysteries that make him who he is, one of a kind and altogether Tristan."

Tristan smiles in deference to his mother, whom he clearly respects and admires. But, being Tristan, he is willing to confront the truth of who he was and who he might still be.

"I chose to be wild," he says. "I was determined to make everyone understand that I am very different from Tyler. But I pushed the wildness too hard. I was out of control. I broke so many rules and never counted the cost to others or to myself. There was a madness in me, I suppose. I wanted to take the world by storm. I was that youth in a painting that I once saw at a museum. That guy was standing on the top of a mountain, his legs astride and his right arm raised defiantly in a fist as he looked out at the gleaming horizon. Beyond the cloud-borne haze, a city of towering buildings, ambitious citizens, glittering treasures, and breathtaking adventures rose up far away in the distance and appeared to be beckoning to him. 'Get ready for me!' I imagined he was shouting. 'I'm coming to get my share of the world, and I'm getting it on my terms.'"

"You make your life sound very exciting," Sandra says. "But even without the wildness, life can be very exciting."

"Maybe," Tristan answers her. "But I'll always want some of the wildness. I'll never let go of that completely."

"Glad to hear that," Kyle says. "Without a bit of wildness, you wouldn't be Tristan Danforth."

"Well, at least not the Tristan that we know and love," Mrs. Danforth says, with her temperate language and maternal affection setting the record straight.

This dance of words, this poise and grace and sometimes extraordinary revelation of feeling—this often-bold expression of syntax, utterance, and meaning, this daring performance of hide-and-seek through subtle nuances and covert deceptions—holds each of us in its spell. We crave to know the truth about one another. We search for hints and clues in the tell-tale creases upon our brows, in the haunted gleam in our eyes, in the vague melancholy that overtakes even the calmest of our faces, in the most spontaneous movements of our hands, and in the most abrupt shifts of our bodies. Our dance of words sparks the air. We choose the words that match the emotions caught inside our faces and the movements of our bodies. Our bodily motions are themselves anchored to the forthright actions we reveal to gain the allegiance of new friends and the wily charades we contrive to reignite the loyalty of old friends who have learned that the sounds and rhythms of our voices and the expressions of our faces and our bodies are sometimes honest and sometimes disingenuous.

My earthbound suspicion of these verbal dances notwithstanding, I have been savoring the words that have floated upon the festive atmosphere that has quickened the spirit of our evening. All of us here at this table, I perceive, have been enjoying this light-hearted repartee with its undercurrents of private mysteries and attempted reformations. At the same time, I am keenly aware that the capacious room around us thrums and throbs with the polite, murmuring voices of other guests and with the upright agility of waiters and busboys who cater with well-learned precision to the requests and the requirements of this stately group of men and women. The young waiter who had brought us our drinks now assists two middle-aged waiters who are equally adept and precise and serve our every need. Though the food is delicious, we women merely pick at our dinners. As it is their habit, the men eat heartily. I admire the menu and decide that I will draw upon it for some of the dinners that I will be hosting when I am a successful career woman and after I am married: red and green cabbage salad with apples, filet mignons with artichokes and *béarnaise* sauce, *Pont Neuf* potatoes, and almond-filled Basque cake.

From the distance, the sandy-haired pianist is still bringing genuine feeling to music both classical and popular. The poignant melodies of Rachmaninoff's "Vocalise" touch our more profound sensibilities. So does the lilt of some popular love ballads of the twenty-first century, including "I Don't Want to Miss a Thing," "Someone Like You," "Can't Get You Out of My Head," and "Don't Go Breaking My Heart."

The romantic promise of the music solaces my senses, but only for a few minutes. It also rouses my yearning for Tyler. It renders vivid all over again my anguish at his absence, my fear of being utterly abandoned by the boy I love, and my makeshift plot to win Tristan's love as a replacement for the love that I have lost because Tyler has drifted far, far away into a sleep from which he may never awaken.

Still the dinner party continues to spark and color the evening. Still the music floats upon the air and stirs our senses. Still the people at this table become pensive when they hear revealing fragments of their friends' histories. Still they laugh with and cheer on their dinner companions who know how to tell amusing stories and how to assess the foibles and other shortcomings of huckstering politicians and glossy celebrities. In this very moment, the Danforths are exchanging anecdotes with Sandra and Matt about their previous year's travel to South Africa. Kyle and Li are asking Tristan and Luna to join them in their visit to Hong Kong during the later part of the year.

I listen to all of them with convincing alertness. I allow neither the sensual lift of the music nor the convivial voices of the guests at neighboring tables nor my quickening interest in Tristan to distract my attention from the conversations that intensify the party atmosphere at this table. Sometimes, I offer a witty remark and throw out a thoughtful question to validate my presence as a *bona fide* member of this gathering. I tell myself I shall bide my time. I shall begin searching for ways to bring Tristan discreetly into my life, our private meetings creating for both of us a romantic scenario of furtive kisses and adventurous journeys and gratifying boy and girl bonding.

No sooner does my secret plan revive my hope and convince me that I am in it again, right inside the lift and boost and swing of a new happiness within my reach, than I discover a chance happening unfolding its possibility before me. Mrs. Danforth, Li, Sandra, and Luna go off to the powder room, to brush their hair perhaps or to apply more gloss to their lips or simply to exchange words about clothes and makeup and hairstyles—topics that would not interest men. Mr. Danforth, Matt, and Kyle pay a visit to the billiards room. Tristan heads for the terrace that overlooks the moon-glowing lake. I mention that I want to visit a classmate who is enjoying the evening with her family at a table not far from our own.

Her name is Kerry Fitzgerald. She was a classmate at the private school that I had attended in North Andover more than a year ago. Kerry was not merely a friend. She was an understanding advocate. She understood, a little at least, why I was always unhappy and why I needed to run away from my family. I haven't seen her in more than a year. But she continued to send me emails even after I left that private school. She was always urging me to follow my heart, to listen to the pulse of my yearnings, and to be true to my dreams. Kerry is a true romantic. She loves life and loves people. But she has a too-trusting nature. She does not yet understand that the world can be a harsh and dangerous place. Nevertheless, I like her very much. She brightens even my dark days with her affirmative spirit.

Tonight, in this very instant, I am making Kerry the ruse in my plot to steal Tristan away from Luna Cabello. She will be the decoy that convinces meddlesome acquaintances that I may, after all, have learned how to be as demure as she is. She is a nice girl that will divert attention from my plan to follow Tristan onto the terrace.

Alone, I make my way along the carpeted path that is leading me to the table where Kerry, at summer recess from her school, is celebrating her father's birthday. On each side of me, the festive tables and the prosperous guests are drinking celebratory toasts or enjoying their dinners or conversing with smooth and sometimes carefree cordiality. With a wave of my hand, I signal a "hello" to mature couples and privileged teens that hold me in careful regard and unquestioned allegiance, understanding that I am the daughter of the estimable Randolph Hayworth. I hold my head high. I keep my glance direct and open. I maintain a straight back posture. I refuse to be intimidated by any memory, theirs or mine, of the months in which I took flight from the rigid rules of my social class and from the deportment that every class requires of its teenage daughters.

I hear the pianist's velvety notes mingling with the partying voices. I arrive at the Fitzgerald table in time to join a table of twenty people as they sing "Happy Birthday" to Kerry's father, whose white hair, big-boned solidity, and low-key assurance, as well as his black suit, allow him a dignified and late-blooming mid-life charisma. Rapt though they are by this special occasion of saluting Sean Fitzgerald on his forty-sixth birthday, several of the guests take a moment to call out a "hello" or to tell me that they have missed me or to say that they are waiting for the time when Doctor Morrison will permit me to receive calls from the friends that have been a part of my life ever since I can remember.

These friends are not taken aback when they learn that Doctor Morrison is now allowing Kerry to visit me, because she has been a friend since we were in the first grade and because she has often proved herself to be a positive influence upon my life.

"You look wonderful," Kerry tells me as she gives me a hug. "I've always said that cobalt blue makes you look very grown up and glamorous."

"You don't look so bad, either," I tell her with the trademark flippancy that she has come to expect of me and that she has always enjoyed. "It's possible that a modeling agency will be calling you."

"Why not?" she answers me, just as breezily. "My future is open. I'll consider any legitimate offer that promises fame and adulation."

Our quips amuse us and please several Fitzgeralds, including Kerry's parents.

"You two are in good form tonight," Mrs. Fitzgerald tells us.

Tonight, Kerry looks stunning. Her flowing Irish-red hair is fashioned with delicate cornrows of triple braids. Her pale skin, blue-green eyes, and bee-stung lips grant her a beauty that casually accepts the last stages of its adolescence. She is wearing an A-line midi dress that has a black crew neck top with long sleeves; a checkered plaid skirt with red, black, and green designer blocks; and a red belt.

Kerry is an honor student and a proficient athlete. At Brooks School, she excels in swimming and tennis. In a year or so, she will begin her undergraduate studies at Princeton University. Afterwards, she will study law at Yale and enter her father's law firm. Already, she is a successful human being. She is the role model that I would always emulate if my character were ethically centered and if I were capable of resisting my self-destructive impulses. In this period when I have been reforming because of Tyler's influence, I have also made Kerry's behavior a template for my better conduct.

The major influence in Kerry's life has been her mother, whom I respect and trust. Though I do not often see her, Mrs. Fitzgerald has been as positive an influence in my life as Tyler, Doctor Morrison, and Kerry. At forty-one, she is the epitome of glamour. Her red hair is pulled back to form a neat coil at the nape of her neck. Her pale skin, blue-green eyes, and full lips grant her a beauty that has retained its youthfulness. But Mrs. Fitzgerald does not court or fabricate youthfulness. Instead, she carries herself with ingrained maturity and a natural acceptance of her motherly station. She is, of course, not a conventional woman. She brings glamour and poise to her motherhood and to her middle years. Tonight, she is wearing a burgundy velvet evening dress that is absolutely right for her figure and for her carriage. With its beaded right shoulder, its long sleeves, and stand collar, she looks very impressive, indeed. It is not surprising that she moves successfully in the corporate world. She is a patent attorney in her husband's law firm, which is one of the most influential here in Blue Ridge.

"I am pleased to see you looking so well," she tells me. "We hope to see you more often now that you are your best self again."

That I am not my best self I dare not tell her. Not only my hidden tensions and my conviction that, without Tyler to guide me, I am losing my way—not only those feelings rankle my certainty about the acceptable person I am right at this moment and the unacceptable person I may choose to become. These months of unhappiness have worn down my hope. My losses have damaged my spirit. I am a drowning girl seeking a lifeline. Within this hour of muted surprises and contrived exhilaration, I have sighted my rescuer. Even now, as I exchange friendly goodbyes with the Fitzgeralds, my mind's eye imagines Tristan (who resembles Tyler so accurately) piloting his rescuing boat toward me. He is not here in the room with me. He is no apparition who has reappeared from some private oblivion to remind me of the romantic pact we made with one another. Rather, Tristan is a new thought, an image pressed upon my awareness. He is throwing out a lifeline to me, some gleaming whiteness that in my clouded vision I cannot accurately discern—a life ring, perhaps, or a life belt or ring buoy. He is waiting for me on the terrace to take hold of it.

I hurry away to the terrace, with its white marble flooring, its equally white marble pillars, its weatherproof tables and chairs, its multi-colored flowering centerpieces and luminous table lamps, and its exquisite view of a lake that, to my imaginative eyes, appears magical and otherworldly. On this mild night in the third week of May, the lake is apparently swallowing the gold rays of the moon and the glittering light of the stars. Its quiet waters and the stillness that has come like a specter to observe the solitary watcher standing in the center of this terrace make this space an ideal setting for clandestine meetings.

That watcher is Tristan. He is in a pensive mood as he looks out at the lake. The cigarette dangling from the right corner of his mouth makes him look a bit streetwise and eager to take on whatever surprises or challenges the whorls and whorls of darkness beyond the lake may be preparing for him. In profile, he appears to my trouble-haunted eyes to be some demi-god, some duplicate or double or living facsimile that a benevolent angel has sent my way to compensate for the loss of Tyler. My searching mind tells me, of course, that Tristan is not Tyler. But he is Tyler's identical twin. He is his mirror image, and that likeness, as skin-deep as it may be, calms my fears, feeds my hopes, and goads my desire to bring Tyler back to me as Tristan.

He has not yet turned to notice me, so quietly have I entered the terrace. I decide not to wait for him to do so. Instead, I make my move.

"You look like a man who is contemplating a new adventure," I tell him.

He turns toward me and gazes upon me with keen and probing eyes. He lifts the cigarette away from the corner of his mouth and takes a few drags on it. Vapors of smoke rise around him and partly conceal his blue, piercing eyes; the cynical twist of his sensual lips; and his guarded smile. He is calculating the deviousness of my character and measuring the contrivance of my appearing here so suddenly within the privacies of this terrace that on this festive evening no other guests have thus far entered.

He moves nearer and with his tall muscularity and ingrained confidence responds to the careful words that I have chosen to begin whatever story between us awaits the push and impetus of our actions.

"Adventures are my stock in trade," he says. "They make my life exciting. They give me a reason for sticking around this crazy world."

"I like adventures, too," I tell him as I return the implicated sensuality of his gaze. "Maybe we can team up and make the world spin faster."

He studies me with an even fiercer interest. At once, I guess that he has ambivalent feelings about my wayward invitation.

"I thought you were on Tyler's team," he answers me. "I've heard that the two of you have already been adventuring. In fact, I heard that you and Tyler are inseparable."

"So we have been," I say. "But not now. Not while Tyler is so far away from me. I'm lost without him. I need someone to fill the void. I need someone to adventure with me until Tyler comes back."

He laughs a hollow laugh. Clearly, he is not pleased.

"You want a puppet, a fall guy that you can manipulate through your plots and your desires. You are trying to find an excuse for dumping your boyfriend. Maybe you don't love him as deeply as you should."

Now I tell him how it is with me. I do not beg for pity. I know better. Tristan does not yet trust me. He would regard any show of emotion on my part as contrived and superficial. Instead, I choose understated words. I stay matter-of-factly.

"I do love Tyler," I tell him. "I love him so much. But he's left me alone. He's abandoned me. I need somebody to save me. I feel as though the real me, the real Rachel

Hayworth, is disappearing. Sometimes, I puzzle even myself. I don't know who I am."

"I don't think I'm the one to help you find yourself."

"I think you could be, if you tried."

"Since we're leveling with each other, I'll tell you the truth without making it sound pretty."

"Go ahead," I answer him. "I'm not brittle."

"You want another Tyler. But I'm Tristan. I can never be Tyler in a million years. At least some of the time, I'd like to be as virtuous as Tyler. I'd like to be kinder, more tolerant of other people's ordinariness, more forgiving of their innate savagery. I'm trying hard, but not all of the time. Not even The Southwestern Texas Military Academy could change me all the way."

"Your father thinks you've changed."

"That's his wishful thinking. That's his way of dispelling his fear that I may turn out to be just another rotten stain upon the earth."

"Your father's no pushover. I find him to be very perceptive. He notices that you are becoming the young man he wants you to be."

"Oh, I'll admit that the Academy has worked its powers upon me. I'm not altogether reprehensible. And I've learned a hell of a lot about trigonometry, calculus, and physics. I did well as a wide receiver for the Academy's football team. I won a few medals for swimming, for boxing, and for running outdoor track—three or four miles every day. I even made sharpshooter at the rifle range, and I know how to take apart the engine of a Maserati Levante."

"Sounds impressive," I say.

My praise of him appears spontaneous, without emphasis or embellishment or any discernible effort on my part to court his favor. Yet I do seek his favor. My low-key strategy nudges me forward.

"I liked working with my Arab bay best of all," Tristan tells me. "The Academy calls it equine therapy. The horse reflects the behavior of the person interacting with it. It's very telling. The horse depends on being able to read you—where you are, what is going on with you, what your intentions are. By working directly with my horse and being responsible for his care, I learned something important, something that was very real to me, about communicating honestly and safely."

He reflects upon the words that he has spoken. Then, as though he is parsing their meaning, analyzing them critically, identifying their relations to each other, he tells me something more.

"I'm not always honest. It's easier to disguise myself, to conceal my feelings, to act very knowing about things when I may not be knowing at all."

I am surprised by his openness. Maybe he sees in me a human being who is as problematic as he is. Both of us have disappointed our parents. Both of us have wrought damage upon other lives. I tell myself that this connection between our tarnished past may facilitate my plan to win Tristan's allegiance. I push forward.

"That military school has changed you," I tell him.

"A little."

"A lot," I tell him.

"My father thinks so. I'll admit that I'm glad that he is pleased. But I don't want to turn into a carbon copy of the kinds of men he finds acceptable. I don't want to be another Tyler or another Clive Danforth. I don't ever want to lose the wildness that's in me—not all of it. I want to be like nobody else except Tristan Danforth."

"I want you to be Tristan, too. I'm asking you to help me through this rough patch. I'm asking you to help me get through these bitter days without Tyler."

"What about Luna? She's my girl. I want *her* to share my adventures."

"Fine," I tell him, even though I do not believe that it is fine at all. Already, I am devising ways to displace Luna. "I can tag along with the both of you—at least some of the time. There'll be no strings. I promise. I simply want to feel Tyler's presence through you. That will help me through some of my darker hours."

"I hope that you are not fooling yourself. I hope that you are not trying to fool me."

"Test me," I say.

"Maybe I'll go a few rounds with you," he says. "Let's see what happens."

He starts guiding me back to the dining room and to our table that is filled with convivial people. Before we leave the terrace, though, he pauses with me on the threshold. A slight frown touches his brow. His levelheaded gaze holds me within its influences. He wants me to know even more accurately how he is piloting this mission, this journey of self-discovery.

"I am trying to change for the better," he says. "I know that I've hurt some people. I don't want to hurt anyone else, not ever again. Change is hard, but I believe that I'm up to it. I can do it. It will be better if nobody sets unexpected traps on my path. But, even if they do, I'll bear up. I'll soldier through. I'll fight back."

I recognize the warning. I comprehend the assertion of strength and the determination behind that strength. Tristan wants to become a good man, but not a sanctimonious one. He has promised to keep some of the wildness that is inside him. He won't be a hermit or a recluse. He loves the world too much for that sealed-off existence. He plans to become a good man in the world, a creditable man who partakes of the world's acceptable pleasures. But being conventionally good is alien to his adventurous nature. He is working hard at conquering his moral weaknesses. He is devising ways to be good on his own terms, without compromising the wild spirit that illuminates and intensifies his existence. His path is rough. His way is sometimes uncertain. But he is soldiering through as well as he can.

I detect the chink in his armor. I recognize the hairline crack in his assurance. Despite his brash exterior, he is sometimes uncertain of himself.

Willful and devious, I move forward with my plan. Tyler may never waken. I'll find a way to make Tristan replace him.

Chapter Eight
DOUBLENESS

A few days later, Kerry Fitzgerald visits me. I am setting in motion my plot to win this new possession—this ambivalent and star-crossed Tristan. Kerry knows the kind of individual that Tristan has been. She knows the scandals that he carries on his back, like a body of death he is condemned to carry for all the weeks and months and years that he lives. I listen carefully to every one of her words.

"Tristan was leading a double life," Kerry tells me while we are alone in the reception room of my family's home in Blue Ridge. "That is why his parents sent him away to that military academy in Texas."

"What do you mean?" I ask her even while I push forward another question. "In what way was he leading a double life?"

Kerry, sensitive and wholesome and honest, is reluctant to tell me more. She is not the sort of person to cast a shadow over a schoolmate's reputation or to find glee in destroying a peer's favorable public image. But my need to know more about Tristan has both impressed and confused her. Kerry knows that it is not my habit to gossip about friends and acquaintances or to ferret out the sordid details of their wrongdoings. Today, she has become guarded in her response to my questions about Tristan and my pleas for essential information that will help me to understand who he is. She is well aware of my tarnished past, yet she has forgiven me my errors. She has become a compassionate advocate because I have worked hard to redress the mistakes that I have made. With Tyler guiding my rehabilitation, I had subdued my willfulness. I had subverted my self-destructive urges.

Kerry perceives the rigorous demands of my reformation. She comprehends the ongoing nature of my struggle. She knows that even now I am striving to become a more reliable human being. For all these reasons, she hesitates to draw me toward the shards and broken pieces of Tristan's volatile past. She does not want me to get hurt or, inadvertently, to hinder Tristan from moving effectively along the hard path that he has chosen to traverse.

In the privacy of our afternoon meeting here within the stillness of this immaculately appointed room that offers refuge as well as solace from a problematic world, I try to ease her apprehension. I want to dispel her confusion.

A few minutes ago, I explained that I want to know more about Tristan so that—like Luna Cabello, the girl whom he loves—I too can help him to adjust to the new and honorable path that he is treading. If the Fates are kind to Tyler and me, if in some distant year Tyler, reawakened and vigorous and life-affirming, marries me, Tristan will become my brother-in-law. Am I wrong in believing that I should know the essential facts of his life so that I can help him to subdue the wildness that is still inside him? My plan to join Luna and him in some of their excursions will often bring me into Tristan's company. Isn't it better that I know more about his past? Shouldn't I have some clues that will explain, at least in part, the mystery of all that happened to him last year?

Only minutes ago, as I brought forth all these reasons why I should know more about Tristan, Kerry agreed to reveal the dark past that brought Tristan low and that, in nearly imperceptible ways, haunts his life even now. But in this very instant, as she at last finds within herself the precise words that tell me Tristan has led a double life, Kerry hesitates once again. A frown touches her brow. Her eyes fill with tears. Her lips tremble.

"What is it? I ask her. "What is it about his double life that is hard for you to tell me?"

Kerry leans into the comforts of the richly upholstered French Provincial chair in which she is sitting and takes a deep breath. Then, while she gazes into my inquiring eyes, she hastens to tell the story.

"Nothing good can ever come from deception," she says. "Nobody leading a double life can ever be truly happy. At school, here in Blue Ridge, Tristan was an honor student and the vice-president of the sophomore class. He pretended to be a clean-cut athlete who was following all the moral rules. In reality, he was carrying on a secret and adulterous love affair with a lawyer's wife. Her name was Madeline Jackson. She was a Caulfield before she was married. She came from a working-class background. She won college scholarships and was graduated with top honors from Connecticut College and from the nursing program in Purdue University. She was known to be gentle and helpful and precision-plus in everything that she did. Physicians trusted her, and patients admired her stamina. She was a beautiful brunette who had a poetic nature. In fact, she wrote a book of poems about life's promises and disappointments. A small university press published it, and critics and readers praised it.

"She was twenty-three when she married Jeremy Jackson, who was a middle-aged widower who had never had any children. He was a cardiologist. Recently, he'd been named to a top post as one of the hospital's administrators. He was obsessed about his work and about his relationship with his much younger wife. He was a perfectionist who was never satisfied with himself either as a surgeon or as a husband. Whether, beneath the assertive style he used to define himself, he secretly fought his insecurity about his career and about his marriage—whether it was that secrecy and self-denial that finally destroyed him, only the few persons who thought they knew him well might accurately answer. Whatever it was, whatever suppressed fear and self-hatred eventually drove his secret fury, the consequence of his final actions wreaked havoc upon the three persons involved in the tragedy."

Now I begin to comprehend the ghosts that haunt Tristan. Now, in this quietly tense moment when Kerry is struggling through her recollection of the tragedy, I imagine with more conviction the apparitions that trouble his dreams, the guilt that wrecks his peace. I find new, accusing words that implicate him in the dark scenario that has left a trail of unease and sorrow.

"Tristan was one of those persons involved in the tragedy," I tell her.

"He was the catalyst," Kerry says. "He was in a special way the primary cause of the wretched things that happened."

"What did happen?" I ask her. "What was so awful that it makes your telling me so difficult?"

"The shootings. The killings. They were the awful things. Tristan was fifteen when all of it happened. But he appeared to be much older, a man who might be twenty or twenty-one. Exceptionally tall, big-boned and broad-shouldered, he wore his masculinity well. You never knew him until a few days ago. You entered Blue Ridge High School in the year that Tristan was enrolled into that Texas military academy. I've known Tristan for several years because of the friendship between our families. I've been told that all the girls at Blue Ridge loved Tristan. He was the prince of every party, the guy whose every move seemed original and daring. Some girls thought him more exciting than his twin brother, Tyler, because there was a dangerous undercurrent to his personality. At teen parties or on sailboat excursions or during kayaking adventures, Tristan could be a daredevil, a reckless adventurer who made all the right moves, a very confident guy who calculated the full measure of his powers before he called out a challenge to his adversaries or to the wide and deceptive world.

"His being at times a powder keg, a loose cannon, a tripwire—his behaving in unexpected and daring ways— appealed to Mrs. Jackson. She first met Tristan when he was a patient in one of the private wings at Blue Ridge Hospital. He'd had his appendix removed and was making a swift recovery. Whenever she attended him in his hospital room, they conversed about many topics, including hockey, sailing, popular music, and deep-sea diving. On the day that he was leaving her hospital care, she gave him a copy of her book of poems. The book became the link that connected Tristan to Madeline Jackson."

"It was an excuse for their secret meetings," I say.

"Yes. That's exactly right. They made love in the Danforths' cabin in Maine when nobody else was around. They enjoyed their sensual pleasures in hotel rooms located at least a hundred miles away from Blue Ridge and usually when Madeline's husband had traveled to some faraway location to attend a symposium that included physicians from around the globe or when he was a speaker at a medical conference being held in California or Switzerland. Always, Madeline and Tristan registered as husband and wife. Nobody questioned them. The Danforth name counted for something. Together, Tristan and Madeline made a very attractive couple. A Danforth had chosen a wife slightly older than he was. That impressed the hotel staff and the amiable guests, most of them visiting foreigners, who observed them.

"Then, Tristan and Madeline grew careless. A few times, when Doctor Jackson had travelled to some far-off location, Madeline invited Tristan into her home. On one of these afternoon occasions, Doctor Jackson came home earlier than they expected. In fact, this time he had not gone away. He and the detective he hired had tracked their whereabouts during the past ten days. Now, without the detective's presence to hinder him, Doctor Jackson quietly entered his home, climbed softly to the second-floor master bedroom, and—with a snub-nosed revolver in his hand—stood before the bed in which his wife and Tristan lay sensual and naked, sated and drowsy after their lovemaking. The afternoon sun was streaming in from the panoramic window and was bringing a calming glow to the oversized bed with its embroidered linens and multi-colored, lavender-scented fabrics. Tristan was the first to notice Doctor Jackson standing there, menacing and desperate.

"'Don't do it!' he shouted as he raised his hand in protest or possibly in petition. 'Don't do it!'

"Madeline, terrified and raising the coverlets over her face, said nothing.

"Without a word, Doctor Jackson shot Tristan and watched the bullet blast into the chest of the young, athletic body while blood shot out of his back, sprayed the pillows, and spattered across the coverlets. He shot him again, the bullet piercing his lungs. Life seemed to vanish swiftly from the body as the impact of the bullets pushed Tristan against the pillows just before he slumped across them, his eyes closed and blood spilling from his chest and trickling out of his mouth.

"Right after that, Doctor Jackson shot his wife, though he could not see her face. He shot three times and watched the sheet become speckled with blood just before it slipped beneath her face and showed her forehead bullet-riddled and blood-smeared and showed, too, her glazed eyes staring with horrified surprise and disbelieving awareness that death, in the person of her betrayed and deranged husband, had come to claim her.

"Perhaps pausing only to consider the consequence of his wrath or to savor the glee of his revenge or to satisfy at last the suicidal thoughts that for a long time had lived concealed yet insistent within himself, Doctor Jackson then shot a bullet into his brain. His body fell at the foot of the bed where, just minutes earlier, his wife had made passionate love with a fifteen-year-old youth."

"Tristan did not die," I say. "We know that much is true."

"Some say he got off easy. He had to have several surgeries because of a collapsed lung and because of some complications from the wound to his chest. But the Jacksons died. There would have been more of a scandal, because Mrs. Jackson had become involved with a minor. But the Danforths paid to keep Tristan's name out of the newspapers."

"How do you know all these details? Or are you merely guessing about what happened?"

"I am not guessing," Kerry answers me. "My uncle is a good friend of the chief of police here in Blue Ridge. He also knows the coroner involved with the case. More importantly, he knows the two detectives who questioned Tristan while he was recovering from his wounds in the hospital. These four persons told my uncle their versions of what happened."

"This scandal explains why Mr. and Mrs. Danforth sent Tristan away to Texas. It also explains why Tyler rarely mentioned his brother."

"Yes. But what I am telling you are merely facts and suppositions. They do not really explain the characters of the people involved. Doctor Jackson was an unhappy man. What he did—the act of revenge that he carried out, the murder of his wife, the killing of himself, and the attempted killing of Tristan—what his mind that was crazed by obsession, revenge, and self-hatred pushed him to do explains only a portion of who he was. His murderous act does not tell us about the man who existed before that terrible moment. He was, from all that I've been told, a brilliant and caring surgeon. He was a compassionate man. But he was also insecure. As extraordinary as he was on every level of his life, he did not believe that he was good enough. That feeling extended even to his relationship with his wife. I heard my mother tell my aunt that Doctor Jackson believed he did not satisfy his wife on several levels. He was not the man of her dreams."

"How does your mother know? Who told her?"

"My mother knows Mrs. Jackson's sister. This sister said that Mrs. Jackson still loved her husband, but that he no longer excited her."

My streetwise perception enables me to understand this tragedy with tough-minded awareness of the bitter ways that law-abiding and promising lives can suddenly crash out.

"This tragedy makes Mrs. Jackson look bad. She had sex with a minor."

"She did, and that *is* a bad thing. But Tristan pursued her. From the beginning, he wanted to sleep with her. I know. The news of this tragedy may not have been spotlighted in the papers or on television or even through social media. But Tristan's hockey teammates and his swimming team buddies knew what was going on. Tristan never told them much. But they knew that Madeline Jackson was making him very happy and that he was making her happy, too."

"His life came crashing down upon him," I say.

"Yes. But Tristan stayed tough. Though this tragedy has hurt him, he has never cried out for help. He's never asked for pity. Still, I believe that deep inside himself he is torn apart. He knows that he is partly to blame for what happened. I am not certain that he loved Madeline Jackson deeply. But he did have a loving feeling for her. Maybe he was using her, just as she was using him. Maybe they were helping one another to get through the rough patches in their lives. Whatever the truth may be, Tristan is trying to change. But it's very hard for him. Not even that military school has subdued all the wildness in him. That's why Luna is important for him. I think that she will make him believe that these first steps he's taken toward reforming himself are just the beginning. He can go on being an even better person."

In my heart, I cannot imagine that being a better person means that Tristan must wash away all of the dynamic qualities that make him who he really is. The wildness that feeds his sensual fury, the rebellious streak that intensifies his individuality—these traits, these attributes, these character prints, these hallmarks of identity—should not be stifled by punishing convention or suppressed by do-gooders who lack the courage to be different and to challenge lockstep rules and regulations. I tell myself that Tristan and I are alike. We cast the same shadow. We *are* rebels. We are wily negotiators. We are double-dealers. We have to be. The world is a dissembling power. Only deceivers, only those clever enough to revel in doubleness, in the guileful personas that dupe ordinary folks and punitive conservatives—only those daring individuals are really alive. Tristan and I belong to each other. So I tell myself, as I begin to jettison all my moral resolutions— every pledge that in this year just past I have made to myself to be worthy of a youth as virtuous and law-abiding as Tyler. Tyler has abandoned me. His death-in-life has wrecked my chance for happiness with him. It has rendered unnecessary my struggle to be an ethically grounded human being.

I listen quietly to Kerry's praise of Luna Cabello. I hold back my protesting words when I hear Kerry pointing to Luna's capacity for making Tristan believe that he will be a happier man when he learns to subdue his wild impulses. I need to keep Kerry on my side. I must conceal my cunning and my wiliness. I stay subdued. With low-key inquiry, I push my game forward.

"Do you think that Luna is the only person who can do all that for Tristan? Is she the only one who can help him?"

"We can help, too," Kerry says. "We are his friends. We can be good influences on him."

"I'll try to be," I say. "After all, he's Tyler's twin brother. I want what is best for him."

"Of course you do. But whatever you do when you are with him, whatever you do for him, tread with caution. His chance to lead a good life is hanging in the balance."

During the next hours and through all of the following week, I reflect upon Kerry's visit. I also keep hearing Kerry's genteel voice advising and warning me about the liabilities of Tristan's duplicity, the downside of his doubleness. I also recall her warning that any wrong move against Tristan will imperil his chance to build a worthwhile life. Behind his tough façade, beneath his hardened exterior, he is striving to become a better human being. I tell myself that I should back away from my devious plan to win him away from Luna Cabello. Far better, I say to myself, that I should maintain my fidelity to Tyler. Far more meaningful will my relationship with Tyler be if, with unabated devotion, I continue to visit him in his hospital room, there to touch his hand, to brush my lips upon his lips, and right after that to call out his name.

I am well aware that my relationship with Tyler, my having fallen in love with all the good qualities that he represents, has been a once-in-a-lifetime revelation for me— a special gift, a heaven-sent reward, a tremendous chance for renewal. I want to believe that our more-than-ordinary love, Tyler's and mine, mirrors accurately the tale of the good prince whom the Fates or his guardian angels cast into a deep sleep until the girl who is worthy of his love will call him back to life. So I continue to tell myself, desiring in fits and starts to carry forward my rehabilitation—the moral reformation that Tyler had been inspiring.

Tyler warned me about the pitfalls of double-dealing. Because of his influence, I experienced the tremendous and happy consequences of my transformation. Through Tyler, I learned that persons who change for the better appear to themselves and to others as human beings who are reborn. They *reappear*. They resolve their problems. They spurn their harmful plots and wrongful devices. They turn away from duplicity, double-dealing, insincerity, and deception. They shed their doubleness.

I might have accepted my loneliness, my feeling of having been abandoned by Tyler or by the happy Fate that brought us together. I might have pledged myself once more to a life without merriment, days and months and possibly years without observing Tyler's blue-eyed gaze upon me or appreciating his gleaming smile or recognizing in his husky voice a deeply felt yearning for me and sensing, too, the meticulous discipline that resists wayward conduct and easy, sensual thrills. I just might have pledged myself to that honorable and walled-in life. But some lack within me, some deficiency of character, some willful and self-defeating impulse pushes me in a different direction.

I go on dissembling. I continue to devise crafty and self-serving plots. I deceive. I lie. I allow my doubleness to propel my wayward life.

It is ironic that my parents draw me into that waywardness. It is they who, even now, invite me to share their duplicity. The success of their artifice, deceit, and guile convinces me that I should live in the present moment. Life is brief. Pleasure may appear as a familiar friend or as an unfamiliar stranger. Whether it is our friend of long standing or an acquaintance both unfamiliar and tentative, pleasure plays its own magic tricks. It often vanishes too quickly.

Unaware that I have reached a crossroad in my journey and that I may be choosing a path that could harm myself as well as others, my parents invite me to share their deceptions.

There will be a trade-off. I will help them push forward their deceptions. In turn, without comprehending the plot that I am weaving, they will help me push forward my own deceit, my inveterate duplicity, and my ingrained double-dealing. They must grant me the freedom to socialize at least occasionally without Sandra and Matt as my chaperones. Alone with Tristan and Luna, without Sandra's and Matt's perceptive eyes to witness my deceit and to recognize the tangled complications of my plotting, I'll have a chance to steal Tristan away from Luna.

So I tell myself as I impersonate the problematic daughter that my parents expect me to be. My capitulating to any demands they make of me in this hour will soften their regard of me and influence them to grant my request. Of that I am certain. I will then be one step closer to rescuing myself from my loneliness. I will be that much closer to replacing Tyler with his double—the twin who is not Tyler, yet in my eyes conveys the illusion of being him, grown wilder and even dangerous.

On this sun-radiant morning in June, my parents have primed themselves for an important photo shoot. *Vanity Fair* plans to place a favorable spotlight upon my father, whom they consider one of the top CEOs in the world, and upon my mother, whose success in films, on stage, and more recently in Netflix mini-series, is very impressive. So the editors of *Vanity Fair* are pleased to tell themselves and to tell the world, preferring as they do to emphasize the more admirable qualities of the persons they choose to spotlight. This stylish magazine often features news and pictures about influential celebrities from varied countries and with diverse *résumés* that include the corporate and entertainment worlds as well as the worlds of fashion, government, and sports. The photo shoot will involve not only my two brothers, who are visiting from London and New Haven. It will also include me, the daughter of the famous Hayworths whose adolescent, speckled past has already threatened to upend the false image that my parents and their public relations staff work assiduously to convey.

"This photo shoot is very important to your father and to me," my mother tells me as we prepare to meet the *Vanity Fair* team in my parents' penthouse on Sutton Place in New York City. "Think of it as a promotional gambit, a business stratagem intended to enhance your father's image as a CEO who also happens to be a successful family man. He wants to impress the conservative corporate executives with whom he does big business across the globe. Regard this photo shoot as a calculated move on my part, too, and on the part of the business leaders who help me run my film production company. My latest film is being released into theaters around the world. I need to draw attention to myself and to my film. I've had a string of successes, and I don't want to break my big box office streak."

My mother's language is matter of fact and self-serving, yet rather temperate. Concealed beneath a veneer of courtesy, though, the words that she speaks and the hint of *hauteur* in her manner suggest that she will tolerate neither rebuttal nor hesitation from me, the daughter who has often disappointed her and whom she has learned to mistrust and disdain.

We—my parents, my two brothers, and I—are sitting in the sunroom that wears its luxuriant amenities with a calming assurance and with pristine aptitudes for pleasing every guest who enters the capacious area. We are waiting for the *Vanity Fair* award-winning photographer and one of that magazine's top journalists to join us for an informal chat that will serve as an attractive preface to the fast-paced itinerary that my parents plan to unfold during these next four days.

This elegant sunroom is perched within the twenty-fourth floor of a Roman-style brick building that is filled with thirty-two penthouses and rises hundreds of feet into the sky. This extraordinary Hayworth room where we are now seated as a family pretending to be happy, this splendid room with its panoramic, sun-misted windows, this room of artifice and insincerity offers an ideal view of the East River and the Manhattan skyline. It also affirms my parents' immense success and, within the pages of *Vanity Fair*, will promote as authentic their fictitious images as ideal and loving parents. The long, comfortable sofa, cream-white and amply upholstered, and four equally impressive armchairs are custom-made Napoleon III reproductions. The armchairs, also cream-white, are clad in a hand-stenciled fabric. A rug with delicate cream-white, blue, and gold designs brings other solacing textures to the room. I imagine that the *Vanity Fair* photographer will include our rehearsed congeniality in the album of Hayworth photos he will create during the busy weekend that my parents have contrived.

Perhaps because she recognizes my suppressed hostility, my mother has more to say.

"Be on your best behavior," she tells me, her voice still controlled, still choosing to nudge me with gentle and accomplished nuances. "Think of yourself as being on stage. Everybody will be watching you."

My father comes into it now. Seated next to her on the ample sofa, he appears to be exactly who he is, her staunch ally who, while sharing her avaricious temperament and her cold-hearted ambition, assists her in devising new strategies for competing effectively in the turbulent race to acquire more and more wealth and to maintain a dominating prestige. To the *Vanity Fair* team, he will conceal his avarice and his hard heart behind the carefully modulated personas of an ideal American businessman and an equally ideal father and husband. That does not surprise me. For most of his waking hours, he is a master of disguise. But here and now, in this sunroom that conceals its tensions behind a solacing atmosphere, Randolph Hayworth unmasks himself. He is blunt. He is caustic. He is—to me, at least—unlovable.

"Don't mess things up," he tells me. "For once, be a straight-shooter. Back in Blue Ridge a few days ago, you promised to cooperate with us. Don't let us down."

My well-honed perversity incites a flash of contrived hostility.

"This is all so unreal," I tell him. "This is not who we really are."

"That puts us right in the groove," my brother Kendall says. "We're playing a smooth game. We stay on our best behavior. We win the gold medals."

Usually affable and often lighthearted when he is in the company of his twenty-four-year-old university peers, Kendall projects a sober demeanor as he addresses me. With a piercing glance, he warns me against devising even a small rebellion. He wants the weekend to be a success. He wants us to keep our father in an agreeable mood. For his next birthday, which is only a few weeks away, Kendall is counting on my father's giving him a penthouse in the Mayfair section of London as well as a Jaguar XL-20. Kendall is my father's favorite. As a first-born son, he has always pleased him. He *has* won a few gold medals because of his supreme athleticism on polo fields, on ice hockey rinks, and in swimming pools.

But the "gold medals" of which he speaks have nothing to do with athletic prowess. Instead, we earn the "medals" through our cleverness and our duplicity. We strive to win every test of endurance, every battle that our destiny heaves up before us on the paths that we are treading, every competition that our ambition compels us to enter. We can't afford to lose. We need to win. It is our stay against humiliation. It is our way of claiming our individuality for ourselves alone and of freeing ourselves for an hour or two from our father's tyranny. We win, and we keep at bay Randolph Hayworth's monstrous tyranny.

"Of course we do," I answer Kendall as he speaks of the importance of winning the game. "The Hayworths always win the gold."

My remark grazes flippancy that no one else in the room appreciates.

"We'd better win the gold," my brother John says, "or there'll be hell to pay."

With his lanky charm, John can be just as hard-hearted as our father. But today he is playing with more subtle calculation and with a keen knowledge of our father's darker moods the role of a twenty-year-old son who is both wise and diplomatic. Like Kendall, he wants to please our father. He, too, as a dutiful and obedient son, wants his share of my father's sometimes-extravagant gift giving. This year, John wants a chalet in Lausanne, Switzerland, where he can ski and play hockey with other athletes and where he can party with his latest girlfriend.

"You are so right, Johnny," my father says. "There will be hell to pay and damnation afterward for any Hayworth who doesn't win."

My father gives his words a stinging emphasis. But on this day his face is not flushed with anger, nor does he raise his gravelly voice. Like my mother, he aims to be temperate. He wants to convince himself as well as the *Vanity Fair* people that he is a solid, fair-minded man. That may be so some of the time, especially when a tremendous business maneuver in China or an exciting adventure hunting red-tail deer in North Dakota or river rafting across white waters in Maine subdues his ingrained tyranny. Against his conscious will, perhaps, he sometimes reveals a softer edge to his personality when he observes with fatherly admiration the same wily characteristics in his sons. Their riding roughshod over adversaries at school or over weak-willed acquaintances in upscale circles pleases my father. Those hostile encounters, harnessed as they are to superficial courtesies and hardhearted dispositions, convince him that Kendall and John will do very well in the morally tarnished, cutthroat arenas of big business.

I remain loyal to my earlier remark. As though I am an advocate of fair play and honesty, I repeat the words that my parents and my two brothers disdain. I am careful to add other words that endorse this family whom I regard as wayward and as self-centered as I am.

"I still say that we should not be ashamed to show these *Vanity Fair* people who we really are. I am proud to be a Hayworth."

My parents and my brothers find my new words pleasing. But my mother quickly sets me straight.

"Of course you are proud to be a Hayworth," she says. "Why wouldn't you be? You lead a very privileged life. But you need to subdue your wilder impulses, Rachel. You also have to learn to play the game with a sharp-witted awareness of the damage any wrong move will cost you. The *Vanity Fair* people are giving us a fair deal. They want to promote the ideal aspects of our family. We must allow them to do just that. We must not get in their way."

Kendall comes into it again.

"For this photo shoot, dear sister, you are permitted to wear an imaginary halo around your head."

My father laughs a scoffing laugh. The image of me wearing a halo amuses him. But it is not one that he can accept.

"Rachel is not the type for halos," he says.

I surprise all of them now. I become acquiescent.

"I'll be whoever you want me to be," I say. "I don't want to let the family down."

My mother is instantly pleased.

"Now you are being sensible," she says even as she approaches with mild skepticism and realistic eyes the demure face that I present to all of them—this problematic family that is used to navigating the shoals and rapids of doubleness.

My father knows the score. He is not fooled by makeshift acts of reformation. There is some part of him that admires my hard edge. Hardheartedness is a characteristic, a quality, a response that will drive my future successes. Nevertheless, he finds it easy to tolerate my acquiescence. It is a sign of my deference, my outward recognition that in this game we are playing my father holds most of the winning cards.

"That's good to hear," he says, "your not wanting to let the family down. You are playing a winning card this time. Besides, you want an Alfa Romeo on your next birthday. That, I think, has a lot to do with your not wanting to let the family down. That's good. You know how to negotiate. You know how to make a deal that brings you rewards."

My mother echoes my father's approval, but with a warning.

"You will have your Alfa Romeo," she says, "if you do your part to make this weekend work for us."

"I will," I say. "It's true that I want an Alfa Romeo. But there is something I want even more than that."

My words rouse both surprise and attention from my parents and my brothers.

John hurries to ask the question that pushes me forward.

"What could be better than having an Alfa Romeo when you are turning seventeen?"

As I answer him, my eyes first scan both of my brothers and then meet directly the inquiring gazes of my father and my mother. Now, without their recognizing it, I set before them the first part of my plan to steal Tristan Danforth from Luna Cabello.

"When I return to Blue Ridge," I tell them, "I want to socialize with my friends without having Mr. and Mrs. Collins chaperoning me. Of course, I love and respect Sandra and Matt. But I want to be on my own some of the time. I want to be in the company of my friends as an independent, young adult. I'm feeling much better these days. I'm ready to get back into the world as an individual. I don't want to lean on anybody, not even on Sandra and Matt."

"You are absolutely right," my mother agrees. "It's time for you to experience some independence. You'll be testing yourself, of course. You will have to make all the right moves."

"I will," I promise her. "I'll know exactly what moves will work for me."

My mother's easy assent to my request might have surprised me, despite my wily maneuvering of double-edged words and inauthentic praise of the Hayworth name. She too-easily grants my request to socialize at least some of the time without chaperones. I know why. She and my father have altered their plans to include me on their excursions to Palm Beach, the French Riviera, Brazil, and Lausanne. My health is problematic. Their schedules are overbooked. Recreational travel will have to wait. Palm Beach, the French Riviera, Brazil, and Lausanne do not presently fit into my parents' schedules unless their thriving careers call them to those places.

So my parents explained to me a few days ago.

Their granting my request to socialize without chaperones makes them feel good about themselves. They tell themselves that they are accommodating parents. They are kind and tolerant and understanding. This time I accept their self-lies. I do not need Palm Beach or any of those other places to initiate my plan to steal Tristan Danforth away from Luna Cabello.

The weekend unfolds our contrived pleasures with sometimes pulsating and always enjoyable scenarios. The *Vanity Fair* journalist, a woman in her forties, matches my mother for her impeccable style, her calculated glamour, and her tireless professionalism. The photographer, a man in his thirties, carries his freewheeling expertise with masculine and ingratiating charm. We get on very well. The photo shoot becomes a winning gambit, a profitable arrangement for all parties.

The next four days move at a fast pace. No sooner do my parents display the various splendors of their penthouse to the camera of the *Vanity Fair* photographer and for the deft choices of the journalist's writing skills, than we hurry forward to some of the occasions that make the Hayworth family appear adventurous and life loving. The photographer and the journalist are always with us, whether we are spending time in the penthouse on Sutton Place or in our cabin in the Maine woods or in a grand hotel in Washington, D. C. Within the first of these four days, after we arrive on a horse farm in Old Westbury, New York, we ride black-bodied Appaloosas, with their black-and-white-spotted coat patterns, striped hooves, and mottled skin, and Arab bays, with their finely chiseled bone structure, concave profile, and arched neck. On other days, we river-raft the white waters on the Kennebec River near our cabin in Somerset County, Maine. We sail my father's Sunreef 100 Power Range yacht in Newport, Rhode Island. We fly to Washington, D.C., in my father's Cessna Citation Latitude Business Jet and attend a summertime ball hosted by a renowned senator and his wife.

All the while, the *Vanity Fair* photographer is recording our best moves, and the glamorous journalist is embellishing our personas with her careful and complimentary words. *Vanity Fair* will publish these photogenic and verbal profiles of my family in early autumn. Both online and print-reading audiences will receive these glossy images, these crafty and painterly renditions of Hayworth family life, as proof of our guarded privileges and a demonstration of our public relations acumen. There may be some resentment on the part of the have-nots. There will be appreciation and emulation from the haves or those young professionals on their way up. There will be awe and hero-worshipping from the dreamers who may never move forward, but who find solace in observing those savvy ones like the Hayworths who do.

So I tell myself, grateful not only because I am one of the haves, but also because I can now move swiftly to claim what I do not have—and not merely a *what*, any possession that comes with a known price tag, but a *who*, a seventeen-year-old youth named Tristan, whose price tag I do not know and have no way of fathoming.

CHAPTER NINE
RACHEL AND TRISTAN

"You are a cool realist," Tristan tells me and then tells me again, this time intensifying his regard of me with a more revealing analysis. "A cool, jaded realist."

We—Tristan, Luna, and I—are standing before a Symbolist print by Edvard Munch in a spacious, second-floor room within the Blue Ridge Museum. Munch was a nineteenth-century Norwegian artist who is famous because of his portrayals of the conflicted relationships between men and women.

I have just made a remark about Munch's portrayals of sexual love as an often tormenting and destructive experience. I have called him a wise historian of the private consciousness, a full-fledged realist. Tristan, in turn, has called me a realist, albeit a jaded one.

Minutes earlier, Tristan joked about the pronunciation of the artist's last name. In the museum catalogue that he is holding, the visual sight of the name *Munch* suggests the action of eating or chewing something. But the *ch* in the artist's surname is pronounced as a *k.* The name itself is pronounced as *Moonk.*

"Looks are deceiving," he said, as he eyed me with penetrating awareness. "If you count on your surface impressions of things or of people, you will always be tripped up."

"You are so right," I told him, in that moment subtly challenging him to find me out in this game of cat-and-mouse we are playing. "Getting to know someone, really know that person, requires patience, insight, and luck."

"I like that," he answered me. "Your mentioning luck, I mean. Luck is an essential element in getting to know a person. But don't underrate experience. We often arrive at the truth of people because of our past experiences with other human beings. We learn from those experiences. We remember. If we are smart, we use those experiences to our advantage."

For a few moments more, he continued to ponder my words. In them, he recognized the invitation I was extending to him. I was inviting him to wait and see. I was telling him to give me a chance to prove myself. Yet the steely glint of his eyes did not bother to conceal his doubt of me. That gaze was giving me notice that I had better always level with him. He'd find me out if I were ever less than honest.

Now, a few minutes later, still affecting a persona that melds demureness with acceptable female self-possession, I stand near but not especially close to Tristan and Luna. We three are not alone. In the left corner of this splendid room that exhibits some of Munch's artwork which is on loan from Scandinavian and Paris museums, two professorial couples, possibly university teachers and probably in their mid-thirties, are bringing their own careful scrutiny to the canvases and prints and aquatints that color and vitalize the walls of this room. The sounds and rhythms of their whispering identify them as visitors from Georgia or Alabama. Nearer than that, perhaps fifty feet away from us, an aged man—silver-haired, gaunt, and well-groomed— comments with a quick-witted, Germanic edge to his appraisal about the art of Edvard Munch. He is conversing with teacherly helpfulness to three middle school children, two brown-haired boys and a blonde girl—tall for their years, straight-backed, studious, and precocious—who are probably his grandchildren.

"Edvard Munch challenges us to find the truth that hides behind mere physical sensation," he tells them. "He is not especially interested in conventional appearances. He is intrigued by the unseen. He finds ways of visually representing abstractions that have no material substance, such as emotions, moods, and ideas."

"We do something like that every day," the older boy says, sounding far wiser and more learned than most boys his age. "We look at the faces of our friends or observe the manner in which they are walking or listen to the words they choose when they are speaking. We try to figure them out. We search for what we cannot always see, the motives and the moods and the truths that hide behind ordinary-seeming appearances."

"Yes. That is something like Munch's approach," the aged man replies. "Of course, we value the seen, all that is clearly visible to our eyes. But we want to know more. We explore what is not seen. We guess at it. Sometimes, we come face to face with it."

The aged man, with his patrician air and his aesthetic inclinations, now guides his grandchildren to the right-hand corner of the room as he carefully examines the catalogue he is carrying and prepares to comment upon other Munch canvases and prints.

The dignified presence of these persons—the two professorial couples and the white-haired man and his three grandchildren—touches my awareness only for the flash of a few moments. Never do I lose sight of Tristan and Luna. Never do I subvert my plan to win Tristan for myself.

The print that is drawing our attention is called *Consolation*. Munch composed its imagery in drypoint and aquatint, which he then printed on Japan paper. The narrative it suggests includes a nude man embracing a nude woman on the edge of a bed. The woman is weeping, though we do not know why. Our not knowing prods our imagination. The print invites us to co-create its meaning.

As I study the print in the company of Tristan, I become uneasy. Against my conscious will, I am emotionally stirred as I look at the naked couple that Munch has brought to life in his print. Though Luna and Tristan are present, they stand apart from me and move closer to the print. They want to study close-up the red, blue, and yellow watercolor; the strands of red hair that glide over the woman's hips; the man's rugged arm wrapped about the woman; and the dark, disturbing shadow that hovers near the couple.

I look at them and at Tristan and Luna from a distance.

It is not the print alone that stirs my emotions—my yearning for the boy who has become lost and my desire to replace him with his brother. It is the presence of Tristan and the influence of his body next to Luna that stirs me, here within the pristine artistry of this room, with its treasured canvases and prints and their implicated flashes of truth. His long, muscular body nearly touches hers. His blue-eyed handsomeness occasionally turns to observe her pensive face. He stands so close to her. He is leaning so intimately into her as they peer into their catalogue to compare the description of the canvas they are observing with the images appearing before them, there inside the colored print on the wall. His left cheek nearly touches her right cheek as though he intends to kiss her. But he does not brush his lips upon her lips. Instead, after taking hold of the catalogue and placing it in a nearby chair, he raises her hands to his lips and kisses them. Clearly, Tristan and Luna are in love with each other. The love that is between them has been growing all the months that they have known one another.

His gesture fills me with awe and with envy. There is so much love in this man, and he is drawing Luna into its powers.

My breathing comes faster. For an instant, I close my eyes. I allow this natural expression of their love to vanish from my sight. Then, with an undercurrent of tension that hides itself behind affability, I proceed to say what I think about Munch's print as I move forward and make a place between Tristan and Luna.

"I like its indeterminacy," I tell them. "I also admire the artist's subtle use of shadow to portray an environment that is as ambivalent as it is sensual. We don't know why the woman is weeping or whether her relationship with the man is ending or beginning."

"Not even the man or the woman may know that," Luna says. "That is part of their mystery."

Tristan smiles. Luna's remark has genuinely impressed him.

"For a girl who has spent most of her time at home with her parents and at church meetings, you know some of the important things about men and women."

"Sometimes I know," she says. "But generally I make my way through the dark, as do most people."

Tristan smiles again. There is no doubt that Luna has captured his heart.

Right now, I am moving through the dark. With ingrained wiliness, I keep my fear at bay. I do not abandon my plot. I search for and find matter-of-fact words and sly innuendoes that call into question Tristan's capacity for fidelity to any girlfriend, even to a girl like Luna Cabello, who comes to him with a *bona fide* halo around her reputation.

"I am surprised that Munch is so honest about the role of the woman in a love affair," I say. "Few men, I think, admit the truth of their relations with women. In this print called *Consolation*, with its irony and ambivalence, Munch exposes the vulnerability of the woman. It is she who loses most in a love affair. She is the one who compromises herself and risks being punished by society."

"Yes," Luna agrees. "There is much sorrow in the truth of what you are saying. Most women love with their hearts and souls. They are willing to give everything for love. Many men refuse to feel as deeply. They hold back. They shun commitment. They are incapable of loyalty."

After hearing her words, Tristan moves away from me. He returns to Luna and takes gentle hold of her hands. Once again, he raises them to his lips and kisses them. Now, as I look on with silent and churning anger, he brushes his lips upon her lips. He looks into her brown eyes. He smiles, with no hint this time of a wily twist at the right corner of his mouth. Then he gives her a long, passionate kiss, right here in this stately room where Munch's troubled figures go on with their anguished lives and where the upright visitors have not taken notice of anything except Munch's art.

"It won't be that way with us," Tristan says right after he withdraws from the kiss. With his direct gaze into her eyes and his voice filled with apparently honest words, he repudiates the duplicity of most men and vows his fidelity to the girl that he has convinced himself he loves. "That's a promise."

"I believe you," Luna says. "I think you are learning to be different from most men."

I don't give up. I won't give in. I summon new words that suggest my grief, my broken heart, my feelings of abandonment and loss because Tyler is not here with me.

"It is wonderful to see you two together," I say. "You make such a perfect couple. It is so good to be with the two of you together. You remind me of Tyler and me. You are a version of all that Tyler and I represented for each other."

My eyes fill with tears. But I bring a melancholic smile to my lips. I play the role of a good-natured girl who is making her way as bravely as she can through a dark time in her personal life.

Before Tristan and Luna can respond to my tearful words, I say more. I want them to imagine that, beneath my brief show of grief, there is a steadfast conviction that the Fates or Blind Chance or a sympathetic angel will grant me my heart's desire.

"I believe that Tyler *will* come back to me," I tell them. "I believe that one day, perhaps when I am not expecting it, a miracle will happen. Tyler will waken and bring me into his life again."

Because she is sensitive and honest and genuinely good-natured, Luna reaches out to me. She breaks away from Tristan and approaches me in a sisterly manner. She pats my right shoulder. She looks with mild and compassionate eyes upon my careworn face. She finds soft words to comfort me.

"Of course Tyler will come back to you," she says. "Of course he will. Don't ever believe that he won't."

She embraces me with the same sisterly manner and the same compassion that drive all the words and gestures that she brings to her friendship with me.

I, in turn, accept those words and those gestures while bringing to my lips a slight tremble and while drawing from my eyes two tears that roll down my sun-tanned cheeks.

Tristan looks on in silence. He is carefully studying me. The ironic twist in the right corner of his mouth suggests to my furtive glance a lack of belief in my gestures and in my words or perhaps only a worldly disinclination to accept as valid my makeshift moral transformation. I share that disinclination. I do not believe in *his* transformation. I cannot foresee a day when he will be satisfied with a life that is sedate and cautious. He and I are meant to go a few rounds together. We are meant to burn both ends of the candle. Better that our lives blaze like a comet and burn out quickly. Better to orbit close to the sun and revel in the danger. Better to ride at the cusp of perilous adventures than to imprison our lives inside the small, airless rooms of safe conventions.

So I tell myself, well-schooled by my first-hand experiences of a time-trapped world—ruthless and rapacious and unforgiving.

I pretend not to notice Tristan. I hold myself steady. I begin conversing with Luna about Edvard Munch's long and productive career. I mention some of his prints, paintings, watercolors, and drawings. As we move into other expansive rooms that hold his work, I tell Luna all that I learned about him in one of my art classes at Brook School. As we stand before them, I offer knowledgeable remarks about Munch's copper plates, lithographic stones, and woodblocks. I keep my posture straight. I stand self-assured and quietly willful. I insist on myself. With silent lips and with my own secret language, I call out my name to myself.

"Rachel, you will win this game," I tell myself. "Be patient. Be wary. Be selfish and cruel if you have to be. Win the prize. Win the fairy tale prince—not Tyler, who is lost forever, but Tristan—his twin, his double, his flesh-and-blood apparition whose speckled nature matches your own."

A week goes by before I see Tristan and Luna again. In the meantime, I spend pleasant summer days with the people who are more often in my life. I sail on the lake behind my parents' home with Matt and Sandra. I swim every morning in the long pool within the south wing of the house. With Matt and Sandra, I attend a fourth of July celebration at the home of the Fitzgeralds, where I am careful to wear a happy face before my friend Kerry and everyone else there. I take long walks with Miss Pearson, the dedicated nurse who continues to monitor the state of my health and who has come to enjoy mothering me. By the end of the summer, she will be moving on to the care of another teenage girl who was involved in an automobile crash. This girl, Miss Pearson tells me without mentioning her name, is convalescing from surgery to her lower back.

My parents are traveling abroad again, busy with their successful careers. My brothers are vacationing with their girlfriends in Hawaii.

With Mrs. Danforth during a rain-swept afternoon, I visit Tyler in his hospital room. I call to him, but he does not answer me. I touch his right hand, but he does not move. I brush my lips across his lips, but he does not waken.

"One day he will waken," Mrs. Danforth says, her gentle voice always encouraging me. "One day he will surprise all of us. You'll see. And you will be ready to use the surprise well."

I devote three hours every morning to academic studies as I prepare for my return to the advanced placement program in Blue Ridge High School in September. I read several classic novels and afterwards discuss them with

Sandra and Matt. We share lively and thoughtful conversations about the strong female protagonists in Willa Cather's *My Ántonia*, Charlotte Brontë's *Jane Eyre*, Henry James's *Washington Square*, and Cid Ricketts Sumner's *Quality*. These protagonists—Ántonia, Jane, Catherine, and Pinky—overcome formidable adversities and willful enemies without compromising their own moral integrity. If I were really trying to be a good girl, I would make them my role models.

Sandra and Matt also guide me through advanced lessons in calculus, trigonometry, French, Spanish, and chemistry.

With Sandra and Matt, I attend Sunday Mass at Saint Michael Church here in Blue Ridge. I listen to the priest's homilies about the spiritual gifts of honesty, of self-sacrifice, of repentance for the wrongs we have committed, and of compassion toward those persons who are less fortunate. I wonder whether my being here in this church is merely another aspect of my duplicity. I feel closed off from whatever God or angels or saints may be observing me. I am more interested in devising the persona of a trouble-haunted girl who is making her journey back to an acceptable and meaningful life. I want my school friends and my teachers to notice me here. I want them to remember the demure way that I pray. I want them to keep in mind the precise femininity in my act of kneeling in my pew when, during the most essential part of the Mass, the priest raises the symbolic wafer. I would like Mr. and Mrs. Danforth, who are sitting two pews behind me, to watch the genteel way that I move to the altar to receive the sacred wafer.

Most of all, I want Tristan to notice me. I want him to forget that Luna is seated next to him. I send a spurious prayer toward Heaven that, because of his notice of me here, Tristan will discover that I am capable of goodness and that I know how to make goodness a partner of the more dangerous possibilities within myself. This pulsating thought, this wild wish, these selfish cravings incite my cunning. They feed my guile. They push forward my deception. Yet in my heart and soul I am aware that I cannot deceive Heaven. Nor do I deceive myself. I am tough-minded, willful, and rebellious. I am not a good girl.

But there was a time not so very long ago when I *was* a good girl. I believed that the saints were watching over me. With all my heart and soul, I told myself that some day one of these blessed saints would appear to me. Hopeful in those years and earnest, I read their biographies. I knew well the lives of Saint Teresa of Ávila, Saint Bernadette of Lourdes, and Saint Thérèse of Lisieux. I regarded them as my friends and my mentors.

I was intrigued when I read that Thérèse, the religious girl from nineteenth century Lisieux, Normandy, within the northwestern part of France, had discovered a spiritual joy in self-forgetfulness and in her need to make other people happy. I was equally intrigued when I learned that occasionally she had visions of Jesus Christ's blessed mother. I tried to be like Thérèse, emulating her self-forgetfulness and her charity, and for a while, in my early teens, I often succeeded.

Bernadette, an impressionable girl from Lourdes, a market town lying in the foothills of the Pyrenees within nineteenth century southwestern France, also saw apparitions of the Virgin Mary. The apparitions inspired her and influenced her to bring Mary's sacred words to the people in her village. Bernadette devoted her life to her worship of Jesus and Mary. She also helped the sick and the poor.

Thérèse and Bernadette were brave and religious girls who were no older than I when they experienced their life-changing revelations. But I felt closest to the little Spanish girl, born way back in the sixteenth century, who later became known as Saint Teresa of Ávila. As a frail yet strong-minded girl, she left her safe, humble home and ventured into the wide, problematic world. She braved turbulent political times and dangerous adversaries. Yet God was always her advocate. Eventually, she founded a commendable order of Carmelite nuns who nursed and fed the poor and the sick and who brought them God's message. On more than one occasion, she saw Jesus, His mystical apparition strengthening always the fervency of her belief.

More recently, I have once again felt a close link to these three teenage girls whose perceptions of the world were influenced by their religious upbringing. They were specially blessed because of their otherworldly devotions. Like them, I too have seen apparitions, though mine have been of a secular nature. I too have been lonely and misjudged. I also have given evidence of my courage and my steadfastness. But no Higher Spirit has visited me. No blessed and sanctified being has conferred with and encouraged me. The apparition that I have seen is a human being whose near-perfection makes him both extraordinary and honorable. As if I am reciting a prayer, I sometimes speak his name in a whisper. Sometimes, while I am visiting my aunt's ocean front home twenty miles way, I stand on the promontory of a white, chalky cliff. I peer at the billowing clouds and azure sky and call out Tyler's name to the Heavens. Nor do I merely call it out. Sometimes I sing it. "Tyler Danforth...Tyler Danforth...Tyler Danforth." The words echo in the air like a melody.

But Tyler never answers me. Only the echoes of my voice answer, as though they are repeating the call to Tyler that I had always been making, here within my silent heart and with my grieving spirit, until a few weeks ago when I met Tristan Danforth for the first time.

I used to be a good girl. Whether the lack of parental love turned me away from goodness or whether it was my perverse, self-destructive tendencies, I cannot say. I do know that, when I turned thirteen or fourteen, I felt lost. I was reaching out for someone or something to save me. My saints did not answer my prayers, because my petitions were always self-centered and self-serving. I began to throw my life away. I became reckless and scandalous. I broke as many rules as I could. I laughed and danced and sang at the parties of my friends who were just as lost as I was. I refused to pity myself or to pity anyone else. At night, just before I fell into uneasy sleep and in the morning when I awakened with unguarded fear and vague apprehension, I felt disoriented, disarranged, despairing. I did not know how to get back the good girl that I had been.

Then, one early spring day fifteen months ago, when the gold rays of the sun became warmer and the pastel colors of the flowers were blooming in every garden, Tyler Danforth came into my life. We Hayworths were guests at a lavish wedding. I had been enjoying the glamour of the ceremony, melded as it was with its churchly subtexts. I had been dancing with boys slighter older than my fifteen years. I had furtively drunk Champagne and Manhattans and was behaving too light-hearted and loose-limbed. Then I saw Tyler and in that precise and magical moment promised myself that I would try to become a good girl once again.

For an amazing year, after Li and Kyle introduced me to Tyler, I fulfilled that promise to myself. Tyler showed me the way. He was my rescuer. He was the Godsend for whom in the most secret corner of my heart I had been waiting.

Here in Saint Michael Church more than a year later, I reflect upon all these things and especially upon the pact that I made with Tyler. It was a sacred pact. It was a mutual promise that we would always follow the path of goodness. For those six months that we shared and for many months afterward, I have followed that path. But these months without Tyler have weakened my resolve. They have battered my peace. They have rendered as null and void the pledge that I made to myself and to Tyler that I would always be true to him and true to my best self. I cannot live without Tyler. But I *can* live with the twin who will replace him.

So I tell myself, fully aware at the rim of my conscience that I am betraying the trust that Tyler placed in me. I am also betraying my promise to myself that I will always be true to all the virtuous qualities that I represented not so very long ago when I used to be a good girl.

When the Mass is finished, Sandra, Matt, and I walk out of the church with Mr. and Mrs. Danforth and with Tristan and Luna. We chat briefly about an upcoming golf tournament and about a summer party that mutual friends are hosting on their yacht in Blue Ridge Harbor. I focus upon my conversation with Mrs. Danforth. I mention the visit we are planning to make to Tyler within the next three or four days. After that, I manage to send a friendly nod toward Mr. Danforth and toward Tristan and Luna. They wave back, though Tristan's salute to me is more reserved than the greeting that Mr. Danforth and Luna send my way.

I bide my time. I imagine that Tristan is suppressing his attraction toward me. I wait for the right moment to team once more with Luna and him. I am careful not to intrude upon their relationship. I do not phone them. My patience will help me win the reward that I seek. My pretended detachment will disarm the wily and distrustful Tristan. It will also strengthen Luna's belief that I am a grieving girl trying to be brave. I am a conscientious girl who fills my days with serious studies and occasional visits to the sleeping Tyler.

During the second week in July, Luna phones to invite me to go horse riding with her and Tristan on the following day.

"You need to break away from your summer studies," she tells me. "Being outdoors and being on a swift horse will spark your day."

"Of course I'll join you," I say. "But only if I'm not intruding. Only if Tristan doesn't mind my tagging along."

"Tagging along? You are not the type to tag along with anybody," she assures me. "Besides, I hear that you are a terrific rider. Tristan will enjoy the competition."

So, without understanding the deceitful underpinnings of my acceptance of her invitation, Luna sets in motion this phase of my plot to steal Tristan away from her.

Or does she understand them?

Early the next morning, she phones me again.

"I can't join you for the horse riding," she says. "The nursing home where I do volunteer work really needs my help today. Two of the nurses left messages on my phone. They sounded urgent. I don't want to let them down."

Instantly, I become uneasy. Is Luna backing away from our meeting because she perceives that my interest in Tristan is more than ordinary? I hurry to impart a casual acceptance of this cancellation of the horse-riding occasion that was going to team me with Luna and Tristan.

"I understand perfectly," I tell her. "Your helping those senior citizens is especially important. We can go horse riding some other day."

"Oh, you will be riding today," she explains. "Tristan is still available. He'll be calling for you around ten o'clock."

Silence enfolds me. I cannot at once find the words that make me sound natural and understated.

Luna dispels the silence and throws out a question.

"Did you hear me? Tristan is still game. He wants to go horse riding. He'll stop at your home at ten o'clock."

"That will be fine," I say while adding a meaningful condition, "if it's all right with you."

"Of course it's all right," she says, all the while maintaining a friendly lilt in her voice. "I hear that you love horse riding. So does Tristan. So do I. But even though I won't be there with the two of you, you must promise to enjoy the day."

"I promise, but I'll miss seeing you and Tristan together."

"All the better," she answers me. "This is a good chance for you and Tristan to get to know each other a little more. But you must do me a favor."

"What favor is that?"

"You must promise not to imagine that Tristan is Tyler. You will only make trouble for yourself. You will only invite more heartache."

"I'll remember that," I answer her, my voice more quiet and almost tremulous.

Just before ten, Tristan calls for me at my lakeside home. Sandra and Matt will not be joining us. But they are pleased that I will be spending the day in good company. Tristan will be providing me respite from my too-diligent focus on summer studies. He will be bringing me into the heft and hurl of a happy day.

I am wearing a white silk blouse, a green cotton jacket, tan breeches, and tan riding boots. Tristan is wearing a cobalt blue, long-sleeve jersey; navy riding trousers; and black rubber boots. On the surface, we appear to be compatible, and our alliance seems natural.

Despite his brooding glance at me, Tristan manages a smile and a friendly "hello."

With Matt and Sandra, he is affable and good-humored. They chat about baseball, the newest Apple phone, and the best gear for deep-sea fishing. To their remarks, I manage to add a few pertinent anecdotes. Then we hurry away to our horse-riding adventure.

On the surface, Tristan appears casual, relaxed, and even-tempered. But I know him better than he imagines I do. Beneath his imperturbable manner, there lives raw and goading his desire to be partnered with my danger. I can be the fuse for his incendiary nature, the spark that ignites his excitement. He is well aware of who I am and who I can be. The danger within me, suppressed yet urgent, teases his interest, torments his dreams, and disarranges his promise to himself that he will walk tall on a conventional path. So I tell myself, convinced that, if we freed ourselves from the rigid laws and repressive rules that stymie the wilder aspects of our natures, we could make the world spin faster.

Yet, back in a mostly unattended corner of my mind, way back so that it does not often disturb my notice, lurks the honest thought that Luna is far better for Tristan than I am. She is a guardian influence. She is the rescuing mentor who teaches him how to live as an ethical human being. Through her exemplary ways, she shows him how to care about and help other people. She inspires him to achieve the highest level of his capacities. She persuades him to find excitement and fulfillment in all the wonderful and ordinary experiences. She is the antidote to his maladies, the cure for his self-hatred, and the remedy for his loneliness.

In this very instant, seated next to him in his cobalt red Jaguar XJ, I am studying his handsome profile as he sits upright and reliable within the cockpit of his vehicle. He enjoys driving his Jaguar, which is impressive because of its gloss-rich oak veneer interior trim; its linear laser inlay; its long-wheelbase, rear-wheel drive; its four hundred seventy horsepower; and its 5.0-liter supercharged V8 engine. He looks like the prince in the fairy tale that haunts my dreams and my waking hours. He looks like my Tyler, though he is not Tyler. He is Tyler's twin, his troubled counterpart, his flesh-and-blood apparition, and the duplicate that confuses and taunts my senses.

No, I am not the girl that the kind Fates have meant for him. I am not the girl who can help him to achieve the honorable levels of his humanity. I am merely the lost girl who is reaching out, panic-struck and miserable, to save not him, but myself—from myself, from my belief that Tyler and my good angels and the kinder Fates have abandoned me, and from the yearning for wildness that has never really left me. Through the flashes of honesty that sometimes attend my awareness, I perceive the dark side of my wanting to team with Tristan. I admit the rightness of his conflicted appraisal of me. He wants to be good, and he is struggling to resist whatever temporary thrills his partnering with me may offer him.

But I can't let go of my plan. I can't deprive myself of this escape hatch—this emergency exit from my problems, this means of evading the whiplashing bruises from my dilemma.

All this while that these thoughts trouble my peace, I chat breezily with Tristan about subjects as varied as the recent victories of the New York Yankees, the cities that offer the best lifestyle for young professionals, and the adrenalin rush of kayaking on Nahuel Huapi Lake in the foothills of the Patagonian Andes.

Along a busy, trafficked highway and afterwards a private road stretching away from that highway, Tristan drives us to Ronan Spenser's horse farm six or seven miles from my family's home. The equestrian section of the property covers only fourteen acres of this four-hundred-acre farmland that fans out to green pastures where sheep and cows graze, to flourishing fields of corn, rye, and potatoes, to ample orchards of apple trees, and to greenhouses where mineral nutrient solutions in a water solvent feed rows upon rows of lettuce and tomatoes.

Today, we do not see Mr. Spenser, who is busy with his wife and their two sons connecting irrigation lines in one of the greenhouses. He is an impressive man. A veteran of the war in Afghanistan, he stands six foot, five inches. His shock of white hair and his slightly weathered sculpted face make him appear older than his forty-seven years. His level gaze and gravelly voice tell me right away that he has taken an accurate measure of the world and is still on friendly terms with it, despite its various depredations and malpractices. I'll miss seeing him today. He is an adult whom I trust. His proven bravery, his earned victories on foreign battlefields and in more trustworthy territories here in The United States, and his steadfast resilience radiate ingrained strength and the staunch power that has made him a survivor. I need to find that kind of strength within my own nature. I need to find valid ways to earn it. Tyler, who possesses so many of Mr. Spenser's extraordinary qualities, was showing me the way to discover my best and strongest self. I am alone now. I must make my own way. Already, without Tyler, I am stumbling on to an errant path. I hurry toward it, willful and bitter.

One of the groomsmen, a wiry, twenty-year-old man named Juan Romero, who is good looking and has brown eyes, dark hair and light brown skin, greets us courteously and brings from the stables the Portuguese Lusitanos that we agreed we were going to ride. These Lusitanos impress with their bay coloring, convex profile, powerful neck and hindquarters, and high-stepping gait. On each horse, Juan has already placed the seat of a Crosby close-contact saddle. Their forward-cut flaps allow riders to keep their legs close to the saddle, while making more secure their positions over the horse's center of balance. Tristan and I put our hard hats on our heads and our gloves over our hands, mount our horses, and are ready to ride.

For an hour or so, we shall ride Lusitanos across the summer flare of the land. Before we begin, it is clear at once to the groomsman and to four other riders who are observing the way that we sit on a horse, hold the reins, and signal him to move forward that Tristan and I are accomplished riders. When we enter the trail, we ride together for half an hour. Then, because I want to surprise him, I break free of Tristan. I am hoping that he perceives my cantering speed as a challenge to his own proficiency. I want him to turn our ride into a racing competition. From the corner of my eyes, I look for his hastening speed—a blur of swift motion, a spectral flash of navy-blue helmet; cobalt blue, long-sleeve jersey; navy riding trousers, and black rubber boots. Within minutes, he is cantering beside me. But only for a moment do I focus on the blur of motion that he becomes. The flare of his swiftness becomes a phantom, a shape-shifter, a ghostly shadow upon my quickened senses.

Now, once again, I break away from him.

Caught inside the exhilaration of my race, I ride with furious abandon. As though I alone am riding, there along the wide, tree-lined trail, I hurry forward to whatever destination the fury of my speed will find for me.

For that brief time, I feel free. I am a girl who has suddenly escaped from the prison I have made of my life. I am racing out of my own body. I am leaving everything behind me—all the grueling hours and days and years that have battered me, and all the rewarding hours, days, and years that I have betrayed. I am rushing away from even this hour, leaving in my wake the flickering imagery of Tristan sitting tall in the saddle and leaving also, as a spun velocity upon my seeing, the gleaming whiteness of the large main house on this farmland property.

Galloping now, I glimpse as careening blurs the meticulous landscaping that enhances the Georgian Colonial architecture of the place: quick verdant slopes and fieldstone retaining walls, ornately paved and planted surfaces, and many tiered, bluestone terraces. I see as flashes of color and animation young men and women picking peaches, pears, and plums from teeming orchards. Paddocks and stables and barns hurl themselves away from me. Guests' houses and workmen's cottages and ample farm fields are another flare upon my senses, rising and instantly vanishing. Trees and hills and lake soar, waver aloft, and disappear. Even the mountains whirl past me, the pale sun tilts, and the cloud-laden sky darts, slopes, and vaults.

I feel freed from all of it. I feel like someone new. I am claiming a totally different existence. The reality toward which I am hastening is another disguise that might hide who I am from all the people coming into my life and maybe from myself.

My Lusitano is galloping even faster now, at full stretch with body and neck lengthening and each leg fully extended as it powers along the winding trail. Behind my horse's neck, I tuck my upper torso precisely and fuse the outline of our forms. I lift myself out of my saddle, so that I can drop my weight down into my heels and push it further back, allowing my upper body to tuck in behind the horse's neck. Onward and more swiftly I go galloping, riding with shorter stirrups to make it easier to lift my weight out of the saddle. I keep my lower legs on the girth and keep my arms extended forward, as my horse stretches its neck within each stride.

Other teeming orchards, colorful brush, and wild-flower fields go flashing by me. Women and men are tending a passing field, and a rugged man is driving a tractor over a northerly hill. Now five or six gray-haired couples canoeing on a distant lake leap into my vision and just as quickly scatter away. Flights of black-backed gulls overtake fleecy clouds, enter their pockets, and then soar above the white cliff that rises out of the lake. I feel myself soaring, too—climbing and rushing out of the reach of the self that I am shedding even as I chase the self that is unknown to me.

Only when I see in the looming distance two horses grazing in a paddock do I push my lower leg forward while still squeezing both legs against my horse's sides. I brace myself against the stirrup, shorten up my reins, and put the hand that holds one of the reins tight into the horse's neck. I use my other hand to keep a strong hold on the second rein, as the horse starts to listen and to slow down. The world that I, alone, have eluded for a quarter of an hour instantly reassembles its imagery for my seeing. My past hovers by me, ghostly and insistent. The brooding thoughts come back to taunt me. But I fight back. I stay tough. My bitterness spurs my resolve. I want to hurry forward to the new, disguised self that I have only begun to devise.

"I'll do all right," I tell myself. "So will Tristan. I've made a plan that can win him and me everything we should have. I'll keep pushing him. I'll make him do everything he needs to do, so we can live life to the hilt. We can make every hour exciting, every day a new adventure."

Now I dismount and lead my horse into the paddock that is filled with perennial rye grass, creeping red fescue, wild white clover, and smooth-stalked meadow grass and is encircled by a cedar wood fence. I am not surprised to find Tristan waiting by the fence. Only a few days ago, Mr. Danforth mentioned that Tristan was just as fine a rider as Tyler. Tristan's horse, frisky and playful, is cantering around the soft turf of the paddock. Tristan watches me with a careful gaze and the suggestion of a smile. Though he stands there, with no words to greet me yet alert in his silence, I imagine that he has an appreciation of my riding skills. After I close the fence, he finds words to praise me.

"You look good in the saddle," he says. "You and that Lusitano are meant for each other."

"I'm pleased to hear you say so," I say. "Your praise is special because you are a terrific rider."

"I always like encouraging my friends."

"Am I your friend?"

"Only for as long as I want you to be."

"Fair enough."

I play upon his sympathy now or upon whatever residue of compassion lives inside him. I speak about Tyler, and my words are not without my genuine yearning for him and my emerging certainty that he will never come back to me. Nor are the tears that well in my eyes altogether guileful.

"This secluded spot has a special meaning for me," I say. "It used to be Tyler's and my private meeting place on all the afternoons when we were riding our favorite Tobianos here."

Once again, Tristan studies me with that brooding look of his. He is not yet ready to accept my show of sorrow and regeneration.

"You need to move on," he tells me. "It's clear that you are unhappy being alone. It's also clear that you lack patience and faith. You don't really believe that Tyler is coming back to you. So maybe you need to meet new guys. Maybe you need to find out whether you can love them as much as you say you loved Tyler."

"What about Tyler? What happens if he does wake up? How will he feel when he finds out that I've dated other guys?"

"He will know more about you then. Maybe you will know more about yourself, too. Maybe you will discover that you did not love him enough."

The truth of his words stings my conscience. I say no more. There is no need to call forth new words that might initiate a bond between us. There are no words that can keep at bay Tristan's doubts of me or that can disguise the ambiguous nature of my being here with him. Instead, we walk side-by-side along the trail that is flanked by lavender fields and scented meadows, accepting the silence between us as a reprieve from his suspicion and from my wily plot. Only when this trail leaves the fields behind and leads us to the top of a promontory do I break the stillness between us.

Standing there with him, upon one of the highest hills in the area, I speak words that reveal more than what his eyes perceive as my spontaneous elation.

"I love this place," I say, as I look out upon a blue mist greenery of hills beyond hills, cloud-laden implications of mountains, and the sun spotted expanse of corridors of space wheeling freely around and below and above them. "Whenever I come here, I believe in myself more than ever. Maybe, that's because the place gives me the illusion of concealment and a promise of safety. Being here gives me time to rally my forces. It convinces me that one day I will be rid of all my troubles. I will be absolutely free."

For this one moment that is different from so many of the moments that I have spent with him, I am speaking the truth. I am not trying to fool him with make-believe talk of escape hatches and easily acquired happy endings. I know that my journey will be a hard one.

Swiftly now, with husky inflections that yoke themselves to gentler words, he reminds me of the way things really are.

"Nobody is absolutely free," he says. "In the end, we always have to pay up."

I gaze at him with casual seeming attention. My blue eyes gleam, and my lips part in a smile, showing—I imagine—my perfect, white teeth and enhancing my demure consent to his words.

"You are so right," I tell him. "The realistic side of me knows that."

My gaze turns back to the colorful panorama that apparently solaces me. Tristan, in turn, studying my every move, sees what with clarified awareness I am observing. Below us, a motorboat is speeding across the lake, leaving in its wake the spume and ripples of blue-green waters. In the faraway distance, at the edge of the sun-tinted forest that stands across from the lake, Chilean willow trees, Scotch elms, and blueberry ash trees are bringing flares of excited color to the summer afternoon. Higher than that, though still within the opaque blue furling of distance, a stray herring gull is curving the dark flash of its wings against the tumescence of ponderous clouds. After an instant's pause, it plummets with wily skill to the consenting lips of lake waters, the better to pluck for its meal a raw, ample fish or a tiny, mackerel-tinted seabird.

Though the vision gives me back what I have not sought, a predatory image shown natural and insistent, I grasp comfortably its familiar message and find again my realistic measure for understanding things.

Turning once more, still toward the east, I am not surprised to sight the zinc-white hang of a wind-bleached cliff glaring like the bones of a devoured world. The limestone solidity of the gargantuan form impresses me, as does the cliff's having endured a wilderness of centuries. The imagery puts me in mind of my own resilience, as willful and time trapped as that is. In a world of uncertainty and violence, my capacity to withstand brute adversaries and wrenching betrayals is, I feel, my most essential weapon. The stark message I take from the cliff quickens my senses more acutely than any of the colors of the earth that surround me.

I notice, too, across and above the disquieted lake and on the crest of sun glanced fertile hills—right there, at the wavering margins of the shadow-laden woods—a gray-blue immensity of swaying larches that apparently grow into the sky and, before my troubled eyes, join all of heaven's restless and eerie motion. The sudden wind is billowing now, like a flare of wings lifted by lower winds and pushing upward against moist, lake-scented air. This feeling of space actively stirring, this sense that here on a sun-hued promontory the wind has come sweeping through the day's intricate layers and, spinning always its rapid coils, has come to claim me—it is this feeling that stops my firm gait and holds me in taut surprise back upon my heels while cliff and clouds and festive summer colors go wheeling by me. The earth itself seems to revolve with visible motion. I notice once more the receding diagonals of the forest across the lake—a shadow flecked welling of foliage and trees, an instant's ambiguity of surface and space.

I notice, too, Tristan's scrutiny of that same sequestered place. I wonder whether in this moment he is maintaining his realistic sense of things. He is even more knowing than I am about the world's equivocal promises and about its bruising, addictive textures.

I turn to him now, eyeing him steadily, as though I am coming back to him after a long absence. His black hair and tan-skinned radiance, partially concealed by the light that shimmers around him, gives him the spectral look of a mirage or an apparition. Then, because the whorls of slanted light begin slowly to recede from him, I see more clearly his enigmatic face and offer, as a subversion of his muted skepticism, my matter-of-fact appraisal of these surroundings.

"I've taken from this place what I need," I tell him. "It has served me well. Maybe it has done the same for you."

"Maybe."

I laugh lightly, giving myself completely to the pleasure of this moment.

"Oh, Tristan, it is wonderful to be happy here with you. Let's promise always to be happy when we are together."

My blue eyes are misty with tears again as I touch his large, strong hands.

"That's an easy promise to make," he answers me, his words as direct as they are even-tempered. "I'm all for that. Just be certain you remember that Luna and I belong to each other."

"You know I will," I say, my voice suddenly tremulous despite my show of exhilaration. "I'll always do everything to make you and Luna happy."

He observes me quietly, but only for an instant. He is not ready to share my exhilaration. His ingrained cynicism requires here-and-now proof of my loyalty to Luna and to him.

I change the subject.

"Let's ride back together," I say, apparently satisfied that this hour has dispelled his brooding at least a little. "We'll go back to Blue Ridge for lunch. I'd be pleased to drive your Jaguar that I like so much."

"You may drive the Jaguar" he answers me. "And I am ready for lunch."

As we walk back to the paddock, something unexpected happens. I trip and fall toward a large, cragged rock at the edge of the road and toward the razor-sharp edges that can cut across my face or slash my shoulders. With quick-as-a-flash agility, Tristan catches hold of me and draws me back to him. He turns the long, slender form of me toward him. For one moment that thrills my senses, our bodies are intertwined. His rugged arms are pressing me to him. His brooding eyes reveal his concern for me. His clean breathing merges with my sweet-scented breath. His lips are nearly touching my lips. For this one moment, his urgent sensuality compels him to hold my body tightly into his rugged and dominating physique. For this one revealing moment, here within the privacy of the woods, he wants to kiss me. I feel the urgency in his touch. I see it in his eyes. I see the need in the fleshy folds of his lips. I have roused him. He wants more than a kiss.

Then, with a swiftness that surprises me, the moment passes. He lets go of me and turns away.

"You should be more careful," he says, the sound of his words more guttural, even raspy.

I do not answer him, charged with mix feelings as I am. I am pleased that I have roused him. At the same time, I am disappointed that a newly acquired moral compunction has influenced him to stay true to Luna.

We enter the paddock and deftly mount our horses. We head back and canter along the trail in unison. Though we speak no words to each other, I impart through my gleaming smile the lighter spirit I permitted to attend me from the moment that Tristan and I reached the promontory. Tristan, too, consents to a modulated variation of this lightheartedness even after we have dismounted our horses outside Mr. Spenser's stables and the groomsmen have unsaddled them and guided them to a nearby paddock.

All during the drive through Blue Ridge and even during our lunch at a fashionable lakeside restaurant often attended by well-groomed patrons in their riding outfits, I join him in good-humored talk of his future travel plans that will sometimes include his Blue Ridge classmates, occasionally his parents, and oftentimes Luna. There will be an exciting trip to Hawaii, occasional trips to the Bahamas, weekends of skiing in Vermont, and his frequent co-piloting of a Piper Cherokee.

Tristan, in turn, listens to my fanciful words that tell him of the exciting trips that Tyler and I have planned after we are graduated from Blue Ridge High School. We have promised ourselves that we will hike through the Larapinta Trail in Australia. We will ski in Lausanne and swim in the Azores. We will fish for marlin off the coast of Cuba, and we will go deep sea diving in Tahiti.

Our lightheartedness, Tristan's and mine, is a subtle complicity, an unspoken agreement that we must not invade each other's romantic territory. But even our temperate language cannot dispel Tristan's distrust of me. In my presence, he will always be on his guard. That is his way of dealing with me. That is how he is going to win these games I am devising every time we are with each other and all the time we are not.

A few days later, a new surprise at first disturbs me. In a phone conversation with Luna, I learn that Tristan will be away for a whole week. He is making a religious retreat at Saint Mark Seminary ten miles away in Westport. The retreat is part of the goal he has set to transform himself into a morally centered human being. I regard his absence as a setback.

I change the subject. I tell Luna about Theo Ryan. This is the first part of my plan to draw Luna to Theo. They will not know that they are propelling my plot forward. My intuition tells me that my drawing them into each other's company will complicate and possibly destroy Luna's romance with Tristan.

"Theo's a terrific guy," I say. "He's had trouble with drugs and alcohol and with many wild escapades. He's even had run-ins with the police."

"I'm sorry that he's going through a rough patch," she says. "I recall seeing him in our school's cafeteria a year ago, but only in the distance. He looked so intense, so wired up, as if he were waiting to make something happen that might change things for him."

"He's making a comeback," I tell her. "He's gone through rehab successfully, and he's doing well in his home schooling. He's swimming and hiking and playing soccer with the friends who care about what happens to him and who are helping him to stay on the right path."

"I'm glad to hear that," Luna says. "I'm glad whenever I hear that the persons who have lost their way are making the hard journey forward to their best possibilities."

"We can help Theo make that journey," I tell her. "Are you in this with me?"

"Of course," she says without hesitation. "What can I do?"

"For a start, we can ask Theo to join us in our horse riding. I know that he loves horses and that he is an excellent rider."

"Let's do it," she says. "Let's help Theo to go forward to the new person he wants to be."

For an hour after my phone conversation with Luna, I withdraw to private brooding and to the stillness of my sullen disposition. I had counted on Tristan's being there to witness this new alliance that Luna will be making, this new and intense friendship that—with my prodding—she will be forming with Theo. Tristan's not being there is a serious setback.

But no sooner does this dark thought hover near me, than I retrieve my hope. I quickly revise my plot. Tristan does not have to be present when I unfold the intricacies of my plan. Only later, when the consequences of my double-dealing scatter his certainty about Luna, will he become involved in its aftermath.

I am not finished. I am ready to subvert even the beneficial effects of Tristan's religious retreat. I refuse to capitulate to the uptight moral conversion that steals away his individuality and his freedom. With subtle craftiness and a familiar proficiency, I weave my plot. I draw Theo into its complications.

CHAPTER TEN
THEO AND LUNA

"Come join Luna and me," I urge Theo when I phone him two days later. "You've always loved riding Lusitanos. Riding will spark your spirit."

"I could use some sparking," he answers me. His words are matter of fact and understated.

There is no fierce wildness in his remark. Something important inside him has changed. There has been a shift of values, a different perception of the world and of his place in it. I noticed these differences during his previous visit a few weeks ago. He is finding his way. He is finding his better self. I envy him. My conscience warns me not to hurt him. I should not draw him into my plot. I should take care. I should not place temptation on his path. I should not make him the catalyst for destroying Luna's romance with Tristan.

But I cannot help myself. Or, rather, I should admit the truth. I don't want to alter my plot. I want to claim the reward that Blind Chance or the punishing Fates have denied me. Since I cannot have Tyler, I want his twin—Tristan, the former rebel, the smooth trickster, and the troubled guy who is trying to convince himself that he is capable of being ordinary and run-of-the-mill.

I coax Theo further. I nudge his interest in a day that will offer him acceptable excitement.

"Of course you can use some sparking," I say, my voice exhilarant and promising. "We can all use some sparking. We'll have a racing competition—you and Luna and I. It will be great fun. You'll see."

Theo hesitates. Silence overtakes our conversation. He is conflicted. Something or someone is prodding his reluctance. Then the moment passes. He swings free of his reluctance. He explains his situation.

"I want to join you," he says. "We *can* have a great time. But I won't be alone. Connor Adams will accompany me. That's a rule I have to follow. Connor makes certain that I follow all the rules. Most of the time, I don't mind. He's been a good influence. He's like a big brother or a young dad or maybe just a helpful Samaritan. Anyway, I can join you and Luna only if Connor is included in your invitation."

"Luna and I will be pleased that he is joining us. In fact, his being with us will make our horse racing even more exciting."

Theo has more to say. His words do not surprise me. I anticipate them.

"I've never met Luna," he tells me. "When I was at Blue Ridge High School, I noticed her. She was one of the good girls. At that time, she wasn't my type at all."

"What about now?"

"Are you setting me up for a date?"

"I'm inviting you to go horse riding. There's no harm in that. In fact, there might be a bit of adventure in it. If you find any other adventure or any other excitement, that will be strictly your choice."

He laughs a husky and quiet laugh. I've put him in a good mood. I am offering him a new friend and an afternoon when happiness, a temporary and once-familiar companion, may also join him. Whether happiness will stay and become a more reliable friend depends upon the way that he meets this new adventure.

"Fair enough," he answers me. "But for now the horse riding is all the adventure I can handle."

For the rest of that day, I try to imagine ways that Connor Adams can, without realizing it, help me to propel my plot. I search my memory. I look for information about Connor that not so long ago I had discovered. Without recalling pertinent facts about him and specific anecdotes, I sense that he is just the man who will help me push forward my plan to bring Theo and Luna together as a romantic couple. I hunt for clues. I ransack the hidden corners of my mind to discover the teller of this information. I rummage through the hidden storehouse of my memory to find the identity of the teller and the specific details that define for my inquiring mind the kind of man that Connor Adams represents. For hours, I cannot remember, so tense am I in my search, so grasping for the telling particulars that reveal the man that Connor Adams has been and the man that he might be now.

And then, quite suddenly, it all comes swiftly back to me.

Only lately have I learned these facts about Connor. I learned them from Kyle Holden, who is one of Theo's loyal friends.

"Connor Adams is the real deal," Kyle told me during that night of Mr. Danforth's birthday party.

That night I told Kyle that I wanted to help Theo to find himself again. I wanted to know the backstory to Theo's efforts at restoring his better life. I needed to know more about Connor Adams, who appeared to be a strict and even militant guardian.

"He *is* strict, and he is militant," Kyle agreed. "He served in the Marine Corps as a top-rated sergeant during the war in Iraq. He saw some of his buddies killed by enemy fire. On one remarkable day, he saved eight wounded men in his squad when, singlehandedly, he took three enemies by surprise and blasted them away before they had a chance to fire their weapons at his wounded friends. Those friends lay on stretchers and gurneys, waiting to be transported to a nearby military field hospital. Connor saved all of them. After that and for several years, he killed many other men, and he saved even more men who, during that brutal and unending war, were fighting alongside him."

I wanted to know more. There was still a gap in my knowledge.

"I thought Connor Adams was a nurse."

"He is that," Kyle answered me. "Later, during his second tour of duty, he became a combat medic. After his military service and after university studies, he became a licensed nurse. It was his work as a nurse that brought him into the rarefied hemisphere inhabited by Theo's father. Mr. Ryan had suffered a broken leg and a dislocated shoulder because of a skiing accident in upstate New York. A medical service agency assigned Connor to monitor Mr. Ryan's convalescence after he left the hospital. Connor did all the right things. He is, from all reliable accounts, an excellent nurse. He is also good company—a first-rate poker player, a jazz enthusiast and fine saxophonist, and a helpful masseur."

"He made a good impression," I said. "He won Mr. Ryan's respect."

"And his confidence. Mr. Ryan rewarded him for his nursing, and he has paid him very well for his other services. He regards Connor as an essential member of his staff. It's no exaggeration to call Connor versatile. He has served Theo's father as a nurse, a bodyguard, a chauffeur, a valet, and a personal trainer. On occasion, he has lied for Mr. Ryan when Mr. Ryan's presence in a hotel room or in a nightclub might have entangled him in scandals. Mr. Ryan has even looked the other way when Connor has calmed his boss's troublesome mistresses by bringing them into his bed."

"He's a front man," I say. "He's always good for an alibi when his boss needs one."

"He's that and more. Now Mr. Ryan has made him Theo's bodyguard and his nurse. But do not imagine that Connor is going to be a bad influence on Theo. In his way, Connor is a man of honor. He is streetwise and trustworthy. He's been doing everything he can to help Mr. Ryan's son follow the right path. In fact, he is treating Theo as if he were his own son."

I do not hold Connor's faults against him. To me, he seems real. He is human. He is fallible. Though he is a war hero, though he has proved his courage while under fire, though he has saved many lives that would otherwise have been lost, he is nevertheless imperfect. He carries a few blemishes within his biography. So do we all.

The following morning, Theo, Luna, Connor, and I arrive at Mr. Spenser's horse farm at ten-thirty. Once again, Mr. Spenser and his wife and two sons are working in the greenhouses. Once again, Juan Romero cordially greets us and allows us to choose the horses that we would like to ride in that hour. The day is sunny, and the breeze is cool. This July morning feels like early April. We are wearing long-sleeved, cobalt blue jerseys; black quilted jackets; gray jodhpurs; black, elastic-sided leather boots; and black hard hats.

Theo gets right into the spirit of our racing competition as we mount our horses and prepare to enter the long, winding trail that will lead us into the wide expanse of this farmland and to the promontory that looks outward to soft layers of gray-blue clouds, the azure blueness of the sky, and the pale, yellow sun that glows like a magical disc inside a circumference too far for our fathoming and too remote for ordinary journeying.

Luna looks assured and moves with precise knowingness as she mounts her Andalusian horse that is especially handsome with its dappled, purplish gray color; its broad forehead and large, kind eyes; its fairly long and thick yet elegant neck; and its long, well-sloped shoulders. This is a horse with a strong body, broad chest, and well-sprung ribs. Its rounded hindquarters are also broad and strong. Its limbs are medium length, and its mane and tail are long and luxuriant. It is an altogether remarkable-looking horse. So adeptly does Luna mount this Andalusian that I understand at once that she has chosen this horse during previous visits to this horse farm. She sits with the weight of her body in the center of the saddle, allowing her hip joints to be open and her legs correctly positioned as close as possible around the horse's sides. She properly relaxes her arms at the shoulder and elbow so that they can move with the horse's head. She holds her gloved hands correctly, with palms facing each other and thumbs uppermost. Without using her arms, she clasps the reins by wrapping her fingers around them and almost closing her hands to make a fist. It is as though arms and reins belong to the horse, the better to follow its motion.

I see Theo watching Luna, mesmerized by her raven-haired beauty and by her inherent decorum. Already, my plan is working.

Theo and I choose to ride Lusitanos. In fact, I am riding the same, excellent horse that I selected a few days ago.

Connor chooses a Palomino, with its golden-colored coat, brown eyes, and white mane and tail.

Before we begin our race, I ask him whether he has had much experience as a rider of horses.

"Enough," he says. "I haven't been thrown from one yet. Actually, my girlfriends and I often go riding whenever we find ourselves near a horse farm."

"Then today we four riders will have a real race," I say.

We begin in unison. We bring our horses to trot. Clever riders that we are, we squeeze both of our legs actively against our horses' sides and soften our hands forward so that our horses feel free to increase the pace and go forward well into the trot. Around us the murmuring chant of the wind, the sunglow greenness of undulating fields and distant hills, and the fleecy nature of the azure sky influence our elation.

Now we ask our horses to go forward into a canter on the left rein. We sit deep and press our right leg on an Atherstone girth, the fine leather band contoured about the belly of the horse to keep the saddle in place. In the next instant, we ask more actively with a squeeze or a nudge of our left leg back behind the girth. Then each of us enters a cantering speed, and our racing competition begins.

From the corner of my eyes, I look at my competitors' cantering beside me. Each of them—Theo, Luna, and Connor—becomes a blur of swift motion, a spectral flash of black helmets, quilted jackets, gray jodhpurs, and black leather boots. But only for a moment do I focus on the blurring motions that they become. The flare of their swiftness makes them fugitive phantoms, vanishing shape-shifters, and ghostly shadows upon my goaded senses. But only for an instant.

Then I break free of them.

My Lusitano is galloping even faster now, at full stretch with body and neck lengthening and each leg fully extended as it powers along the winding trail. Behind my horse's neck, I tuck my upper torso precisely and fuse the outline of our forms. Once again, as in other racing competitions, I lift myself out of my saddle, so that I can drop my weight down into my heels and push it further back, allowing my upper body to tuck in behind the horse's neck. Onward and more swiftly I go galloping, riding with shorter stirrups to make it easier to lift my weight out of the saddle. I keep my lower legs on the girth and keep my arms extended forward, as my horse stretches its neck within each stride.

As they were during my ride a few days ago, other teeming orchards, colorful brush, and wild-flower fields are caught inside my swiftness. They float up before my seeing and go flashing by me. Young women and men are working in a passing field, and a rugged man is driving a tractor over a northerly hill. Now five youths canoeing on a distant lake leap into my vision and just as quickly scatter away. Flights of herring gulls overtake fleecy clouds, enter their pockets, and then soar above the white cliffs that rise out of the lake. For just a brief moment, I feel myself soaring, too—climbing and rushing out of the reach of the self that I am shedding even as I chase the self that is unknown to me.

Only when I see in the looming distance four horses grazing in a paddock do I push my lower leg forward while still squeezing both legs against my horse's sides. I brace myself against the stirrup, shorten up my reins, and put the hand that holds one of the reins tight into the horse's neck. I use my other hand to keep a strong hold on the second rein, as the horse starts to listen and to slow down. The world that I have eluded for half an hour instantly reassembles its imagery for my seeing.

Now I dismount and, with precise and knowledgeable movements, lead my horse into the paddock that is filled with perennial rye grass, creeping red fescue, wild white clover, and smooth-stalked meadow grass and is encircled by a cedar wood fence. I am not surprised to find Connor waiting by the fence. Aware of his proficiency in so many fields, I have already imagined that he is an excellent horseman. His golden Palomino is cantering around the soft turf of the paddock with a Tobiano, one of ten horses that are cantering or grazing here. Connor watches me with a polite gaze and the shadow of a smile. Though he stands there, with no words to greet me yet receptive in his silence, I imagine that he has an appreciation of my riding skills. After I close the fence, he finds words to praise me.

"I think that you and this Lusitano have had a long acquaintance," he says. "You and he have learned to be friends who respect each other."

"I am happy that you think so," I say. "We are friends. We are *sympatico*. We are like-minded. We are sympathetic to each other's needs. We have cantered along many trails."

Before he can say more, Luna and Theo return. They dismount at a gate to the paddock that is forty or more feet away from where we are standing. Laughing and chatting at the same time, they begin leading their horses into the paddock. So captivated are they by each other's presence that they do not at first give us any attention. Nor do they seem aware that Connor and I can hear all that they are saying.

Luna is more effervescent than I have ever seen her. Her brown eyes light up as she speaks with Theo. She moves closer to him and is enjoying the light-spirited repartee that they are sharing. It is clear to me that she has already opened her heart to him.

"I beat you by a mile," she is telling him. "My Andalusian and I left you and your Lusitano behind us ten minutes ago."

Theo is open and hearty the way he had been years ago when he had just entered his adolescence and believed that he could make happiness a permanent friend. As he looks at Luna, his eyes also gleam. His breath comes faster, and he makes of his walking beside her a most remarkable occasion.

"You couldn't have left me behind," he tells her. "I would never permit it. Now that I've met you, I'll never let you go."

Luna pauses. She guesses that Theo is unaware that she is Tristan's girl. She does not want to hurt Theo's feelings. She finds a diplomatic way to establish the boundaries of their relationship.

"Of course you won't let me go. Nor will I let you go. We'll always be friends."

Theo ponders her words. Then, still affable yet more reserved in his rejoinder, he tells her more about what he is feeling.

"True friendship is important. It can be the beginning of something else—something more."

To this remark, Luna adds a gentle observation.

"Well, nothing more than friendship is happening now. We don't need to let it happen."

"If you say so," Theo answers her. "After all, our friendship is just beginning."

His sensual gaze upon her undermines his pretense that his feeling for her could ever be merely platonic. I know those sensual eyes. I remember that look filled with yearning and passion. It was a gaze of desire. It was a telling awareness that made me feel I was the only girl in the room and even in the whole world. For a long time, Theo has carried a torch for me. Now, his flame burns even brighter for Luna.

Why Luna doesn't tell him about Tristan is a mystery that I cannot readily solve. Perhaps, she does not want to hurt his feelings. Possibly, because I have made her aware of his recent troubles, she does not want to upset Theo. Her keen intelligence tells her that there will be another time when she can inform Theo that she is Tristan's girlfriend.

But, just as I am musing upon her motives and her reluctance to mention her romantic attachment to Tyler, Luna rethinks her hesitation. She tells Theo how it is with her.

"There's something you should know about me," she says. "I have a boyfriend. His name is Tristan Danforth."

Theo holds himself steady. He is disappointed, but he is not defeated.

"You're not married to him," he says. "There's still a chance that you may change your mind."

Luna lets him off easy.

"You are a charmer," she says, "a cool, fantastic charmer."

Leaving their horses to graze now, Luna and Theo turn toward Connor and me, aware for the first time that we are standing at the farther gate to the paddock. They call out words to amuse us. Their faces are beaming with happiness. Together, they *are* sparking. They throw a few quips our way.

"You two are the winners of our race," Luna says, merrier than I have ever seen her. "That's very clear, and your victories are well-deserved. But do I get a consolation prize?"

Before Connor and I can answer her, Theo—as lighthearted as Luna—has something to say.

"Do I get any points for trying hard to win?"

Connor lobs a quip back. He enjoys seeing Theo looking genuinely happy.

"We are willing to console both of you. But you don't get any points until you try harder to win the next time."

Everybody laughs. Everybody is having a good time.

Connor and I follow Luna and Theo into the paddock.

To my eyes, they appear to be a romantic couple, so convivial and compatible are their responses to one another. Observing them there in the paddock, fully immersed in their exhilaration, I seize the moment. I recognize the opportunity. I push my plot forward, heedless of the damage that I may wreak upon Luna or upon Theo.

Quickly, I bring out my Apple phone from the pocket of my jacket and capture their romantic pairing on video. At home, I will select a revealing frame, pause the video on that frame, press the home and sleep buttons simultaneously, and with this screenshot create a still photo. I intend to post both the video and the still photo on as many social media sites as I can find, including Pinterest, Facebook, Tumblr, TikTok, Snapchat, WhatsApp, and X/Twitter. I want the whole world to believe that Theo Ryan and Luna Cabello have become a romantic couple. I want Tristan to see the postings. I want him to see the hundreds of "likes" that the video and the photo will win from Blue Ridge students and the thousands of "likes" that my photo and video of them will draw from persons who do not even know them.

To cover my tracks, to avoid suspicion, and to convince these three companions that I am casually making a video as a way of recording this happy time, I make a video of Connor with Theo and another of him with Theo and Luna. Then I hand Connor my phone and ask him to take some pictures. Before we leave, he takes more photos and videos of Theo and Luna. He captures their genuine affection for one another. He also records pictures and takes videos of Luna, Theo, and me together as a carefree and upbeat trio. We return briefly to our horses—the Andalusian, the Palomino, and the two Lusitanos that made our riding exciting. Connor, Luna, and Theo mount their horses, and I take their pictures and make a video. Then, after handing my camera to Theo, I mount my Lusitano and he takes my photo and makes a video of me with my Lusitano.

After that, after we dismount and leave our horses cantering about the paddock, Theo and Luna move deeper into the paddock. Connor and I follow them, but we keep our distance so that they can enjoy their special moment alone together.

Theo guides Luna toward a Criollo that has captured his attention. The friendly and gentle manner in which he approaches this fine horse quickly draws my attention. His manner draws the attention of Connor and Luna, as well. At the moment, the Criollo is standing alone—docile yet supreme—by a fence in the northerly area of the paddock. As he approaches the horse, Theo begins whispering to it, offering calming words that validate his affection for this tough breed of horse, this amazing animal favored by sixteenth century *conquistadores*. With his large, steady right hand, he rubs the horse's back and its crest, the upper part of the neck where the mane grows. The Criollo accepts his show of friendship and accepts, as well, the cubes of sugar that Theo offers it. Then, when Theo steps away, the horse breaks into a trot and circles the wide expanse of the paddock.

Watching Theo standing with the horse as he initiates a mutual trust and a strong bond between them, Luna is very moved. Perhaps her awareness of Theo's capacity for loving intensely stirs her emotions and feeds the desire for him that has already found a place in the most secret corner of her mind. Perhaps it is that stirred emotion, that secret desire that compels her to call out her appreciation of his inherent sensitivity and his tremendous capacity for loving.

"You really love this horse," she says. "I see it in the way that you whisper to it. I notice it in the way that you touch its back and its crest. How wonderful it is to meet someone my own age who loves so honestly and with so much intensity!"

Now Connor comes into it.

"Is there a story behind your affection for Criollos?" he asks. "Is there something in your past that makes every Criollo very special for you?"

"There is," Theo says, without any other words to explain his preference.

I nudge him now. My intuition tells me that whatever memory Theo can revive for us will inspire and increase Luna's admiration.

"Tell us about it," I say. "We'd like to hear about the first Criollo that won your respect and your allegiance."

Now, as we four walk beyond the home fields of Mr. Spenser's farmland and head for Theo's Jaguar in the parking lot, Theo tells us about his first encounter with a Criollo.

"Two years ago, my Uncle Roderick invited me to spend the summer at his ranch in Buenos Aires. My uncle knew that even then, at the age of fifteen, I rode very well. It was he who introduced me to my first Criollo. He even persuaded me to enter a polo tournament in which, as a teammate of young and hardy gauchos, I could prove my mettle. All during that visit and weeks before the tournament, I spent time riding and caring for the Criollo. More than once, when I was in the stables feeding it or cleaning its stall or brushing its coat, I noticed the sturdy and compact body of the horse. To my uncle and to some of the workhands, I praised its strong, short limbs; the size of its bones below the knees; and its solid feet."

"Criollos sure give a guy a terrific ride," Connor says.

"They do that and more," Theo says. "They also come with an impressive history."

"Tell us about it," I say. "I'd like to know what makes the history impressive."

Now Theo is more willing to open up about the Criollo.

"Criollos are descended from Andalusian and Barb horses," he tells us. "Long ago, they adapted to the harsh environment of the pampas. There, the extremes of climate—intensely dry, hot summers and severe winters—proved intolerable to all but the most vigorous specimens. Even the coats they had developed were a form of self-preservation. Dun-colored with dark points and often with a dorsal stripe, the coats protected them from their enemies by rendering them inconspicuous against the dry pasturelands they inhabited."

Connor has something to say.

"You like Criollos because they are tough."

Theo nods his head in agreement. His face brightens, and his eyes glow as he speaks of them.

"They know how to survive," Theo answers him. "They know what to do when they are in a tough situation."

Luna's eyes glow as well. I watch her peering at this human being that she is beginning to regard as wonderful—this troubled youth, this strong-minded adolescent that only today she has had the good fortune to meet. I imagine what she is thinking. I guess at her feelings. Theo's love of a horse that can endure hardship and danger enthralls her. His easy compatibility with the horse's movements and his elation because the horse returns his affection inspire her respect for him and the early stages of her devotion.

I know what love is. I love Tyler Danforth. I recognize the spirit of love when it brightens a girl's face or leaves a boy's face flushed with wonder.

In this special moment, Luna offers Theo an insightful remark about his empathy with Criollos.

"You share an affinity with him," she says. "You belong together."

He smiles at her, pleased because she has searched his heart and found something—some inclination, some need, some impulse or desire or propensity—to her liking.

We have nearly reached the parking lot when Connor draws me aside and asks me incisive though understated questions.

"What is it with you? What plot are you devising?"

"There isn't any plot," I say. "I just want Theo to be happy."

"He told me that you were his girl a year or two ago."

"We had a thing going," I answer him. "We had a lot of fun together. But it was never anything more than that for me."

"What about Theo? How does he feel?"

"Theo doesn't need me. He needs a girl who will really love him."

"You think Luna's the answer? You think a girl who says that she loves Tristan Danforth is going to make Theo happy?"

"She's already making him happy. Maybe that's all he will need. Maybe Luna's loving him even a little bit will be enough."

"I don't want him get hurt."

"Everyone gets hurt sometime. You know that. Theo's tough. You know that, too. He'll get over it. He'll get past the hurt, if there is any."

"Maybe. Maybe not."

For a moment, he ponders the situation. Then, more certain of what he needs to say, he tells me more.

"Anyway, the experience just might be a good test for him. Maybe it will show him whether he's ready to get back into the swing of things."

The four of us stay in a buoyant mood. We lunch at The Blue Ridge Country Club, and all goes well.

Then, at precisely eight o'clock the following morning, I post photos and videos of Theo and Luna on all of the social media sites, including Instagram, Tumblr, Snapchat, Facebook, WhatsApp, Pinterest, TikTok, and X/Twitter. I send six images of their intimate pairing to my six hundred friends, most of them classmates from Blue Ridge High School and from the friends that I made at Brooks School. I do not send any of the photos or videos that include Connor or me.

My friends will assume that Theo and Luna were having a good time, without any companions to intrude upon their privacy. They will see Theo smiling with heartfelt affection at Luna while he guides her into the paddock. They will observe her elation as he whispers to the Criollo in the north section of the paddock. They will notice the love in her eyes as he stands near her at the paddock fence. When they look at the other photos and videos, my friends will perceive Theo's and Luna's happy laughter, their easy compatibility, and their quiet joy.

By ten o'clock, the photos and the videos have gone viral. By then, I am well aware that I have created a wellspring of conjecture, a seedbed of malice, and a firestorm of rumor.

"What happened to Tristan?" several of my cynical friends—a few males and many females—ask in their postings. "I thought Luna and Tristan were a couple who were going to last a long time."

"I've never seen Theo looking so happy," many other viewers of the photos and the video remark. "Take another look at the way Theo lights up because he is standing near Luna. Is it love at first sight?"

"Aged philosophers say that love is for the very young," one girl writes just before she clicks *like*. "Looking at Theo and Luna, I'd say those philosophers were on to something."

A particularly vicious group of girls sends out this posting: "First Tristan. Now Theo. Who will be the next guy for Luna?"

More and still more messages of surprise or malice or disappointment flood the social media sites. The viewers exceed the friends in my own group, their numbers spawned by the groups who are followers of my friends' social media pages. By the end of the day, more than thirty thousand viewers have commented on the video.

Through all that night and into the early hours of the following day, I revel in the success of my plan. Surely, when he returns from his religious retreat, Tristan will hear about these postings from some of his loyal friends.

Probably, they will advise him to ignore the mean-spirited remarks and even the well-meaning responses. But his curiosity may goad him to seek out these social media sites that, even when they are well meaning, intrude upon the privacy of his relationship with Luna. As for the naysayers, the shallow classmates and vicious strangers who have made sport of Luna and him, he will have to summon all the discipline of which he is capable to suppress his anger and his desire for retribution. He will have to turn away from the malice and the envy and even the sympathy. I know Tristan. He will know what to do. He will maintain his proper bearings. He will navigate his voyage toward a safe harbor.

I wait, held steadfast to my own uncertainty. I resist the apprehension that churns within my conscience. I push myself into the familiar obligations that grant me a steady equilibrium.

With Sandra Collins, my kind and wise teacher and counselor, I swim across the viridian-blue waters of the pool located within the south wing of my parents' home. I practice the front crawl, always striving to perfect my flutter kick, my rotating arm stroke, and my rhythmic breathing. I give special attention to the breaststroke, with my whip kick starting in the glide position, and the sidestroke, with my scissors kick bringing both legs together with a forceful snapping motion, like closing a pair of scissors. I move swiftly through the butterfly stroke as my legs perform a dolphin kick. My legs stay straight and together as I kick them in a manner not unlike the way a dolphin's lower body and tail move. My body achieves a fluid, wave-like motion. Over and over, I repeat these swimming movements. Sandra, an excellent swimmer and a college medalist a few years ago, swims alongside me, providing the competition that helps me to hone my swimming mastery.

"You are improving every day," she tells me once we have completed a steadying hour at the pool. "You'll help your team when you return to school."

I answer her with genuine enthusiasm.

"I can hardly wait. I am ready to be in it again. I've been missing my school friends."

It is ten o'clock on this sun-filled morning in late July. But nobody has phoned me yet. Nobody has left me a text message or sounded the alarm about a scandal-in-the-making that involves Theo and Luna.

I move forward with my summer studies. Matt and Sandra are guiding me through rigorous weeks of study that will enable me to pass the entrance tests into the senior class's advanced placement program at Blue Ridge. This morning, we focus on trigonometry, as we review cosines, tangents, right triangles, and half-angle formulas.

At eleven o'clock, the Collinses—Matt and Sandra— discuss some poems by Emily Dickinson, including "Because I Could Not Stop for Death," "There's a Certain

Slant of Light," and "Safe in Their Alabaster Chambers." I mention that I admire Dickinson's trenchant observations about loneliness, despair, and death.

"I like her ambivalence," I remark as we discuss the poems. "In her view, faith does not come easy. Loneliness is an emotionally painful burden from which we cannot be easily rescued. Death belongs to that other side of existence whose mystery none of us can really fathom."

"Spot on," Sandra tells me. "You are becoming more than a little acquainted with Emily Dickinson."

Now my academic morning comes to a close. Today I welcomed its challenges. I tried to disappear inside its tasks and its intricacies. With scrupulous exactness, I met each one of its tests—my strategy for holding my senses upright and calm.

At noon, we three enjoy lunch on the patio. Or, rather, I pretend to enjoy it. The food is delicious. Our cook, Mrs. Durand, who was born in Paris and is schooled in the *Cordon Bleu* tradition, serves us a lunch that includes trout braised in Riesling wine and a pear and honey tart. The Collinses enjoy a glass of Chardonnay, and I find a glass of unsweetened almond milk quite palatable. Sandra, Matt, and I speak of their future travel to France and Italy. I mention that my parents have placed on my schedule for next summer a trip to China. I do not mention that they have included me in their plans because my presence enhances their image as conscientious parents. China is a big market for both of them. They have already experienced major successes there in the fields of film and big business.

"You will like China," Matt tells me. "When Sandra and I visited there two years ago, we were well-treated. There are so many splendid places to see and so many adventures to enter."

"Maybe I will like China," I say. "I'll know when I am actually there. I'll find out when I'm inside the experience."

"You are an empiricist," Sandra quips. "You base your opinions upon facts and upon the actual experience of doing."

I laugh, glad that I can break at least a little all the tension I am harboring.

Now, while Matt and Sandra hurry to our lakeside dock to prepare for our hour of sailing, I take out my phone. This is the time, after my lessons and after our lunch, when I am permitted to send or receive phone messages.

With bated breath, I enter my social media sites. I become aware of the hundreds of messages that are waiting in my cue. As I begin to read some of them, I become more and more uneasy. The abrasive remarks that friends and strangers have directed against Luna would baffle a rational person. There is something ugly, some grievous soul-blemish, in their eagerness to cast stones upon a girl whose conduct has always been above reproach. Besides, whatever kind of relationship that Luna and Theo are creating between themselves is nobody else's business.

THE REAPPEARING

Trouble is brewing. I sense it. I expect it. Not only Luna and Theo will be caught in the ricocheting forces of its consequences. I, too, will be caught by the caroming effects of this scandal and by all the tangled images that I have so willfully devised.

Not even the bracing sail across the lake eases my tension. Not even the sight of black-backed gulls standing poised and confident on the breeze-touched waters of the lake or the sounds of their hoarse, trumpeting calls can rouse my happiness. Nor does the immensity of the white stone cliffs rising out of the water as though they are the remnants of a world devoured by time and accident—not even these prodigious and monumental rock formations can dispel my uneasy feeling that I have murdered Luna's reputation. In the faraway distance ahead of us, I see two pairs of rugged, adolescent boys and lithe, proficient girls skiing adeptly on the rippling waters of the lake. Tethered to twenty-nine-foot open-cockpit daysailers, they appear to my eyes to be levitating above the lake. They look more-than-ordinary. They look otherworldly. They look magical. The sun also looks magical, a giant golden disk skyborne and celestial. Yet not even my sighting the water skiers or the sun has solaced my senses. When Matt invites me to take my turn piloting our craft, I eagerly accept the opportunity. Suddenly, without anticipating the restoration of my spirit, I feel in command. Quite suddenly, I am once more in control of what is happening in the unpredictable moment that I am now living. Hope, though still a vague and nebulous thing, infuses my outlook.

I sail around the lake with genuine exuberance. I share humorous chatter with good-natured Sandra and equally trustworthy Matt. Today, I do not pause at any friends' docks or jetties. That is not part of the agenda that the Collinses and I have planned. We simply want to experience the sheer velocity of the boat's speed. More than that, I want to know once again the nearly out-of-body sensation that my piloting offers me. For a while, my dark thoughts scatter away. My self-recrimination vanishes into the hidden storehouse of my troubled thoughts. After a while, Sandra takes over, and I am free once more to reflect upon my wayward behavior and the plotting that I have devised against three friends who have never wronged me.

What I have done to Luna is wrong. I have also wronged Theo and Tristan. I have cast shadows over their reputations. The photos and videos that I have posted suggest that Theo is willing to steal Luna's affection away from Tristan. Those postings also suggest that Tristan's brooding romanticism has failed to inspire Luna's fidelity. As far as I know, my postings do not represent the truth. They are devious. They are dishonorable. They are destructive. Yet something good, some beneficial outcome, though unintended, may come from my shameless plotting. My postings will serve as a test not only for Luna, but also for both Theo and Tristan.

Will Theo find the courage to back away from his love for Luna? Will Luna find the strength of will to resist her attraction to Theo? Will Tristan express his trust in Luna, despite the rumors of her infidelity? There is still a chance that Luna and Theo and Tristan will fail the tests that the Fates and I have placed before them. There is still a chance that Tristan will then turn to me.

CHAPTER ELEVEN
MANY VISITORS

During the next afternoon, at a quarter past three o'clock, after I have successfully completed another session of academic studies with Matt and Sandra, Luna visits me in the patio of my parents' home that overlooks the tranquil lake glowing with summer brightness. She is wearing a sun-yellow jersey shirtdress that accentuates her tall, slim figure and her long, shapely legs. Enhanced with utility-inspired details, the dress has button front pockets, sleeves that she has rolled up to three-quarter length, and a self-tie belt. Her deeper yellow ballet flats perfectly complement her radiant appearance. Today, Luna is wearing a new hairstyle, a raven-haired lob with fringe bangs. This new look modifies her identity. It alters my earlier impressions of her. She still carries with assurance her wholesome look and the appealing smile that, even when it is touched by a hint of melancholy as it is in this moment, is very appealing. But today she has acquired a more sophisticated air. She is a girl who knows herself well. She is, I think, a girl who will never compromise her beliefs or betray her friends. In all these ways, she is different from me. Always, every morning, she will wake up and know that she will respond to the day's rewards and betrayals with a brave heart and a disciplined mind.

I am wearing a floral polyester long sleeve blouse, beige slacks with matching slim beige belt and gold buckle, and beige clip toe platform sandals. My clothes give me a look that is summer-fresh and casual. But I do not feel casual. Nevertheless, I suppress my tension.

We take our places in comfortable patio chairs, and Mrs. Durand, our housekeeper and cook, brings us a tray filled with frosted glasses of lemonade and, fresh from her oven, delicious carrot and walnut teacakes.

To express her appreciation of our hospitality, Luna sips the lemonade. But she is not really interested in either the lemonade or the teacakes. In this hour, she has come to talk over things with me. Though disappointment and anger are allies of her melancholy, she holds herself steady. She remains even-tempered and matter of fact.

"Your posting the photos of Theo and me was no accident," she says. "You want to make trouble for me. You want Tristan and me to break up."

I carefully weigh my words. I decide not to disguise my motives. What good would that do for me? Luna sees through me. She recognizes a devious girl when she sees her.

In this moment, though, I want to tell her the truth. I want to tell her how it is with me. Suddenly, it is important that she knows how unhappy I am. I feel a frown creasing my brow. I feel my lips become tremulous, and I hear my voice quaver. Sorrow rushes out of me, but I hold myself steady. I do not cry out my pain. I do not lament my fate. I tell her what she already has guessed. I tell her with different words and morose emphasis that I am like a drowning girl who suddenly sights a safe harbor. Tristan stands in that harbor. Maybe he is waiting for me.

"Yes," I explain, admitting as I do that I want Tristan and her to break up. "That is what I want. I need Tristan to replace Tyler. I need to be happy again. I can't bear my life. I don't want to face the prospect of waking each morning and knowing that the boy that I love is lost to me. Tristan could replace Tyler. He could make me happy again."

Luna is carefully studying me. She witnesses my anguish. She probably sees the faint evidence of sleepless nights and daytime brooding.

"Tristan would have to love you to make that happen," Luna answers me. "I believe that he does not love you. He's not a perfect individual. Your flirting with him *has* intrigued him. He is, after all, a healthy male. But what do you expect to get from a romance with him? It would never last. I believe that it will not even begin. I know Tristan well. He will never betray his twin brother. He will never come between Tyler and you. Even if Tyler never wakens, Tristan will not want to carry that burden of replacing Tyler's love for you."

I resent her words. They carry possibility and truth that are too wrenching for me to bear. My own words become blunt, traveling as they do on the edge of caustic.

"You don't really know what Tristan is going to do," I tell her. "You are not as certain of him as you pretend, or you wouldn't be here now trying to convince me that he could never love me."

Luna remains unafraid of my words. She parses their meanings, analyzing their implications and their relations to one another. Then she speaks her mind, open and forthright.

"There *is* a possibility that I am misreading his character," she says. "But I believe in Tristan. I believe his love for me is genuine and good. Our relationship—his and mine—is not a will-o'-the-wisp confusion, a flickering light or aspiration that leads us on but can never be reached. He and I are soul mates. I think that our souls have known one another long before he and I met."

I bristle. I express the rising anger that is part of my sorrow and part of my fear.

"You make it sound all so easy. But it's more complicated than that. Tristan may love me in a way that he could never love you. There's wildness in me that attracts him. That same wildness is in him. He'll have a more enjoyable life with me."

"It would not be a better life. With you, the troubled and devious girl that you once were and that you are becoming again, he would repeat the mistakes that he has already made. He would miss the chance to be a truly good man."

"I won't believe that," I tell her. "Tristan *has* to love me. He has to. I don't know what will happen to me if he doesn't love me. I need him to replace Tyler. Maybe, gradually, I can learn to love him for himself."

Luna rises from her chair and looks out at the lake. From my place at the table, I observe what she sees. Three sailboats are gliding with undulating swiftness over the rippling water. Their passengers are middle-aged couples dressed in colorful sailor hats, waterproof shirts and jackets, bellbottom trousers, and boat shoes. They are laughing or chatting or singing merry ballads. Above them, the blue sky still contains floating clouds and a golden sun and a gray-backed gull swooping down to the lake's watery ripples to scoop up an olive-green bluegill.

Luna ponders all these images and then turns to face me once more. This time, she confronts me with incisive questions. Never does she raise her voice. But her words are pressing and heartfelt. In spite of the way I have treated her, she is concerned about my wellbeing.

"What has happened to your courage?" she asks me. "Where is the strength that you showed when you were working with Tyler to become a better person?"

In an instant, I calculate my losses. I search my mind, heart, and soul. I tell her the truth about myself and about the courage that has sometimes propelled my behavior.

"It's disappeared," I tell her. "It's vanished. I lost that courage when I lost Tyler."

Luna presses further.

"Have you really lost Tyler?"

I hesitate. I waver. With bitterness and anxiety, I find the words that tell her what I am feeling.

"Yes. I think so. He has been locked inside that sleep for such a long time. I don't think that he will ever awaken."

"Where is your faith? Where are your trust and your hope?"

Tears fill my eyes. There is something about Luna that has disarmed my envy of her—my resentment that she is happy with the boy who could replace Tyler for me. Suddenly, I hate myself for mistreating her. She is better than I am. Unlike her, I do not know how to hold on to trust and hope.

"I've lost them," I say to her. "I've lost myself. I don't really know who I am. I've disappeared."

"You must try to find yourself," she gently tells me. "Your best self. The self that you were creating when Tyler was here rooting for you."

"He's not here now," I say. "I am alone."

"I don't think that Tristan is the answer for you," she tells me. "But I won't stand in his way. I love him very much. I want him to be happy."

"What about you? What if Tristan does choose me?"

"I'll get by. I know how to stand alone, if I have to."

She pauses, pensive as she reflects upon the meaning of her remark. Then she has more to say.

"You need to learn how to stand alone, too," she tells me. "You need to stand tall and courageous. You need to rely on yourself even when a boyfriend is standing beside you."

Her words sound honest and lived-in. I find myself in awe of her.

"That's what you are doing," I say. "You are standing tall even though some of our classmates are saying mean things about you."

"Their malice is irrational. It can also be dangerous. But I'll rise above it. I'll go forward. The people who know me well, the ones who are loyal and kind, will walk tall beside me. They are like me. They are confident and self-reliant. We don't allow mean and foolish people to break our spirit."

Once again, a wave of regret washes over me. I have not behaved well.

"You are so good," I tell her. "I am sorry that I have acted badly."

She smiles and at first says nothing more. It is time for her to go.

Only after I accompany her to her aquamarine blue Audi A5 and after she enters its plush interior does she offer me another heartfelt thought.

"We might have become close friends if we'd met a year before Tyler's accident or a year after his recovery. If Tyler does recover and if Tristan and I stay together, we will be seeing each other quite often. As it is now, I don't know whether we can ever be close friends. But at least we know a little more about each other. That's always a good place to reestablish a troubled friendship."

Having said so, she waves goodbye and drives away.

For the rest of that day and all through the night, I think about Luna's visit. I am surprised and even astonished that she can respond to my betrayal of her trust with composure and patience. She *is* the right girl for Tristan. But, despite my self-recriminations—my accusations against myself and my awkward confession of my wrongdoing—my hope that Tristan will choose me over Luna still lingers in a dark corner of my mind.

I toss and turn, and in the middle of the night I wake up screaming.

I am relieved that nobody in the house has heard me, here on the second floor of the east wing—not Matt and Sandra, whose bedroom is located on the second floor of the west wing of the house, nor our cook and housekeeper, Mrs. Durand, and her husband, the groundskeeper and manager of the place. Their room is located on the first floor of the west wing.

I scream because my latest nightmare has shown me an appalling image of myself. I am standing before a judge in a courtroom. He is reading aloud the verdict of the jury that has heard detailed revelations about my lies, my plots, and my wildness. Before he speaks, I look back at the jury box and see once again the unfriendly faces of the twelve jurors who have heard damaging testimony against me.

The jurors include my parents and my brothers, Theo Ryan, Tristan and Luna, Zhang Li and Kyle Holden, Kerry Fitzgerald, and Mr. and Mrs. Danforth. They glare at me, their rheumy eyes glazed with dismay, disappointment, and even contempt. They are merely vaporous shadows now—shape-shifting specters, haunting apparitions, luminous wraiths who ignore my urgent and impetuous pleading—my call for mercy and forgiveness.

"Speak to me," I urge them, though a spectral bailiff who looks like Doctor Bronson tells me to stand before the judge in silence.

I ignore him and go on petitioning the jurors.

"Tell me that you will forgive me," I say, while my voice becomes a raspy lament. "I am sorry that I failed you. I am truly miserable because I hurt every one of you. Oh, please forgive me. Don't condemn me to disappear forever."

But the jurors will not answer me. Instead, they place the index finger of their right hand upon their lips. They are signaling me to be quiet. With this gesture, they are also advising me that they will not speak to me.

Distraught and fearful, I turn to the judge. I am not surprised that she is Doctor Morrison, to whom I have revealed my innermost thoughts and my most secret wrongdoings. At this very moment, the bailiff calls the courtroom to order. Only after that does the judge deliver the verdict of the jurors.

"This court finds you guilty in the first degree. You are a killer and a traitor. You have murdered the reputation of your friends, including Luna Cabello. You have betrayed Mr. and Mrs. Danforth's trust in you. You have refused to forgive your parents and your brothers for their errant ways. You have worked against Tristan's reformation—his worthy attempt to lead a good life. You have used Theo for your own devious purposes. You have broken the pact that you made with Tyler. You have murdered that relationship because of your lack of courage and your lack of faith in Tyler's reappearance, his coming back to you as a renewed and healthy young man.

"In just these recent weeks, you have abandoned your best self—the self that with Tyler's help and my help and the help of Miss Pearson, Mr. and Mrs. Danforth, and Mr. and Mrs. Collins you had reclaimed. You have abandoned your faith in goodness, patience, and fidelity. For all these wrongdoings and for your self-centered willfulness, this court declares you guilty. You are condemned to eternal disappearance."

"No! No!" I cry out. "Give me another chance. Don't make me disappear!"

My cry becomes a scream. I jump up from my pillows. My entire body is trembling. I am soaked with perspiration.

Quickly, even though my hands are still shaking, I light the lamp on the night table. My haunted eyes search the room for the ghost jurors who condemned me to eternal vanishment. My lips are quivering. My mind is reeling. There are no unforgiving jurors here. There is no punishing judge.

I slump back against the pillows. I stare at the canvas on the wall opposite my bed. It is a painting by Berthe Morisot, a gifted French artist of the nineteenth century. Her Impressionist canvas shows a titian-haired, adolescent girl peering at a bluebird as she sits surrounded by lustrous greenery and the distant blueness of the sky. On many occasions, when I was ten or eleven years old and still believed, despite my home troubles, that the world would treat me with kindness, I saw myself as that girl.

I used to be a good girl.

I keep that thought. I concentrate on the canvas that so often solaced me. The girl and all that she represents for me enables me to send my dark thoughts scattering. I am solaced once more. I fall into sleep again.

In the early afternoon of the next day, after I have completed my academic sessions with Matt and Sandra and after I have shared lunch with them on the patio, Zhang Li and Kyle Holden visit me. They look absolutely right together. They also look terrific in their casual summer clothes. Li is wearing a sea-green cartoon cat print t-shirt with long sleeves and an asymmetrical silhouette. Beige bell-bottom pants and green pumps with a buckle strap and chunky heels complement her easy-going appearance.

With his tall and lean physique, Kyle wears well a viridian blue, loose fitting short-sleeve shirt with linear patterns of miniature triangles, squares, and circles; gray soft flax trousers; and navy lace-up sneakers with white trimming.

I notice at once the irony of their casual appearance. Their clothes are casual, but Li and Kyle do not feel casual. Worry and uncertainty chip away at their optimism and their buoyancy.

I pretend not to notice their nearly concealed uncertainty. I, too, am wearing casual, summery clothes. My long-sleeved, azure-blue blouse, cream white slacks, and azure-blue block heel sandals with cream white accents enhance my contrived lightheartedness. Seated with them on the patio, I enter the conversation with brisk enthusiasm and genuine interest in all that Li and Kyle have to say to me.

We speak at first of their recent stay in Camden, Maine, where their grandparents—the senior Zhangs and Holdens—own ocean-front summer homes. There, in Camden, they enjoyed many days of swimming, water skiing, and sailing in breeze-swept Atlantic waters. We also mention the many hours that we are devoting to our studies of chemistry, calculus, trigonometry, and world literature in preparation for our forthcoming school year.

At this time, Mrs. Durand hurries in with a tray of lemonade as well as cinnamon teacakes. With precise and attentive courtesy, Li and Kyle sip the lemonade and nibble at the teacakes.

But my watchful eyes notice something more than their courtesy. Their poise and their outward calm cannot suppress the tension that lives within their minds and souls. Only after their courteous gestures of accepting the lemonade and the cakes do Li and Kyle reveal their uneasiness. Only now do the tension and dismay touching almost imperceptibly their faces and their voices push them to mention the primary reason for this visit.

"We have come here for a special reason," Li tells me. "We need to talk with you about something important."

I guess what is coming. But I hold my ground. I stay calm, and I manage to sound a bit flippant.

"Well, out with it," I tell them. "I want to hear all about your main purpose for visiting me."

Kyle comes into it.

"We don't want to upset you," he says, with no condescension, but with genuine caring for the way things are with me. "Li and I realize that you have gone through your own nightmare ever since the car crash. But we believe that you are a tough cookie. You are strong enough now to face a few hard truths."

"What truths might those be?"

Li hurries to say more.

"It's about Tristan and Theo," she tells me. "We don't want them to get hurt."

She hesitates. She doesn't want to hurt me, either.

Kyle speaks the words that need to be spoken.

"Your posting those photos of Luna and Theo wasn't a good thing," he says. "Those photos made Luna and Theo look bad. They don't do much good for Tristan either. They give the impression that Luna has dumped him."

"Most of our classmates are calling Luna a playgirl," Li says. "They are saying that she plays around with every available guy."

"It's not true, of course," Kyle says. "Luna's closest friends know that. You know that, too."

"It doesn't really matter whether you remove those photos," Li tells me. "The damage has already been done. But you could still fix things. You could set the record straight."

"What do I have to do?"

"You can post *all* the other photos that you made that day, the ones that show that Luna and Theo were sharing an afternoon with you and the Collinses. Luna and Theo were not on a date."

At first, I do not respond to their suggestions. The rebellious and trouble-making part of me resents their good thoughts about Luna. I know that Kyle and Li are right. I also know that, despite yesterday's self-recriminations and good intentions, I am not ready to do the right thing. Instead, I throw out hasty words that may help me to push aside Li's and Kyle's petitions.

"Why should the gossip of foolish and malicious people matter? Why should Luna and Tristan and Theo allow it to matter?"

"That gossip does matter," Kyle says. "Those malicious comments are casting shadows upon the lives of good people."

"You need to keep in mind how it is with Tristan and Theo," Li says. "They are fighting fierce battles. They are fighting against the worldly temptations that made them altogether different persons last year. They are trying to follow moral paths. They are doing everything they can to get their best selves back. They want to find the Tristan Danforth and the Theo Ryan that disappeared. They want their best selves to reappear."

I resist their advice. I don't want to relinquish my plan to win Tristan's favor. I scoff at their talk of "best selves."

"Their best selves?" I ask. "What selves are those? Do they really want to become guys who resist all their natural impulses and every daring adventure that proves they are really alive?"

Now Kyle offers even more pressing advice.

"Don't get in their way," he says. "Don't make their battles harder than they need to be."

Li shifts to the heart of the matter, their primary reason for visiting me. She talks of Tristan and Luna.

"Kyle and I know that you want to move in on Tristan's relationship with Luna. That's a mistake. They really love each other. You could never destroy what they mean to one another."

I protest. I balk. I defend my devious point of view.

"Maybe I can shake up things," I say. "Maybe those photos will test this extraordinary love that Tristan is supposed to feel for Luna. Maybe he loves her, but not enough to trust her when she's in the company of any other guy."

"That's wishful thinking on your part," Kyle answers me. "Besides, you should be thinking about Tyler. What has happened to the love you once felt for him?"

The question strikes like a whiplash against my conscience. It compels me to pause. Once again, a frown creases my brow. Once more, I fight the tears that begin to fill my eyes. Against my will, my lips begin to tremble.

"I still love Tyler," I say after a while. "But what good does that do for me? He's not coming back. He'll never open his eyes to look at me. He'll never hold out his hand to touch me. He'll never speak to me. Not anymore. Not ever."

Both Kyle and Li notice my sorrow. They sense my genuine anguish. But it is Li who moves toward me and, with her hand, pats my shoulder. In my mind, her kind gesture makes her a spiritual sister to Luna.

"You are very unhappy," Li murmurs, "and we are sorry for that. Try to believe that Tyler will come back. Try to be faithful to the pledge you made to him. Once, you told me that you and Tyler promised that you would always be true to each other, no matter what happened."

"That seems like such a long time ago. That's when I believed that, with Tyler there beside me, I was learning how to be a good person again."

"That's a lesson that never ends," Li tells me. "We learn how to be good over and over again when we do the right things that need to be done."

Kyle leaves me with this thought.

"Think about what we've said. Think about doing the right thing for Tristan and Luna."

Then, after hugging me, they go forward to their busy summer afternoon.

Their visit has left me shaken. Their matter-of-fact words have bruised my willfulness. Their ingrained compassion has nudged my remorse—my lacerating regret that I have brought harm to Theo and Luna and even to Tristan.

Bitter and guilt-ridden, I push away all thoughts of what I have done. I close off my memories of Tristan, Luna, and Theo. I put away my phone.

I take refuge in the music room within the first floor of the south wing of my home. Here, canvases by Pierre Bonnard, Edouard Manet, and Berthe Morisot adorn the walls, and an array of red, yellow, and white roses in an Art

Nouveau vase by Emile Gallé collaborate with the splendor of the Steinway French Provincial console piano. A twenty-foot cloud ceiling, parquet flooring, and gilded antique *boisserie* paneling and columns are other French Classic emblems that suggest a refined luxury as well as the prestige of my parents who live here only intermittently and who value music and art as accessories that enhance their reputation as wealthy people who can afford such luxuries.

From my seat at the piano, I can see past the columns into the exquisite ballroom. I also see the second-floor mezzanine that overlooks the music room and the ballroom. That mezzanine leads, beyond my here-and-now seeing, to the master suite that has French doors opening to picturesque views of the lake.

Here, at the Steinway, I play the first nocturne in Chopin's collection of nocturnes. It is a nocturne in B-flat minor. There is no one in the room to listen to my playing. The Collinses are still sailing on the lake, Mrs. Durand and her assistant are busy with their housekeeping and their preparations for our evening meal, and her husband and his team of assistants are bringing their well-honed skills to their care of this six-acre property.

I enjoy the freedom of being alone. I also enjoy the rhythmic freedom of Chopin's nocturne in B-flat minor, the first in his collection of nocturnes. My left hand plays an unbroken sequence of eighth notes in simple arpeggios throughout the entire piece. At the same time, my right hand moves with freedom in patterns of seven, eleven, twenty, and twenty-two notes. I revel in the sumptuous notes that float upon the sun-glanced atmosphere in this room. I embrace my seclusion. I give my complete attention to the music.

My regret disappears. My disappointment and fear scatter, disperse, and dissolve.

For nearly an hour I practice. Over and over, I play this first of Chopin's nocturnes. I test myself within its intricacies. I search for different approaches to the challenges it presents to me. I permit the music to make a friend of my intuition. I allow it to cleanse and to solace my spirit.

No sooner does this solace wash over me, no sooner does my spirit waken to thoughts of new, rescuing possibilities, than I am brought down to earth once again. Quite suddenly and just as unexpectedly, Mrs. Durand hurries into this room of music and escape to tell me that Theo Ryan and Kerry Fitzgerald have come to visit me.

I notice that Connor Adams has not accompanied Theo, who has apparently earned back some of his independence.

There is no visible tension in either Theo or Kerry. Their direct and honest gaze suggests to my searching eyes that they have come to terms with the trouble I have caused. Already, they are moving on to the next sequence of happenings.

Kerry looks radiant in a coral-colored jacket and coral cigarette pants. The jacket has white button details and, like the pants, is made of a lightweight stretch fabric. Asymmetric clear-detail mules with open back, square toe, and coral heels complete her summer-fresh appearance.

With his lean muscularity, Theo looks tanned and sturdy. He is wearing a smoky-red polo shirt, navy pants, and matching caramel-colored belt and brogues.

They greet me with words that sound natural, unassuming, and friendly. I summon my own reserves of cordiality as I respond to their greeting.

Now I guide them to the comfort of a French Provincial sofa, and I take my place in a matching chair opposite them.

"I'm here to let you know how I feel about what's happened," Theo says. "I'll lay it on the line. I don't intend to make it look pretty. You played a dirty trick on Luna and me. We trusted you, and you broke that trust. But I'm willing to forget about it. I've made a few mistakes in my life, so I don't have the right to cast stones. I'll soldier through this mess.

"In fact, this scandal about the photos hasn't treated me badly at all. All of the social media craziness has revved up interest in me. Girls think that I've decided to be dangerous again. Guys are wondering what my secret is. What have I got that drives girls toward me? In some ways, this thing about the photos has brought me back to life. I'm in it again.

I'm really interested in coming back and getting it right this time."

Kerry listens to every word he is speaking. She smiles in agreement with everything that he is saying. In her gaze, I see not only a romantic gleam. I see respect. I see mature admiration for a young man who is learning how to conquer his inner demons. I see in her steadfast look at Theo an emerging comprehension of all the good qualities that he has been retrieving.

"Of course you are coming back," she tells him in a voice that is both lilting and encouraging, "and you *are* getting it right this time."

Her words delight him. But only the momentary flash of affection for her that glows in his eyes tells me how he feels. I know Theo. I remember how he brightened whenever a person or an experience pleased him.

Their new solidarity impresses me. Theo's tough-minded response to the social media madness directed against Luna and him has influenced Kerry to see him with new eyes. Already, they are becoming a couple, a unity of two persons who understand and admire each other. I envy them. They possess the same kind of happiness I enjoyed with Tyler. They have what I have lost.

I hurry to say the words that tell them how it is with me.

"I'm sorry that I made trouble for you, Theo. I did not mean to bring harm to you. I know you well. I know how tough you can be. I believed that you would bear up. You would be okay."

Mrs. Durand comes into the room, carrying a tray of frosted glasses filled with lemonade and her freshly baked apricot teacakes.

"There is nothing better than cakes and lemonade to make a visit more enjoyable," she tells us, her motherly inclinations sparking her good-natured personality.

We thank her for her thoughtfulness while she places the tray on a coffee table that stands before the sofa, and she quickly leaves us to our conversation.

In this moment, none of us is interested in lemonade or teacakes. Instead, Theo finds new words to push away my false reasoning, my feeble excuse for my wrongdoing.

"Your posting the photos did hurt me," he says. "It felt like a punch to my gut. I felt betrayed. I felt that you set me up to make your plot work. You want Tristan for yourself, and you don't care what happens to Luna. You didn't hesitate to cast a shadow on her reputation. You want to break up her romance with Tristan. Nothing about your plotting makes you looks good. But you can still set things straight. You still have a chance to make everything right."

Now Kerry comes into it again. Her words are equally sensible. She intends to be helpful. She wants me to do the right thing.

"Do what Luna has asked you to do. Post all the photos that you took that day when you went riding with Theo,

Connor, and Luna. Let people know that Theo and Luna were not on a date. They were simply involved in a gathering of friends."

I hesitate. I am still not ready to do the right thing.

"Do you really believe that my posting all the other photos will make a difference?" I ask her. "The social media crowd prefers to believe the worst of everybody. My posting additional pictures won't really make a difference."

"Maybe it won't change their unjust responses," Theo says. "But your posting those other photos *will* make a difference for you. It's a chance for you to make amends. It's an opportunity for you to redeem yourself."

Once again, my fear hurries into the room and hovers by me. Once more, my terror of losing Tyler, the only young man that I will ever love, pushes away whatever courage I possess. I need to replace Tyler with the young man who looks exactly like him. I am not ready to abandon the plot that might bring Tristan to my side.

"I don't want to post those other photos," I say. "Let Tristan be tested. Let him show Luna that, despite the romantic implications of those photos of her and Theo together, he trusts her. Let him prove that he really loves her."

"What you are doing is wrong," Kerry says. "It's so wrong."

"I know," I tell her. "God forgive me. I know."

Theo has more to say.

"Kerry and I are going to do our part to set things straight," he says. "We are posting photos of her and me on all the social media sites. We are letting people know that we are going steady."

"The photos will be telling the truth," Kerry says. "We *have* decided to go steady. Our photos will override your pictures of Luna and Theo. The word will quickly get around that Luna was never anyone to Theo except a new acquaintance, a girl he had just met and toward whom he behaved with courtesy and respect."

"Why are you telling me all these things?" I ask them. "Why do you think that it is important for me to change my mind about the pictures I took? Your photos will set the record straight."

Kerry tells me more.

"Your posting those photos of Connor, Luna, Theo, and you is important, more for yourself than for Luna and Theo."

"You can make amends," Theo tells me. "You can do the right thing."

"I don't know what I'll do," I say. "I'll have to think about it."

Whether Theo takes my hesitation as a promising sign, I cannot tell.

In this moment, though, he changes the mood of our meeting. He sparks the atmosphere with his optimism. Taking hold of the tray that contains the lemonade and teacakes, he hands a glass to Kerry and me and, before returning the tray to its place on the coffee table, takes hold of a glass for himself.

"Let's drink a toast to your doing the right thing," Theo says while directing his words to me. "Let's drink a toast to your finding the Rachel Hayworth that Tyler Danforth loves."

We drink the toast. We return to our places and enjoy the lemonade. We partake of the cakes. We turn these closing moments of the visit to a nearly festive occasion.

Then, after our little party is over, Theo and Kerry rise from their places on the sofa and cross over to me. I rise, too. They surprise me by taking hold of my hands. They offer me smiles that express their good will and their best hopes for me. As I accompany them to his Porsche Taycan, Theo says something more. He leaves me with words that will echo in my thoughts for many days afterward.

"Do the right thing," he tells me. "You'll never have cause to regret doing the right thing."

Obstinate and unhappy, I do not post the group photos that will alter the implications of the earlier postings that showed Theo alone with Luna. I can't let go of my plot. I am still hoping that Tristan will leave Luna and turn to me.

I return to my playing of Chopin's first nocturne. Once again, I lose myself in the pulsing rhythms of the music. My spirit ascends with each note. I make my escape. I forget the trouble and disappointment that may lie in wait for me.

On the following afternoon, quite suddenly and with no anticipation on my part, Tristan pays me a visit.

I greet him with surprise and appreciation.

He looks like someone new. He looks as though he has been reborn, so beaming and affirmative is his smile. Gone is his brooding personality. His conflicted self-centeredness has vanished, too. The religious retreat in which he took part has worked its wonders.

As he greets me in our large reception room on the first floor in the east wing, he sounds confident with no suggestion of arrogance. With a quickened glance and aesthetic appreciation, he surveys the well-appointed room. Frescoed walls and ceiling, a blend of pale yellow and beige, brighten the room. Gilt-wood antique chairs, a London Chesterfield rolled-armed sofa with tufted back and cream white color, a gold patina and bone cocktail table with scrolled apron and legs with ornamental detail, and a needlepoint carpet bring subdued formality to this room where so many prominent guests of my parents have often gathered. On one of the frescoed walls, foil bouquets flank a seventeenth-century Flemish painting that draws Tristan's special attention. This painting portrays six mariners in a boat who are held mesmerized by the apparition of an angel descending from out of the clouds.

"I'd like to meet that angel," Tristan says, serious and reflective. "Maybe he'd tell me how to build a good life and how to keep it."

As I guide him to a chair, he moves with assured agility and with none of his former swagger.

Today, he is wearing a gray polo shirt, deep indigo jeans, and chestnut-colored penny loafers.

I match his summer-casual look. I am wearing a white three-quarter sleeve top with a V-neck and azure-blue *appliqué*, azure-blue high-waist twill pants with tapered legs, and white wedge sandals.

I wait for him to begin our conversation.

Though his face never loses its brightness and its suggestion of good will, he maintains an understated and earnest manner.

"I want you to know that I forgive you," he says. "You made a mistake. You hurt some people. But Luna and Theo and I have weathered the storm. Maybe we were wounded, but we did not fall. Nothing has changed between Luna and me. It will take more than social media nonsense to destroy what we feel for each other. We are moving forward to new days and happier times. So is Theo, whom I regard as a buddy—a friend who has travelled some of the same, self-defeating roads."

Made tense and unhappy by this news of his loyalty to Luna, I stay silent. Not even when good Mrs. Durand brings us a tray of lemonade and apple teacakes do I find words to deflect my disappointment or to disguise my apprehension that I am once again being abandoned—first by Tyler, who gave me his honest love for six wonderful months and now by Tristan, who never loved me but who was my last hope for retrieving my lost happiness. With Tristan by my side, I could have come to believe that I had not really lost Tyler. Tyler had come back to me. He had reappeared in the bodily form of Tristan. But no longer will I be able to believe that fantasy. Tristan will never belong to me. He belongs to Luna, and he is not Tyler.

Tristan drinks the lemonade as he waits for me to tell him how it is with me. I do not keep him waiting. I tell him exactly how it is with me. I make my confession.

"I can't pretend that I'm not disappointed," I say. "I was counting on you. I thought that you were unwilling to let go of the wildness that was in you. I thought I was better for you. Together, we could have many exciting adventures."

"You were testing me," he says.

"You passed the test," I answer him. "You proved that you love Luna more than you love your wildness."

"With Luna, I can tame the wildness," he says. "She and I will share many adventures. But we'll live on the realistic level. We won't throw away responsibility and common sense."

"Your religious retreat has made a difference for you," I tell him. "You have learned some important lessons."

"A few," he says. "I learned especially from Father Donnelly's homily about one of Saint Paul's letters to the Corinthians. They were the people in the first-century

Greece to whom he was bringing a message about the best way to live."

"Saint Paul's letter impressed you. It must be very special."

"It is. Father Donnelly asked us to memorize the Scriptural passage. At the end of our retreat, he gave each of us a card on which the passage was printed. He wanted us to keep the card as a reference that will remind us of Saint Paul's message. I asked Father Donnelly for an extra card. I'd like you to have it. I hope the words help you as much as they have helped me."

He hands me a white card that is five inches wide and three inches long. On it, embossed in gold letters, are Saint Paul's words. I scan the words without really processing their meaning. Instead, I echo some of the words that Tristan has spoken to me.

"The words on this card helped you."

"They helped all of us. They gave everyone who was making the retreat a clear idea of the kind of life Saint Paul asks us to live."

"What kind of life is that?"

"It has to do with loving and accepting other people, just as we want to be loved and accepted."

"I love you, or at least I want to learn to love you. Doesn't that count?"

"You don't love me, even though your fear is persuading you that I am the answer for all your problems. If you really loved me, you would understand that I belong with Luna. If you loved me in the right way, you would also love Luna. You would not want to hurt us. When Saint Paul speaks of love, he is not speaking only of romantic love. He is not even speaking especially about being *in love*. He is speaking of the experience of loving every human being because of their humanity and, yes, because a Higher Power has created them. It is this kind of love, influenced by the spiritual rather than the carnal part of our natures, that helps us to become the best persons that we can be."

"You sound like a priest or a minister or maybe even a rabbi."

"I'm not good enough to be any of those," he says. "Besides, that is not my calling. I have not been chosen for that. I'm like them only in this way: I have come into this world to make it a bit better. I've come here to be the best person that I can be."

"Tyler was helping me to be that kind of person. Without him, I am lost. That's why I was counting on you. You are his twin. You could help me, too. You could help me to become the best that I can be."

"I'll always try to help you," he says, "but not as your boyfriend. If you really love my brother, you should not stop loving him now when he needs you most of all. You say that Tyler has abandoned you. But it is you who are abandoning him. You've lost your hope and your courage. Nobody can get those back for you except yourself. Tyler told you not to be a leaner. Stand tall. Stand bravely as an independent young woman who is willing to face the world's challenges."

He finishes his glass of lemonade and samples one of Mrs. Durand's apple teacakes. I sip the lemonade, but I have no appetite for the teacakes, though they look delicious. Then Tristan rises, his full-fledged masculinity validating his princely assurance. It is time to leave. He surprises me once more by giving me a brotherly hug. Then, as he makes his way to his Jaguar, he studies my face even more keenly.

"Find your courage," he says. "You won't go forward until you find your courage."

After he leaves, I take up the card that he gave me. Sad of heart and at the edge of despair, I read Saint Paul's message to the Corinthian people.

"I may speak in tongues of men or of angels, but if I am without love, I am a sounding gong or a clanging cymbal. I may have the gift of prophecy and know every hidden truth. I may have faith strong enough to move mountains. But if I have no love, I am nothing. Love is patient. Love is kind and envies no one. Love is never boastful, nor conceited, nor rude. It is never selfish, nor quick to take offense. Love keeps no score of wrongs. It does not gloat over other people's sins. It delights in the truth. There is nothing love cannot face. There is no limit to its faith, its hope and its endurance. There are three things that last forever: faith, hope, and love. But the greatest of them all is love."

Over and over I read the words. I memorize them. I probe their meaning and, probing, find myself insufficient. I declare myself guilty of self-centeredness, anger, impatience, deviousness, and envy. I lack faith. I lack courage. I have lost the virtue of making hope my friend. I am in danger of losing the gift of love that Tyler taught me to value.

After this visit from Tristan, a blur of days passes swiftly. I fall ill again. My nerves are jangled once more. Depression gnaws at my pride. Fear eats away at my confidence. Regret consumes my hope.

Doctor Bronson, the physician who has always monitored my health, examines me in his office within Blue Ridge Medical Center.

"You are run down," he tells me. "You have been trying to do too much. For a few days, you need to stay away from the excitement of being with your friends in Newport, Vermont, and Maine. Relax at home. Go sailing with Matt and Sandra. Once in a while, play tennis with Sandra, if you are up to it. Take walks with her and her husband. Get plenty of fresh air. And, just as important, arrange some meetings with Doctor Morrison."

Hearing of my setback, my parents drive in from their New York penthouse.

My father has little patience with my setback.

"Don't pamper yourself," he tells me. "Hayworths who are worthy of their name never pamper themselves. Bear up. Get on with it."

"Doctor Bronson wants me to rest."

"Nonsense!" he fires back at me. "He doesn't understand Hayworths. You can bear up. You can fight whatever it is that is trying to bring you down. Move on. Find a new path. Make a new adventure for yourself. Just get on with things."

My mother treats me no better.

"This latest episode of depression is a sham," she declares. "It's fake. It's pretense. It's your way of getting attention from people who are not especially interested in you."

I answer her in kind. My words are just as bitter. They cut just as deeply.

"You and dad are among those people," I tell her without raising my voice. "You don't have any special interest in me."

My father comes into it again.

"Of course we are interested in you," he says. "You are, after all, a Hayworth. You are our daughter. We want you to stand tall. We want you to solve your problems without running to doctors or even to us. It's high time that you faced the world with the same courage that was in you when you ran away last year."

"That wasn't real courage," I say. "That was rebellion. That was rage. That was my cry for help."

"Well, don't cry," he says. "A true Hayworth never cries. We fight back. We punch our way out of every mess that the world is pushing in our direction."

"Do try your best," my mother tells me.

"You are leaving again. You are going back to New York and then hurrying on to all the places across the globe that keep you away from me. You are always abandoning me."

"Don't talk that way," my father tells me. "It's not true. We are not abandoning you. We are placing you in the care of Matt and Sandra Collins. Doctor Morrison will be helping you, too. If anyone can help you get on with things, she's the one."

"You must help yourself, too" my mother advises me. "Never rely on other people to find happiness for you. You must find it for yourself."

"Don't worry about me," I tell her. "I'll find it. And I won't ask you or Dad to hold my hand while I'm looking for it."

"Your mother and I are glad to hear that," my father says. "I like the way you tell us that you'll find happiness. Your voice sounds steel-true—as hard as the hardest nails."

After he has said so, he finishes drinking his scotch. Then he and my mother hurry away to New York and to their flourishing careers. They have no intention of including me in their forthcoming trip to China.

The next afternoon, Doctor Morrison stops in to see me. Hers is an unusual visit. Ordinarily she meets me in her office. But, because of my setback that keeps me confined to these six acres of my parents' Blue Ridge home, she visits me in the library.

She wants to know everything that has been happening to me since our last session two weeks ago. I tell her all of it. Call it a confession, if you like. I don't hold back. I reveal all my secrets and all my plotting. I explain with specific details my plan to win Tristan away from Luna. I describe my scheme for pairing Theo with Luna. I disclose my need to replace Tyler with Tristan.

"I'm at loose ends." I say as I finish telling her the wretched way things are with me. "I don't know what to do."

"I think you do," she answers me. "You are learning that double-dealing and wiliness will never bring you happiness. They are not the solution for your problems. You have to tread a different path. You have to become interested in helping other people. Maybe, as you help other people, you will get to know a little more about Rachel Hayworth."

"How do I do that?" I ask her. "Where do I meet these people that may need my help?"

"Be a volunteer in hospitals and in nursing homes. Last year, you were a very good volunteer. This year, you can also pay attention to your schoolmates who may need your help."

"I don't know," I say. "I don't know whether I'm good enough or giving enough for that."

"Try it. Try to be giving. Keep in mind that famous philosophers have said that the best way to find yourself is to lose yourself in the service of others."

"How can that help me? I'm already lost."

"Not to yourself. Not yet. You need to lose your old self. You need to reappear as a new person. You will do that when you stop feeling sorry for yourself. There is a world of good people out there. Some of them need your help. Do it. Find them. Help them. Then, maybe you will find your new self. You will reappear. You will come back to the wider world and to your friends as a new person—the best person that you can be."

For many hours after our session, I reflect upon Doctor Morrison's words. I ask myself whether I have the will or the courage to change. I rack my mind. I search my soul. I can't find the answer. At night, I fall into a restless sleep. Then, shortly before dawn, I wake up, startled and tense. There, across my bedroom—right there, beneath the canvas that shows within a field of colorful flowers the innocent girl that I once imagined was my alter ego, my natural counterpart—precisely there, Tyler or his life-like apparition suddenly appears to me.

"You are here," I exclaim. "You haven't abandoned me."

I hurry out of my bed, gathering my silk robe around my quickened figure. Yet, though my will keeps pushing me forward, something—some supernatural power—holds me back. This power prevents me from moving close-up to Tyler. Nevertheless, I see him clearly. His body is celestial. The entire muscular form of him glows in this bedroom into which the rising dawn is sending its rays. These rays disappear inside the effulgent light that envelops Tyler's body. He is wearing the same prince's uniform that he wore in the Blue Ridge High School play about a sleeping prince and the good girl who rescued him from the spell that had been cast upon him. Yet he looks otherworldly. He looks like a princely angel. He looks like the Tyler that I know well. He glows with the radiance that was always inside him, an emblem of the spirit that guided his every move.

Inside this radiant dawn and within my bedroom, Tyler speaks to me.

"I have not abandoned you," he says. "I still believe in you, despite the mistakes that you have been making—your devious plots and your willful trouble-making. The plots and the trouble-making are not worthy of the better self that you were discovering when we were together."

"We are no longer together," I say. "I am alone, and I don't know which way to turn."

"You must find that way on your own. Remember what I told you. Don't be a leaner. You are better than that. You can be brave when you give yourself a chance."

"It's hard to be brave when you are standing alone."

"Yes, it is. But you can do it. Do it for yourself first of all. Then do it because it is the only way that I will return to you."

"What if I can't do it? What happens if I try and if I still can't be brave?"

"Then one day some brave girl will come to the hospital and kiss me. That is the day when I shall awaken."

"I don't want any other girl to win your love. I want to be that girl."

"You must find your courage. Discover your best self. Then, when I hear your voice, I shall awaken. I shall open my eyes and see you. You will not merely appear as the self you once were. You will reappear as the better self that you have become."

"I'll try," I promise him. "I'll try to change. I'll do everything that I can to become a good person."

No sooner have I spoken these words, than Tyler vanishes and the light that was his own radiance vanishes as well.

I return to my bed, propped against a galaxy of colorful pillows. I recall every word that just passed between Tyler and me. I carefully weigh the heft and heave of their meaning. I make new resolutions. I create new plans that will guide me onto new paths. I will bring my care-giving skills to the sick and to the needy.

I am ready to change. I begin again.

CHAPTER TWELVE

THE REAPPEARANCE OF RACHEL HAYWORTH

I reappear.

Not to myself first of all do I reappear. Those persons who are frequently connected to my life notice the change before I do. My body and soul and disposition rematerialize in subtle and gradual increments. My face becomes more honest, more open. No longer is the calm that it shows a mask for my concealed anger and my inveterate schemes. The calm is authentic. Without displeasure or resentment, I accept the quietly emerging life-alterations that keep unfolding about and within me. Slowly and to my eyes at first imperceptibly, the anger drains away, and the schemes vanish like smoke after a fire has burnt itself away. I walk with a more quickened pace. I respond to others with patient and respectful words. I offer encouraging smiles to those persons who are shy or uncertain. I pay courteous attention when the knowledgeable persons with whom I am working offer me corrective words after I have misjudged my capacities and have attempted to complete tasks for which I am not ready. I bring fresh energy and well-honed skills to new assignments and new challenges. The soul sickness that has long plagued me withdraws in defeat, its powers evaporating after a fierce battle against its formidable adversaries, hope and virtue.

Miss Pearson, my trustworthy nurse, guides me along the path that will lead to my reappearing. She continues to guide another girl as well. That girl, whose name is Martha Ford, suffered serious injuries last summer in a car crash not unlike the one that has imperiled Tyler Danforth's life and that stole away the reformation that I had been achieving because of Tyler's positive influence upon my life.

Martha's boyfriend, Drake Bradford, had been driving his Lexus LC 500 with careful attention to the night-darkness of the country road that was leading Martha and him to her parents' home in Blue Ridge. They had been returning from a rowing competition that had taken place earlier that day on a lake in nearby Westport. Drake, who is the captain of the rowing team at Blue Ridge High School, had guided his team to a trophy in that summer competition that brought together not only teams of high school students who were primed with youthful muscularity, but also teams of country club adults who had maintained their physical prowess.

On this evening of the accident, after the triumph of Drake's team and after the exuberant party at which high school teenagers drank nothing stronger than almond milkshakes and soft beverages, Martha and Drake were feeling elated as he drove his Lexus along the dark country road. When he saw the headlights of the BMW-M2 that was rushing toward his vehicle, Drake swerved to avoid the crash. He veered the trajectory of his Lexus. He accelerated its speed so that he might elude the oncoming BMW. But though he was an adept a driver, he could not elude the speed of the out-of-control BMW with the intoxicated middle-aged businessman behind its wheel. The crash sent Drake's Lexus catapulting and spinning and flipping past the tall elms that stood at the side of the road. It sent it plunging down into the darkness of a ravine.

No one died that night. But all three persons were grievously injured. The middle-aged driver has recovered from his broken legs, fractured pelvis, and concussion. He is serving a two-year term in a Connecticut prison. Drake suffered a fractured shoulder and a broken leg. He has recovered and is slowly returning to his athletic regimen. Martha suffered a concussion, a broken arm, and a broken leg. She has recovered from the injuries to her body. But she has lost some of the spirited enthusiasm that she had always brought into her life. She has also lost some of her confidence.

"She has often spoken of wanting to ride a horse again," Miss Pearson explains to me. "I've been told that she was a very proficient rider before her accident. She would like an experienced rider to help her get back her confidence. She keeps telling me that, if she could ride her beloved Arab bay with the assurance that she always brought to her riding, she might believe in herself again. She might not feel so completely lost."

Now Miss Pearson enlists my assistance in turning Martha's wish into a reality. Months after the car crash injured Drake and Martha, Miss Pearson wants to accommodate Martha's wish to return to horse riding.

It is in this way that Miss Pearson initiates my new period of reforming. Martha has recovered from the injuries she sustained in the crash of her boyfriend's car. But she believes that she has lost something of value, some characteristics that define who she is to herself and to all the persons who are important to her. She has lost some of her confidence. She needs to prove all over again that she is self-possessed and unafraid of the unexpected. She needs to reappear to herself, her transformation reviving and advancing her spirit of adventure. She wants to rediscover the girl that she had always been—enthusiastic, self-reliant, and a bit daring. She wants to discover in a new way the girl that she can become.

Miss Pearson would like me to be her teacher.

I readily agree. At Blue Ridge High School, I had been aware of Martha Ford's presence. But I had usually seen her from a distance. We were never students assigned to the same classes, because Martha is two years younger than I. For that reason, we had never become friends. Time and chance have changed that. I feel a spiritual connection to Martha because of the car crash that threw her happy days away, swooping them up and scattering the happiness into fragments.

We both have suffered because of the powers and the consequences of those nearly fatal accidents. For the first time in a very long time, my heart reaches out to a fellow human being who has suffered a great deal and who, in the aftermath of her bodily pain, suffers now in a different way. Having been tossed about by Blind Chance, a careless driver, and a car-wrecking accident, Martha Ford is fighting a new battle. I want to show her how to fight it well. Eventually, she may come to understand that I, too, am fighting a battle. My enemy is myself. I need to conquer that enemy. I need to find the new Rachel Hayworth. I need to reappear.

Martha is petite and very lovely. She stands at five foot, four inches. I am guessing that when she wears stylish mules or more formal high heels, she appears much taller than she really is. Her straight-back posture helps to create that impression. With her flowing titan hair, blue eyes, turned-up nose, and bee-stung lips, she has, I imagine, no trouble in attracting the steady gaze of male admirers. The love of her life is, of course, Drake Bradford. For her, there is no other boy. Until a few weeks ago, I could have made a similar remark about myself. For me, there was no other boy except Tyler. Even months after his accident, there was no other boy for me. Then I lost hope. I lost faith. Panic-struck, abandoned, and lonely, I reached out to Tristan. In that way,

I betrayed Tyler. For that reason, the possibility has diminished that Tyler will answer my new calls when I stand by his hospital bed. Maybe that possibility has burned itself to the socket.

I tell myself that I want to help Martha for no other reason except to bring ease to her troubled soul. I would like to help Martha revive her belief in herself. Yet my new, honest way of looking into my own soul tells me more. By helping Martha to reclaim the self that disappeared in a life-threatening car crash and to alter that self for the better, I may also discover and authenticate my new self. Perhaps one of the more temperate Fates or a kinder angel will notice my careful efforts to help a fellow teen who wants to be nudged forward onto a more promising path. Possibly, in noticing my efforts, the more temperate Fate or the kinder angel will make my own struggle if not easier, then steadier. So I tell myself, reluctant to make self-centered petitions to any of the Fates and to my favorite angels.

From our very first meeting, I come to regard Martha as a spiritual sister. We share the same kind of suffering. We have experienced similar losses. We know how it feels to become disoriented and sullen after a nearly fatal car crash. We know what it means to fall in love with the only boy we will ever love.

"You are the perfect teacher for Martha," Miss Pearson reassures me. "Because of your accidents, because of your good fortune in meeting Tyler, and because of Martha's good luck in meeting Drake, the two of you share some important and similar experiences. I know you will help her. I am certain that, with your assistance, Martha will ride a horse with confidence again and renew her acquaintance with all the riding skills that she learned when she was ten years old."

An hour later, when we arrive at Mr. Spenser's horse farm, Martha and I greet each other with a natural friendliness as well as with keen-minded anticipation.

"Let's have a go at it," I tell her. "Let's reacquaint you with horse riding. Let's make you a first-rate rider again."

"I'm game," Martha says. Her eyes sparkle with enthusiasm and with hope.

Miss Pearson, Matt, and Sandra are there to cheer us on. They, too, will be riding.

"We'll join your team," Matt says, handsome and rugged as usual in his riding clothes.

"We promise not to get in your way, even if we try to outpace you," Sandra teases. Even in her attractive riding outfit, she looks demure, assured, and very pretty.

"We are in this together," Miss Pearson reminds us. "Let's do what a good team does. Let's ride together."

So I begin again.

Matt, Sandra, Miss Pearson, and I have a splendid riding experience that day. Each one of us is wearing a navy-blue protective hardhat and chin harness, cobalt blue long sleeve shirt and jeans, and navy-blue leather boots. Our clothing, similar in style and color, gives us the appearance of a team. We ride like a team. We as a team do not race. We canter at a leisurely pace. Always, we keep our studious eyes upon Martha, whose riding experience today is not splendid. We sense at once that she sits uneasily in the saddle. The brightness in her eyes has dimmed with apprehension. She has not yet rediscovered the language that exists between her body and that of the horse. The experience of riding a horse seems alien to her. The expertise that she had once mastered now eludes her.

By the time we return to the stables, Martha is weeping.

"I've lost it," she says. "I've lost my trust in my beautiful Arab bay. I've lost me, and I don't know whether I'll ever get back the person that I once was."

Miss Pearson comes into it now.

"Be patient, Martha," she says. "Give yourself time. You will find your way back."

"Or find your way forward," Sandra says, visibly moved by Martha's weeping.

"That's the thing," Matt says. "Don't look back. Look ahead. You are more likely to become new by looking ahead."

I come into it now.

"Before we ride again," I tell her, "we'll visit the stables and the paddock. You can get to renew your friendship with the horses in that way."

Martha dries her eyes with a lace handkerchief that is monogrammed with the letter M. The handkerchief enhances her femininity. So does her sensitive awareness that she is a long way from being the Martha that she understands.

During the following week, at precisely eight o'clock every morning, she and I visit the stables and the paddock on Mr. Spenser's farm. At first, Martha seems shy and apprehensive around the horses. But, gradually and perceptibly, she grows comfortable in their presence as she pats their backs and feeds them sugar treats.

Then, a few days after this routine of visiting the horses, she and I begin riding again. Though Miss Pearson, Matt, and Sandra are always present, they stay apart from us. They have decided that my fostering a one-on-one friendship with Martha may encourage her to trust herself while she is in my company.

For the next two weeks after that, as Martha and I ride cautiously along the long, winding trail within a mix of the August-gold cypress, white ash, and silver birch forest that stretches out and away from Mr. Spenser's farm, I review with her all the rules that a good rider heeds. Martha continues to retrieve her riding skills. Each day, she is finding the confidence that she lost and bringing new powers to it.

When we are not riding or reviewing all that we have accomplished during our session for that day, Martha tells me about her happy life with her father, who is an Episcopal minister, and with her mother, who is a pediatrician. She speaks admiringly of her two older brothers who are students at Cornell and Dartmouth and are headed for careers in corporate law. She shows me their photos that she has placed in her iPhone. She also shows me a photo of Drake Bradford, a red-haired, muscular youth with freckles lightly touching his good-looking face and with a winning smile.

"I'm looking forward to the day when my life will be as perfect as it was before the accident."

"Was it perfect?" I ask her.

She ponders my question with interest, taking her time to seek out an answer.

"Nobody's life is really perfect," she answers me. "But my life seemed to be perfect. There wasn't any problem that I felt I couldn't handle. I have a wonderful family. I have many friends. I do very well in all my classes. I'm involved in many activities at school, in my community, and in my church. I'd be a fool to think that I should ask for more."

"Maybe your life is nearly perfect now," I tell her. "Maybe your wanting it to be absolutely the same is preventing you from seeing it as it really is. Nothing has changed for you at home or at school or in Blue Ridge. You and Drake have survived your accident. You are still in love with each other. What more could you ask for?"

"I don't want more. I just want it to be the same."

"It won't ever be the same," I tell her. "Life changes every minute that we are really alive and are truly in it."

"I feel that I am not in it, not since the accident. I want to be in it again."

"You will be in it the way you want to be. Just give yourself time. Give yourself a chance."

"That's what Doctor Morrison has been telling me," she says.

"She's counseling you."

"Yes."

"She's my counselor, too. I find her very helpful."

"So do I. I like her very much. She makes sense out of my confusion. Whenever I see her, I feel better that day. I believe that I will change my life for the better. I will be in it the way I want to be."

"I'm sure you will be."

Martha pauses. Her gaze upon me is steady and direct. She is trying to figure me out. When she resumes speaking, she describes how she perceives me.

"I can't imagine that there was a time when you weren't in it," she says. "A girl like you has always been in it. You have always done the right things. You have always felt the correct feelings. You have never lost yourself."

Now I tell her how it is with me.

"I've made a mess of my life, and I can't blame the accident. My life was a mess before the accident. I was a wild girl then—willful, disobedient, and self-destructive.

Then something wonderful happened for me. It wasn't just something. It was someone. His name is Tyler Danforth. We fell in love. He guided me to the right path. I changed for the better. I was disciplined. I was hopeful. I was ambitious. I was kind. Then the accident crashed into our lives. I've lost Tyler because of the accident and because of the problematic girl that I am. I am trying to change. I am trying hard to rediscover the faith that I once had that Tyler will waken from his deep sleep. I still love him. But I no longer feel good enough for him. I've made too many mistakes before and after the accident. I'm not giving up, though. I'm staying in it. I'm building a new person whose name is Rachel Hayworth. It's tough going, but I'm hanging in there. I'm fighting my battles. Maybe I will turn things around and do all of it the right way this time."

"You are already doing so," Martha says. "You are already making things work for you and for me."

"I'm glad that you think that I'm helping you," I tell her. "But it is you who can help yourself more than I or anyone else can."

"How can I do that?"

"Just stay in it," I say. "Just stay in the battle. Stay in the exciting and unpredictable world. Keep telling the world that you are here and that you want to help people."

"I'll keep trying," she promises. "I want my life to go forward. I want it to be new. I want to feel that I'm really in it."

On the bright summer day of our next meeting, Martha and I are riding our favorite roan-colored Arabian bays along the horse trail that stretches across the wide expanse of the flourishing green land of the Spenser property and fans outward to the colorful woods with their giant trees and glistening foliage. Matt, Sandra, and Miss Pearson are riding behind us, but never do they intrude upon our conversation.

Once again, I hear the murmuring chant of the wind, and I see the sunglow splendor of undulating fields of scented grasses and the ascending emphases of Connecticut hills.

I am riding side by side with Martha, observing her emerging ease and confidence as she rides her horse. She is dressed protectively—as I am—in a hard hat and a chin harness, in a quilted jacket and comfortable breeches, and in boots and gloves. Today I notice that Martha is sitting with the weight of her body in the center of the saddle. She is allowing her hip joints to be open and her legs positioned as close as possible around the horse's sides. At the same time, she is relaxing her arms at the shoulder and elbow so that she can move with the movement of the horse's head. She holds her hands correctly with palms facing each other and thumbs uppermost. Without using her arms, she clasps the reins by wrapping her fingers around them and almost closing her hands to make a fist. It is as though arms and reins belong to the horse, the better to follow its motion.

We have been riding at a leisurely pace while enjoying the August warmth and the pleasure of being together on a summer day when we are both free of school and other cares. But, after twenty minutes, Martha wants her ride to be more exciting.

She calls out her challenge to me.

"I'll race you to the edge of the forest," she exclaims. "That way, we'll make this ride very special."

"All right," I reply to her, caught up in the free-spirited lift of the moment. "We'll have a race. Let's go!"

Instantly, we ask our horses to go forward into a canter on the left rein. I watch Martha's every move as I ride beside her. She sits deep and presses her left leg on the fine leather band contoured about the belly of the horse to keep the saddle in place. Then, once again Martha and I make the same moves. With a squeeze of the right leg back behind the leather band, we ask our Arabian bays more actively to go forward into a canter.

Martha and her horse shoot ahead of me.

I see, as a vivid memory that I imagine will print itself forever upon my mind, how skillfully Martha collaborates with the kinetic energies of her horse. As I come cantering behind her, I can see the Arabian bay lengthening out its body and neck and fully extending its legs as Martha powers over the winding trail. Riding with the seat taken out of the saddle, she tucks her upper body in behind her horse's neck and extends her arms forward as with each stride the horse stretches his neck forward. She fuses the outline of their forms. This afternoon, she is riding with shorter stirrups to make it easier for her weight to be lifted out of the saddle. Through the reins, she is always keeping contact with the horse's mouth in order to help balance him. Onward and more swiftly she goes galloping.

So, also, do I ride swiftly onward, cantering and galloping toward the forest that is looming upward toward the August sun and the parallel waves of puffy, blue-gray clouds. Teeming apple orchards, colorful brush, and wildflower fields go flashing by me. Adolescent youths harvesting a passing field and a rugged man driving a tractor over a southerly hill leap into my vision and just as quickly scatter away. On and on I gallop, while trees and hills soar, waver aloft, and disappear. Even the radiant sun tilts, and the cloud-laden sky darts, slopes, and vaults. So it seems to my excited senses as I ride swiftly toward the forest, always keeping in my sight Martha's fast-moving race toward the edge of the woods.

Minutes later, when I reach the entrance to the woods, I am caught by surprise. Martha does not pause there to bring her horse race to a close. She does not push her lower leg forward while still squeezing both legs against her horse's sides. Nor does she brace herself against the stirrup, shorten up her reins, and push the hand that holds one of the reins into the horse's neck. She does not use her other hand to keep a strong hold on the second rein, as the horse starts to slow down. Martha does none of these things. Instead, she races along the clearing into the woods.

I quickly follow her.

But only for an instant do I see her riding her roan-colored bay even more swiftly toward the receding distance, before she disappears in the midst of a towering array of white ash trees, with their fluttering green canopies and late summer promise of autumn bronze, gold, and copper. Nor do I see her when she reaches a circuitous turn in the clearing and passes by ornamental cypresses, their leaves already tinged with blue-gray and yellow-gold hues. Riding now in search of her, I hear as a faraway sound the strong, slurring notes of a tawny-colored ovenbird. I witness as blurring motions or animated flares upon my senses the sprint of a horseshoe hare and the scurrying motion of a red squirrel. I see a whitetail deer leaping with athletic ease into the shaded, receding space that is the forest path beyond me. Still I ride briskly forward, my keen eyes looking for Martha or for any sign that she and her Arabian bay have powered through the area.

But there is no sign. There isn't the slightest evidence that Martha has ever arrived here. Even when I dismount and, while leading my horse into the deep folds of the forest I search all the byways and the unexpected intricacies of the trail, I cannot find her. Then dark clouds overtake the sky, covering the forest and shadowing the trail that twists its paths before and behind me. All too quickly, the forest and the trail disappear to my casual seeing. Not only Martha, but also Nature itself is disappearing. The thought comes to me that both Nature and Martha are playing a game of hide-and-seek. I laugh a joyful laugh and for that moment remember how it feels to be very young and very carefree.

Nevertheless, I continue to call out to Martha. The laughter has embraced my voice. I am thoroughly enjoying this moment, just as I imagine Martha is enjoying her merriment.

"Martha! Martha! Where are you? Call out to me. Let me hear you, so that I can find you."

At first, only the wind answers my call, though. Then in the flash of an instant and as though some mystical being has waved a magic wand, the cloud darkness that for a few minutes has been hiding the sun inside its murky prison and covering everything else disappears. Nature, brighter and more vivid than ever, reappears.

So does Martha.

When I reach the end of a long path that is nearly concealed by the wind-billowing trees and the flowering bushes that border the trail, I see her. At once, I understand that Martha has not been playing a game of hide-and-seek. She has not been hiding from anyone. She is standing on a promontory that juts out to the tremendousness of space that keeps unfurling its sun-touched splendors: the gold disc that is the sun, the confluence of blue sky and white clouds, and the blue-backed gulls soaring above the breeze-tossed waters of the lake below us.

At first, Martha does not notice me, so intent is her gaze upon the beauty of Nature that suddenly, after vanishing inside a threat of storm-darkness, has reappeared. In profile, she looks calm. She looks happier than I have ever seen her.

I move toward her, and with that movement my feet step on some fallen leaves with their withering yellow-brownness and the crinkling sound they make under my feet.

Martha turns to me. Her eyes are shining. Her face is beaming. Her smile glistens with bright teeth and unrestrained joy.

"I'm in it again," she says, "and I have you to thank for my being able to see it. I'm in it, and I see it clearly. There's a whole world out there, and it's inviting me to be a part of it."

"Of course the world is inviting you." I tell her, channeling all that Doctor. Morrison, Matt and Sandra, Miss Pearson, and my own experiences have taught me. "It will invite you whenever you are ready to meet it with hope and courage."

Now Martha laughs an exhilarating laugh.

"I'm ready for the world as it exists today," she says. "But the world keeps changing, and so will I. I'll always be ready for the world as long as I keep changing for the better."

"So must we all," I answer her. "You and I and everyone else. We must all keep changing for the better."

Martha laughs again. But this time her laughter is anchored to serious reflection.

"Let's do it," she exclaims. "Let's keep changing for the better."

"That's a terrific promise," I say. "Let's keep it alive."

We shake hands, and with that handshake we make a pact. Call it a bond or an accord or an alliance, if you prefer. This alliance involves ourselves, Rachel and Martha, as we exist today. It also includes all the Rachels and Marthas that we have yet to become.

We leave the promontory after a few minutes and ride back to the main forest path where Miss Pearson, Sandra, and Matt are waiting as they sit with straight-back posture and natural assurance upon their sturdy Arab bays. They are pleased that Martha and I are compatible. Without saying so, they believe that I am doing the right thing. I am being a positive influence upon a troubled and decent girl.

A few days later, Doctor Morrison, the wise psychiatrist who has always guided me toward the best paths, confers with me about the progress that Martha has been making because of her friendship with me.

"You're a positive influence upon her spirit," Doctor Morrison tells me. "I see how Martha lights up whenever she mentions you. She trusts you. She sees something of herself when she observes you. You are both waging similar battles. You are trying to conquer your fears and your doubts. You are trying to subvert your regrets for things that you have lost. You are trying to make yourselves new."

"I don't think that I have done so much," I say. "Martha has been a better person than I have been. She doesn't need to regret things that she has done wrong. She's an innocent. She's pure-white. I'm a blemished creature."

"You mustn't be too hard on yourself, Rachel," she advises me. "Right now, you can keep remembering the past if it's a way of staying on a proper course. But don't let your memories chain you. Don't let them get in the way of your becoming the new person you want to be."

A few days later, Miss Pearson discusses my next volunteer assignment.

"You have made a strong start," she tells me. "You are a better person for having helped Martha Ford. Now I'm asking you to meet new challenges. Do you think that you are ready?"

"I do," I answer her. "From now on, you can count on me. I'll always be ready."

"Let's see what happens," she says. "Let's see how well you meet the next challenges."

"I'm no stranger to challenges," I say. "I'm not old enough to vote. But challenges and I have had a long acquaintance."

"You are ahead of the curve," she tells me. "You live on the realistic level. You understand the way things are. You know firsthand a basic secret of the universe. There will always be challenges for you and for the rest of us. And you and the rest of us have to be ready and willing to stand up to them in brave and honorable ways."

Miss Pearson pats me gently on my right shoulder as she offers me a benevolent smile.

"Go forward," she says. "Do your best for all the children that you will be meeting."

For a moment, I consider the weight of her remark. Then I proceed to ask her a question.

"Will there be many children?" I ask her.

"There will be," she says.

"How old are they?"

"Five years; six, seven, eight, and nine years; some even ten or eleven."

"I'll do my best," I tell her.

"Of course you will," she answers me. "And Matt, Sandra, and I will always be here if you need us."

So I continue my new adventures. Perhaps I should call them my further explorations. I keep on searching for ways to help other human beings. I try to connect the Spirit-life that activates my best impulses with my honest efforts to bring some moments of happiness to the children who are confined to hospital beds that are not the beds they sleep on at home. Some of these children are suffering from leukemia. A few of them have broken their arms or their legs in athletic competitions or because of the roughhousing that seems so natural an ally of childhood exuberance. Two of them are recovering from pneumonia, and one other is recuperating from an appendectomy. These same innocent and afflicted children have to endure the long, lonely days and nights that are crowded with good doctors and nurses who, nevertheless, are not their fathers and mothers. These brave and apprehensive and anguished children find themselves trapped inside a shadowland of endless days and nights with needles that pinch them and medicine that sometimes makes them feel weaker and sicker.

These are the children for whom I work to bring a happy memory, a remarkable occasion, and afternoons of useful learning and spontaneous exhilaration.

There is Dewayne, the eight-year-old African American boy who is struggling bravely through a fierce battle with leukemia. His brown eyes shine with love and appreciation whenever I read him a story and every time that he joins other children and me in a game of Scrabble or a card game for children that offers funny questions and hilarious answers.

One afternoon, he tells me about the future that he envisions for himself.

"I'm going to be a doctor," he says with the firmest conviction. "I want to help sick boys and girls get better."

"You will be a very good doctor," I tell him, "because you care about people."

Hearing my words, he beams with satisfaction. My belief in his wish makes the possibility even stronger.

In this moment, I experience true happiness. My brief, ordinary exchange of words with Dewayne brightens his afternoon. It also brightens my spirit. It sparks my awareness that even in small ways my service to the children in this hospital intensifies their hope for recovery and reacquaints me with the better person I used to be. In these exchanges, I focus on the children. I no longer make myself the center of things. I forget about my problems, my regrets, my needs, and my goals. I concentrate on the children. I work to allay their fears and their sorrows. I begin to understand what Doctor Morrison meant when she told me that, in order to find my better self, I must lose my self-centeredness. By offering my helpfulness to these children, I am shedding my old, troubled self. Gradually, I am becoming new.

I regard these children here in Blue Ridge Hospital as a blessing that my kind angels have sent to me.

There is Diana, the ten-year-old Dutch girl whose pale face sparkles with joy when, while participating in "a brain game for kids," she successfully tests her logic, language, and physical coordination. She especially likes challenges that test her mathematical skills, her knowledge of English grammar, and her quick-witted awareness of facts that pertain to nineteenth-century American history and to the famous astronauts of the twentieth century. Diana has been waging her battle against viral meningitis and its after-effects, including headaches, exhaustion, and memory loss.

"When I'm well again," she tells me, "I want to go skiing. My mom and my dad taught me to ski when I was five years old. When we visited Massachusetts, we skied on Wachusett Mountain and in Nashoba Valley. It was really thrilling."

"Sounds like adventure," I tell her.

"I'd like you to come with us. I want to show you that as a skier I keep improving."

"Of course I'll join you," I answer her. "We'll have a great adventure together—you, your parents, and I."

Hearing my promise, Diana is elated.

"I can hardly wait," she says.

Once again, I learn more about kindness and connectedness.

I learn so much from these children.

There is Esperanza, the nine-year-old Latina who finds a special elation in acting out clues in intricate games of charades. Enervated still by her bout with pneumonia, she nevertheless moves with balletic grace and charms her peers as well as me with the creative variations of her clues.

Esperanza also loves languages. She speaks fluent Spanish, English, and German. So do I. On the afternoons when she is feeling well, we choose the language that we will speak during our meetings.

"Let's do a Spanish Monday," she tells me.

"That will be music to my ears," I answer her. "What about a German Wednesday?"

"Exactly right," she says, bright with the promise of quickening each afternoon with new thoughts and foreign phrases.

"We can preface each meeting with the familiar sounds of English."

"Absolutely," she agrees, as her smile brings a glow to her pale face. "We'll be international. We'll be our own small United Nations."

Her remark stirs my laughter. She joins in. Once more, I understand the gift that my kind angels or Blessed Chance is giving me. I understand at least a little more what it means to bring happiness to another person.

There is Kaito, the ten-year-old Japanese boy whose wan face lights up whenever I join him in science-oriented card games that introduce the players to elementary chemistry and physics and that require them to use their logical and strategic thinking skills. Kaito has endured two surgeries to remove tumors that were growing at the cusp of his brain. He is winning his battle. He has not allowed his grueling months to crush his spirit.

Kaito's father is an astrophysicist who works for NASA—The National Aeronautics and Space Administration. Through his father, Kaito has learned so much important information about our universe. I am not surprised that Kaito is planning to become an astrophysicist.

Whenever I visit him as a hospital volunteer, my joining Kaito in challenging science-oriented games pleases him. His sharing the knowledge that his father has imparted to him pleases him more. I understand the language of physics and chemistry, because I have studied these subjects in advanced placement courses at Brooks School and at Blue Ridge High School. But Kaito's knowledge of these subjects is far more complex.

I enjoy listening to him. He speaks about black holes, dark energy, dark matter, and gravity. He tells me about the origin and evolution of the galaxies, stars, and planets that make up our universe. He talks about the planets around other stars and mentions future explorations that might discover whether those planets harbor life. He summarizes what he knows about NASA's Physics of the Cosmos program that addresses questions about neutron stars, gravitational waves, matter, energy, space, and time.

He is looking forward to joining NASA's Space Camp for Kids. In that program, while working with a team of peers, Kaito will train like an astronaut on the one-sixth Gravity Chair, the Five Degrees of Freedom simulator, and the Multi-Axis Trainer. He will construct and launch his own model rocket. He will learn what it is like to live aboard the International Space Station.

Kaito's knowledge becomes his gift to me. I, in turn, bring as my gifts genuine interest, meticulous attention, and quiet gratitude for the privilege of knowing and learning from him.

There are so many other children here in Blue Ridge Hospital, and all of them are patient, hopeful, and courageous. All of them come to trust and to like me. For many of them, this liking grows into a love that is both innocent and spontaneous. It is this affectionate bond that connects our spirits. It is this spiritual bond that is our gift to each other while we are living. It is this same, extraordinary bond that may live in our memories until we die and, possibly, in all the eternal days after that. The kindness, affection, and courage that we share with others create the bond that connects our here-and-now world to that faraway and mysterious world we shall one day enter.

So I begin to understand, drawing upon the friendship that these steadfast children and I share.

Again and again, I work to ease their suffering. I bring respite from their hospital routine. Not only do I bring board games and card games and video games. With the games, I also bring instruction to these children. I coax their confidence. I nudge their trust. I nurture their exuberance.

I join them as they put together intricate puzzles.

I show them how to sculpt with play dough and clay.

I urge and guide them to write poems and stories on their computers.

I teach them how to play the guitar. They learn quickly, and they revel in the astonishment of producing the sounds that create "The Wheels on the Bus Go Round and Round," "Smoke on the Water," "You Are My Sunshine," "Puff the Magic Dragon," and "You've Got a Friend in Me."

My afternoon hours on Mondays, Wednesdays, and Fridays at Blue Ridge Hospital pass swiftly.

All my other summer hours are filled with academic preparation for my senior year at Blue Ridge, as well as with sailing with Sandra and Matt on the lake behind my home and with occasional excursions to Newport, Rhode Island; Bar Harbor, Maine; and Martha's Vineyard in Massachusetts, with fun-loving Kerry Fitzgerald, newly reliable Theo Ryan, and my loyal advocates, Sandra and Matt.

Most of the late summer is sun-filled and warm. I experience days and days of nearly adequate contentment.

Only in the last week of August does the warm sheen of the sun fail me. In that week, the rains come, disturbing my conviction that I have at last located my proper equilibrium and the steady course that will guide me to good health, worthwhile journeys, and reputable harbors.

The inclement weather stirs my sorrow. It quickens my regret. It goads my longing for all the good days that have hastened away to ghostlier demarcations inside the secret recesses of my memory.

I am not really happy. How could I be? Tyler is not here with me. Nor am I very often there, in the west wing of Blue Ridge Medical Center, calling out to him as I petition him to come back to life—come back to his family and come back to me. I no longer feel worthy of his love. I no longer believe that I am good enough to bring him back to life. Perhaps one day I shall feel worthy. On that day, I shall believe that I have made amends for my past wrongdoing. I wonder, while apprehension hovers near me, whether Tyler will still be there, sleeping the long sleep that has made him its prisoner.

The following day, after seven days of steady and sometimes turbulent rainstorms, the sun returns. It glows with extraordinary brightness. Its radiance touches the galaxy of clouds that blend their immaculate whiteness with tinges of red and blue.

This morning, as I awaken, everything in my bedroom looks different. The rays of the August sun illuminate my cantilevered oak bed and with delicate traceries reveal its juxtaposition of crisp angles and rounded corners, its lush peach and gold fabrics, and the medley of cream white, pale orange, bright yellow, and azure blue pillows. The sun lends its sheen to the integrated nightstands, a gilded metal bench standing in front of my bed, the pale gold and tufted upholstery of two wingback chairs with their flared arms and tapered legs, and the needlepoint carpet. Sunlight also touches the opposite wall and the Impressionist canvas of the pensive girl in a flower-filled garden—the good girl that I perceived as my *alter ego* when I was very young and had not committed any mistakes.

The day itself awakens, and I hurry out of bed to meet it.

I bathe and dress, and I sing as I comb my hair. My face in the mirror gleams with good health, and my eyes sparkle with carefully earned hope and the fervor of anticipation.

"Something grand is going to happen today," I tell myself. "Something unusual. I am not certain that it will happen to me. But I will be there to witness it."

No sooner do these private, unspoken words quicken my spirit, than the scenario that I am just now imagining begins to unfold. Mrs. Danforth hurries in with news that complements my anticipation. Her exuberance has coaxed her to do what she has probably never done before. Without our invitation yet with our wholehearted pleasure at her arrival, she joins Sandra, Matt, and me at the breakfast table to tell us her news. She declines our offer of orange juice, waffles, and blueberries with a wave of her hand and with warmhearted words that declare our breakfast looks delicious. But she accepts a cup of coffee before she proceeds to the exciting details of her news.

"I've had another dream," she tells us. "It has come to me every night for a week. I feel it's important. I believe that it is more urgent than all the other dreams that have visited me."

Polite and attentive, I listen to all that Mrs. Danforth is telling us. But I say nothing. If Tyler's mother is the bringer of the grand happening that I am expecting, I do not care to tempt the anger of the unpredictable Fates with an easy show of my happiness. I do not want them to mistake my elation for the arrogant pride that expects rewards that it may not have yet earned. But I know that the Fates are here with us. Quite suddenly, they have entered the room to stand hovering by me, visible only to my intuition and to the Spirit-awareness of my imagination.

I am grateful when Matt speaks his own thoughts.

Matt is especially interested in Mrs. Danforth's words. He is currently reading psychological case studies about the ways that dreams sometimes predict future happenings and also prepare the dreamer for the startling behavior of persons that they know and about whom they care a great deal.

He asks Mrs. Danforth probing questions.

"What dream did you have? Is it the same dream that has often come to you—the one that Rachel has sometimes mentioned to us?"

"It was the same dream, yet more than that."

"What makes you believe that this particular dream is so important?"

With no hesitation, Mrs. Danforth answers him.

"In all the other dreams I have had before this week, Tyler was speaking to Rachel. She was standing by his hospital bed, and he was speaking to her. 'I heard you calling my name,' he always said. 'I heard you, and I have come back to you.'"

Sandra comes into it now. Already, tears are filling her eyes.

"It is a beautiful dream, Mrs. Danforth. It is so beautiful. How wonderful if it could come true!"

"It will, my dear," she says. "This morning, I am more certain of it than ever before."

Matt wants to know more.

"What is different about the dream that came to you all last week?"

"This time Tyler wasn't speaking to Rachel," she answers him.

Her words take me by surprise. Instantly, I wonder why, in this most recent series of dreams, Tyler is not speaking to me.

"To whom was he speaking?" I ask. "Was some other girl standing there by his hospital bed?"

"No," Mrs. Danforth answers me. "There was no girl there. Without you or without any other girl, the hospital room seemed incomplete. It was as though an artist had revised a painting and had left out something or someone important."

Sandra asks another question.

"Is that what made your dream different—Rachel's not being there."

"That and something else."

For a moment, a taut stillness enters the room. We three who have been listening to Mrs. Danforth wait for her to tell us more.

"What is especially different about this dream is that Tyler directed his words at me. 'Ask Rachel to visit me,' he said. 'Ask her to come to my hospital room and stand by my bed. Ask her to call my name.'"

I come into it again. I am eager to verify what I think I have heard her say. I ask an even more urgent question.

"Are you certain he asked for me?"

"Of course he asked for you," Mrs. Danforth answers me. "I wasn't really surprised. I believed that one day he would ask for you. My earlier dreams told me that he would."

I sense the frown that creases my brow. I grope for words that will reveal my doubts.

"It doesn't seem possible," I tell her. "Not after I failed him. Not after I stopped being the good girl that he'd influenced me to be."

"That's all changed now," Mrs. Danforth says. "*You've* changed. You have been doing all the right things. You have shown that you care about persons less fortunate than you are. You have worked hard to make those persons happy— if not forever, at least for a day or a week or a year. You have influenced Martha, Dewayne, Diana, Esperanza, Kaito, and so many others to believe in themselves again and to work toward making themselves new and well."

"I didn't do anything special," I say. "You are making a big point out of my small efforts."

"I am making a small point out of your large efforts. Tyler may know all about them, even though he is caught in that magical sleep. If so, he must be very proud of you."

I summon my confidence. I tell myself that I must stay strong. Today especially I must do the right things. One of these things is my asking Mrs. Danforth for some instructions.

"What do you want me to do?"

"I want you to come to the hospital with me. I want you to visit Tyler."

I hesitate. I am not certain that Tyler will answer my call. I don't want Mrs. Danforth to be disappointed if he does not answer me. I wonder if my visiting Tyler will merely defeat her hope. I wonder, too, if my calling to Tyler and receiving only the silence as my answer will wreck my own newborn hope.

But enough of my feelings, I tell myself. Have courage. Take a leap into the unknown. Believe in tremendous possibilities. Believe in other good people. Go forward with them if you can, or go alone if you must. Whatever you do, work to change things for the better.

Now I speak the words that Mrs. Danforth is waiting to hear.

"I'll go with you," I tell her. "And I'll call Tyler's name as clearly as I can."

"You are making a wise decision, Rachel," she tells me. "You will see."

Hearing my words, Matt and Sandra become elated.

"You are doing the right thing," Sandra tells me. "It's the best thing you will do today."

"Go for it," Matt says. "It's your chance. Take hold of it."

Now Mrs. Danforth directs new words to Sandra and Matt.

"I'd like the two of you to come with us," she says. "I'd like you to see what happens."

Sandra looks at Matt. He nods his assent.

"We'd love to join you," Sandra says. "We want to see what happens."

So, right after we finish our breakfast, we hurry onward to Blue Ridge Medical Center.

Once again, we enter the long, polished corridors that lead us to Tyler's room. Once more, a motherly nurse greets us. Her name is Florence Blanchett, and her reputation as the supervisor of nurses here in Blue Ridge Medical Center is impeccable. Her silver hair, weathered face, and kind smile serve as emblems not only for her age and experience, but also for her compassion. Dressed in white, she might be mistaken for a dedicated nun who is not required to wear a veil.

She greets us with words that are both heartfelt and informative.

"I'm so pleased that you are here," she tells us. "I felt that you would be visiting today. Something in the air told me—some fresh brightness, perhaps the steadier rays of the sun gleaming across the room and casting a glow over Tyler in his bed. And something more than that told me—something more than the fresher air and the more radiant sunlight."

"What else was it?" Sandra asks. "What else convinced you that something important was going to happen today, here in this room that has known mostly silence and the sleeping presence of Tyler Danforth?"

Mrs. Blanchett takes a moment before she answers. She is weighing the importance of her words and their possible alliance with the extraordinary things that will happen today. Then, having given her thoughts a careful review, she proceeds to tell us why she believes that today may be a milestone for Tyler—a turning point in whatever is going to happen to or for him.

"Last evening, Tyler moved his head as it lay against the pillow. He moved it several times during the nighttime hours. He continued to be restless through the first part of this morning. He'd never done that before. Always before, we nurses and perhaps a physician's assistant have moved him out of his bed when we changed the bed linen. Sometimes, we placed him on a gurney and then guided him into the operating room for new surgeries. But all that is different from what happened last night and through the first hours of this morning. He moved by himself. He summoned a power within himself that enabled him to move his head and to shift his body ever so slightly."

Matt has another question.

"What does Tyler's primary physician say?"

"He isn't making too much of it. Not yet. He doesn't want to raise the Danforth family's hopes until he studies further all that has been happening with Tyler in these recent hours."

Matt probes further.

"Yet you have raised your hopes," he tells Mrs. Blanchett. "You have been raising our hopes, too."

"That I have done. That I am doing," she answers him as she directs her words to all of us. "Something important has happened. I don't know whether it will happen again. But I believe that if it does happen, if Tyler does move his head on the pillow or shift his body beneath his coverlet, some extraordinary change is going to take place."

Mrs. Blanchett's words quicken our anticipation. But it is Mrs. Danforth who receives these words with the greatest enthusiasm.

"I know exactly what you mean," she says. "I, too, believe that something different is going to happen today. It will happen here, and it will be wonderful."

Now Mrs. Blanchett guides us to the bed where Tyler is sleeping.

The sunlight that flows through this spacious room imbues the entire area that includes Tyler's bed with otherworldly brightness. It infuses the entire bed and the night tables and the visitors' chairs that stand in an out-of-the-way corner with magic-seeming luminosity. Poster-size photos of Tyler cover the walls behind and beside him. Vibrant with life, he appears as a prodigious reality, a dynamic youth, and an altogether charismatic presence. In these poster-size pictures, he is an agile horse rider, a formidable goalie for the Blue Ridge High School hockey team, a fleet-footed second baseman for the school's baseball team, and a proficient water skier.

Not only do the posters show these vivid images. They also reveal other aspects of Tyler's remarkable vitality. They show him as a middleweight boxer and a medal-winning swimmer. They parse his identity. They probe the meaning of each image. They scrutinize his masculinity. They consider with care and with accuracy all the physical characteristics and the keen-eyed alertness that make him who he is.

More than one of the posters identifies him as the dashing prince in our school's play who belongs to a magical realm. In none of these posters that show him as a prince is he sleeping. In fact, he is looking out at the viewer. He extends his right arm and his right hand toward that same viewer, who might be you just as it is I who stand observing him in this very moment. In the palm of his hand he holds a diamond ring. It is a ring of betrothal. To the males who observe him and who have already been dreaming of girls, he as the prince may be showing the ring that belongs to the girl *he* is seeking. Perhaps he is telling these male viewers that each one of them may be a prince, if their actions merit that rank. They, too, are looking for the girl whom destiny or the kinder Fates may grant them. To the female viewers, the image of Tyler as a prince holding a ring of betrothal in the palm of his hand is sending a different message and even a challenge. He wants to meet the right girl. He is searching for the girl who is meant for him. Is she the one?

As I move closer to his bed, I study Tyler's handsome face. Today, as on other recent days when I have come to the hospital to call out Tyler's name, I notice that his face shows him to be a youth who is not at peace. Some pressing motive, some compelling desire has ransacked even the hidden corners of his peace. Tyler's face reveals his discontent. He seeks escape. He is waiting for some miraculous thing to happen. He would rescue himself, if he could. But the magic spell that the punishing Fates have cast upon him prevents him from activating his own rescue.

He keeps waiting for the special girl who will be his rescuer.

With all my heart and my soul, I want to be his rescuer. But my past wrongdoings still cast a cloud over me. The recent good works that I have accomplished may not be sufficient expiation for my past errors. I am not certain that even the more favorable Fates will take pity on me. I do not know whether I merit so magnificent a reward as Tyler's love. Though loyal Sandra and Matt are here standing behind me, though I am aware of good Mrs. Blanchett's motherly advocacy, and though I am grateful for Mrs. Danforth's warmhearted acceptance, I nevertheless hold back. I have not accomplished enough. I want to do more. I never want to stop doing the right things. I never want to refrain from helping the downtrodden, the sick, the needy, and the sorrow-laden.

I change course. I will myself to reflect upon my life with more hope and more optimism. I remind myself that I have come here for a special reason. I want to help Tyler if I can.

As though she has a magic link to my thoughts, Mrs. Danforth coaxes me forward.

"It's time, Rachel," she gently reminds me. "It's time to do what you are meant to do. It's time to do the right thing."

"Do it," Mrs. Blanchett whispers. "Do it now, and do it well."

"We are rooting for you," Sandra tells me. Her warm voice is tremulous and caring.

"Do what you are meant to do," Matt says. "Do what you were born to do."

So I take the power that is in me, prod my tenacious will, and move even closer to Tyler, as he stays locked inside his sleeping in this immaculate hospital bed.

I call out to him. I call his name. My voice is crisp and even melodious.

"Tyler," I say. "It's Rachel. I am here for you. Wake up! Wake up! It's time for you to come back to me. This is the day that you must come back to all of us."

Tyler does not stir.

Mrs. Danforth prods me further. She will not permit my dismay to prevent my success here today.

"Kiss him," she tells me. "Kiss the young man whom you love."

I will myself to do as she asks. I lean forward and lower my face so that it meets Tyler's sleeping face. I brush my lips against his lips. I feel the life in his lips. That pulsing life startles and pleases me. I break away from the kiss and study his face once again. With no hesitation this time, I lower my face and kiss him once more. This time, I do not merely brush his lips with my lips. I press my lips firmly upon his lips. I feel tears welling inside my eyes. Still, I hold the kiss for a few moments longer.

Then something startling happens—something wonderful and vibrant and miraculous. I feel Tyler's lips returning my kiss. I experience the love and the truth and the passion that are alive in that kiss.

When I break away from the kiss, I look with astonished eyes upon Tyler. His searching eyes are wide open. He is awake, and he is speaking to me. His voice is wavering and raspy and yet stronger with each word he speaks.

"Rachel!" he calls out to me. "You *are* here! I've been waiting for you for such a long time."